Lock Down Publications and Ca$h
Presents

I0658707

Ran Off On Da Plug 2

RELENTLESS AGAIN

Written By
PAPER BOI RARI

First Edition 2025

Printed in the United States of America

This is a work of fiction. Names, characters, places, and incidents either are products of the author's imagination or are used fictitiously. Any similarity to actual events or locales or persons, living or dead, is entirely coincidental.

Lock Down Publications
P.O. Box 944
Stockbridge, GA 30281
www.lockdownpublications.com

Like our page on Facebook: Lock Down Publications
www.facebook.com/lockdownpublications.ldp

Stay Connected with Us!

Text **LOCKDOWN** to 22828 to stay up-to-date with new releases, sneak peaks, contests and more…

Like our page on Facebook:
Lock Down Publications

Join Lock Down Publications/The New Era Reading Group

Visit our website:
www.lockdownpublications.com

Follow us on Instagram:
Lock Down Publications

Email Us: We want to hear from you!

Dedication

I dedicate this magnificent artistic craft to the Westside Ambassador of Dothan, Alabama. Freak Zeenie! God blessed me with the gifted words and creative thoughts, so I must empower them. Check out the word play, bruh.

Make sure you keep that light shining for God, bruh. God is watching, and everybody else too. Everybody gon' pay! I'm coming soon, 2025 right round the corner!

Welcome home, Freak Zeenie!

Author Notes

Psalm 142

1) I cry aloud to the LORD, I lift up my voice to the LORD for mercy.
2) I pour out before him my complaint. Before him I tell my trouble.
3) When my spirit grows faint within me, it is you who watches over my way. In the path where I walk, people have hidden a snare for me.
4) Look and see, there is no one at my right hand, no one is concerned for me. I have no refuge; no one cares for my life.
5) I cry to you, LORD; I say, "You are my refuge, my portion in the land of the living."
6) Listen to my cry, for I am in desperate need. Rescue me from those who pursue me, for they are too strong for me.
7) Set me free from my prison, that I may praise your name. Then the righteous will gather about me because of your goodness to me.

AMEN!

Acknowledgments

First, I'd like to give my thanks to God, in Jesus name, Amen. I also want to give thanks to my mothers. Amand Faulk, and Charlotte Fogle. I love y'all women way more than words could ever express. I want to send my love to my god mom Mary too, and my aunt Shea. i miss yall heavily. RIP Pop. Man...You left me too soon old man, but you produced a real one when you made me. I got it! You'll be forever missed and loved. I wish you could see how they carried it, but I can hear you saying to me, Lee I told you so.

Next up, my first lady. Lady Bugg, I love you, daughter. You are swift now. Keep your mouth closed and ears open. You gone be a force to reckon with. To my daughter Cupcake, stop being so mean! To my son Trell, get your butt off that game! LOL. To my future wife Esha, thank you for being you. I have a clear understanding about our love now. I love you forever in this life and will do it all again in the next one if we could do it again.

To LDP, thank y'all for giving me a chance of a lifetime.

Last, but not least, to all my readers and supporters, sorry for the long wait, but due to my circumstances, things became difficult, but with God I managed them, and I hope y'all enjoy this great story. There's more to come. Stay tuned! I'm working. I appreciate y'all and I send my love to you all.

The things I had to go through, just to get to go through the things that I wanted to. Everything is a blessing though, and it's up to you to find out in which way they benefit you.

Check this novel out. I'm 'bout to take you through hoods you never been to where shit gets deep, cause I'm in the streets like a pothole!

Turn the Page …

Chapter 1

A Week and a Half Later—
Dothan, Alabama

If money brought mo' problems, it's safe to say that Freak Zeenie would need night classes to solve all the different quizzes life was presenting towards him. It's laws to the universe. It's believed that you get out, only what you put in it. Ambiguous, ambitious, and with a stamina that never perished. Freak Zeenie relentlessly faced life rebelliously.

Freak Zeenie had become a tycoon in just under a year of being free. He had inherited the position instead of earning it through good ol' hard work. Accumulating a large amount of money, power, and drugs simultaneously without instructions could cause a variety of actions to take place ambiently.

It took Freak Zeenie all but four days to empty out all the kilos at the construction building. Transporting 'em out to his stash spots, out in Kinsey, Alabama with the help of Cartier Jay, Boo-Boo, and Kal-Kal. His secret was now exposed, but he hadn't had a choice in this situation.

Now Freak Zeenie was sittin' on his sectional trying to console Khashia. She had been crying, weepin', and throwing up for the last week straight. All the way to Detroit, Mich., and back. Right after the Mexicans left. The Atlanta police department contacted Khashia, who Denise had down as her next of kin. Once Khashia viewed her step sister's headless body, this has been her condition ever since. They had Denise cremated and spread across Lake Michigan just as she requested. Khashia had a court date to go get her step nephew from out the group home in Atlanta, Georgia next week to be exact. Khashia was upset with herself. She'd claimed that she had just planned to go spend some time with Denise right before she had come down with COVID-19.

Freak Zeenie couldn't believe none of what had just took place before his eyes. Denise claimed that her son was his. Then Khashia, being her step sister, and both of them were fucking with his ops. *Damn . . . How come this is happening to me, Lord? Not like this!* He sat there thinking as he rubbed her back.

"It's gon' get better, bae, it's gone get better. Trust me. Time will heal it in due time," Freak Zeenie whispered in Khashia's ear softly. Gettin' up, Freak Zeenie went and ran a tub full of warm water, droppin' some scented pebbles into the water for her. After completing his task, he went and retrieved Khashia. "Come on, let's get you freshened up and laid down before I go to work," he said. Khashia sniffled as she allowed Freak Zeenie to lead her into the bathroom.

30 Minutes Later—

Khashia laid in their king-size bed as Freak Zeenie went and took a quick shower himself. *Dear God, how would I ever forgive myself? I was trying to save us both, but things became too complicated for me once Mark disappeared on me*, she thought to herself as she continued weepin', rubbin' her red puffy eyes.

Freak Zeenie dried off. He was rushin' because today was the day Zacatecas' shipment landed. *Fuck ass bitch! Got too much goin' on.* His face balled up, bringin' crinkles across his forehead. Freak Zeenie shook his head out of frustration. *I got to get the fuck away from this bitch, fuck all that!* he kept sayin' over and over again in his head as he dressed.

Freak Zeenie came out the massive bathroom. "I'm on my way to handle this business. You good, right?" He looked Khashia deeply in her eyes and waited.

"Yeah-yeah . . . I'll . . . be fine," she claimed.

"You need somethin'?"

"No, thank you."

"Alright. Call me right away if you do, a'ight?"

"Okay." Khashia pulled the covers over her head.

Freak Zeenie stood there a few seconds before making his way out the house. He crunked up and pulled out en route to the construction building. He picked his phone up, about to call Khashia, then disregarded it.

Two minutes hadn't passed before Khashia's phone lit up. Throwing the covers off her, she reached over grabbing her phone. "Hello?" She looked at the phone and saw the screensaver still showin' but still heard ringing. "Oh shit!" she said, jumpin' out the bed, runnin' towards the dresser. Snatchin' the bottom drawer out, she reached her arm deep in the hole, drawin' out the phone. Fumbling a second, Khashia finally had the phone unlocked. "Hello?" she answered, soundin' out of breath.

"You have a collect call from—"

Khashia pressed five, knowin' already who it was.

"What's up, baby? Damn, you gone leave me in this bitch forever, ain't it?"

"Nooo, I'm workin', Trae! You don't understand. It's so much shit that then happens! Right when I had enough info on Mark, he disappeared. Then I could never do my step sister like that. I was tryin' to save her too, but now even she—"

"Dead! Yeah, I know. Do somethin'! Fuck! I got to get the fuck out this bitch!" he stressed. "Khashia?"

"Yeah?"

"I love you!"

"I love you more!"

"Show me then! Fuck all that!" Trae said firmly.

"I—" the line went dead. "Will. I will, just watch!" she said. Khashia put the phone on silent, placed it back in the hole, and replaced the bottom drawer in. She got back in bed. *I know what I got to do bae, but you gone have to chill a minute. I got you.* Khashia kept formulating her plan until she finally drifted off to sleep.

Chapter 2

A Week Later—
85 South
Atlanta, Georgia

Freak Zeenie sat in deep thought while Khashia made sure her nephew was mentally stable, knowing he had just endured a ton of adversities very early on in life. Freak Zeenie had a mega-ton of his own problems too, to be concerned with, than the pre-teen who sat next to him in the back of the Cullinan Rolls-Royce. While Freak Zeenie stared out the window in thought, the pre-teen hadn't said much of anything. Khashia was the one who was controlling the conversation.

"Deshawn? Deshawn, you hear me talkin' to you?" she asked, looking at the back of his head.

"Huh? Oh. Nawl . . . Auntee. What were you saying again now," he answered, turning back around, giving her his undivided attention. Deshawn didn't hear her because he was too busy in his own thoughts staring at the back of Freak Zeenie's head.

"I said, family is everything. Ain't you glad that me and your uncle came and got you from out that nasty ass place they just had you in?"

You saying the wrong shit, Tee! This ball headed ass nigga ain't my fuckin' uncle. Deshawn shielded his thoughts by presenting a Colgate smile. "Hel—I mean yes, Auntee K', man, it's messed up in there," he said then sat back and directed his attention to his tablet that Khashia had bought for him.

I got to consult with Freak later about getting him a psychologist. Ain't no way he okay. The boy never knew his dad and now he has lost his mother too. Khashia kept her thoughts concealed, but shook her head at the situation. Khashia glanced over at Freak Zeenie.

Freak Zeenie's mind was going faster than a Bugatti with all three keys turned on. He had been waiting on Lil Fed and Carlos to quickly flip the load he dropped on them days ago. They hadn't checked in, but he was sure they would be sooner than later with the plan he gave them. Freak Zeenie had too many bricks to be trying to serve 'em for forty thousand apiece. So he took 'em down to twenty-eight thousand.

Freak Zeenie had to take risks he didn't want to take, but took 'em anyway. When you are under pressure these are the types of situations that can occur. You could make decisions way too fast that you know should have taken you more time to make. Freak Zeenie was trying it all right now.

45 Minutes Later—
Brentwood
Dothan, Alabama

Soon as the Cullinan truck pulled into Freak Zeenie's driveway, they all knew something was wrong. "Man, what the fuck!" he bellowed, looking over at Khashia. He opened the door about to get out.

"Hold on, bae! We need to call the police first, don't we?" she said, pickin' up her phone.

"Who?" He looked at Khashia. "You can call. I ain't calling no one." Freak Zeenie got out, headed towards the mansion. He wasn't trippin 'bout a loss because he kept no money or drugs where he laid his head. He stopped at the door that hung off the hinges. Freak Zeenie stood there, puzzled. He looked back at Khashia and Deshawn. "I wonder why *SafeTouch* didn't contact us or nothing," he said, lines formed across his small forehead.

"Me too! That's a good thought," Khashia responded, as she connected with the dispatcher. It was all fascinating to Deshawn.

3 Minutes Later—

A Dothan police patrol vehicle pulled up. A male and female got out holdin' a clipboard. Walkin' as stiff as a board.

Khashia greeted them. "Hi, this is just how we found it. We haven't even entered yet," she said, explaining before they had a chance to ask one question.

"Oh, okay. So—"

"Damn . . . y'all got here fast! Fuck, y'all was next door or something?" Freak Zeenie said. "I guess it's about the zip code you live in, huh? Let this had of been the bottom! Y'all would have asked us to come in to file a report without even coming out," he said, shaking his head at the truth he spoke.

The two officers looked at each other. Their eyes acknowledged that Freak Zeenie had spoken facts.

"Like I was about to say, well, let's go in and see the damage first," the female officer said, walking toward the broken down door. Her partner followed her with Freak Zeenie 'em behind them.

The house had been ransacked from the kitchen to the back door. Cabinets opened, washer and dryer flipped over. Deep freezer moved. Curtains snatched down.

"If I had to guess, whoever it was must have gotten startled and left probably as y'all pulled in," the female officer said, writing on her clipboard.

"How you figure that?" Freak Zeenie questioned her.

"Because," she pointed to the open back door.

"Right."

"Well, we took down everything. We will put some extra security over here. I suggest y'all change the locks, and get an alarm system too. This house is too big for y'all—"

"We do have one!"

"Well, what happened? Because we never received a call," the female said, staring at them both.

"Let's see," Freak Zeenie went and looked in the open cabinet. "The got damn box cord is cut!" He spoke at the sight of the mutilated cord.

"It should have still sent a signal out though. This is just the horn," the male officer spoke for the first time.

"It's because they disconnected the main box on the outside too!" Deshawn blurted out. They all looked at him at the same time.

"How you know this, lil' man?" the male officer asked him.

"I ain't here for all that now," Deshawn said, remaining silent. Freak Zeenie laughed a little.

Damn, boy, sounds like some shit I'll say. Freak Zeenie's thoughts formed, but never made it vocal.

20 Minutes Later—

A silver 600 Benz pulled up into Freak Zeenie's driveway no sooner than the police had turned off the block. A tall man stepped out, putting a pair of cranberry box-toe gator boots on the ground, matching a three-piece tailored suit. Freak Zeenie thought his uncle would beat them there, but unfortunately, he was late.

Freak Zeenie walked outside before his uncle could make it to the front door. "You late!" Freak Zeenie said sternly.

"Man . . . What happened to your front door?" Pastor Barber said, ignoring Freak Zeenie's sarcasm.

"You late, Pastor Barber! You are cutting into my check. Do I need to cut into yours? Time is money!"

"Nigga, I just had revival, baptized a nigga, buried another, christened a child, and married a couple. Hal-le-lu-jah, praise God." Pastor Barber took his handkerchief out and patted his forehead, wiping away the beads of perspiration that quickly had formed. Pastor Barber was high as a kite. He'd snorted an eight-ball of coke on the way down.

Freak Zeenie busted out chortling. "Unk, you hell now! How I beat you here coming from the A', and you coming from Birmingham?"

"Freak, fuck all that! Nigga, come on! Time is money! I got shit to do. I need to hit this highway and get it my way. After this, me and your aunt heading down to Mississippi to Biloxi to get our gamble on!"

Freak Zeenie smiled and kept his thoughts to himself. He scratched his bald head, looked around, then jumped in his black Jeep Wrangler. He cranked it up and pulled out with Pastor Barber trailing him.

Nigga ass going straight to hell, playing all them games with God like that, Freak Zeenie thought, as he led the way to the construction company. He had to call his uncle in to help traffic some of the work for him. Since he was a pastor, and had a church van, Freak Zeenie felt like his uncle would be a perfect road runner. On top of that, Pastor Barber had a heavy gambling appetite that he would even use the church's money to feed his craving every once in a while. So when Freak Zeenie presented the opportunity to him, Pastor Barber jumped on it like a diving board.

10 Minutes Later—

Freak Zeenie let the door down behind the church van as Pastor Barber pulled in. Pastor Barber got out, opened the side doors, and the back one in a blur. They both worked diligently to load the kilos inside the van.

Minutes Later—

"Here. Half now—"

"I know. I know. The other half when I come back through, right?"

"You better say it!" Freak Zeenie said, giving him the money, then patted the top of the hood, signaling for Pastor Barber to pull out. Freak Zeenie would pay Pastor Barber $75 dollars per kilo, sending him on the highway with a hundred at a time. Pastor Barber could make up to $7,500 a day at times. Pastor Barber was always ready to drive.

Even though Freak Zeenie had the big rigs at his disposal, he chose to move the work how he felt safe to do so. He didn't trust Zacatecas either. During his time of incarceration, Freak Zeenie had the chance to see it all when it came to the game. Plus, he'd never forget his own past situation either. So he moved how he moved in order to get the same job done in a different way.

Freak Zeenie got in his jeep headed back home to tell Khashia and Deshawn to pack up. They were moving; there was no way he could lay his head, or his family's head, in a home that had been invaded. He also had to find out who the snake was, so they could slither their way face up in a casket in somebody's church.

Chapter 3

Tuesday
Yazoo FCI
Yazoo, Mississippi

The BOP had finally started back transferring inmates through the system again. The pandemic had put all prisons on hold, coming down straight from CDC, trying to keep down the spreading of COVID-19 and the thousands of lawsuits coming from the inmates themselves.

Trae was up early this morning due to his celly having finally transferred. Trae had just finished an intense five hundred count of navy seal burpees. Perspiring and breathing hard, he put his radio on the station to listen to the Rickey Smiley show.

The doors popped at 5:30 a.m. to 5:45 a.m. in the mediums. No sooner than the CO cleared them to come out, Trae rushed out, headed straight to the 180 (hot water tank). After making his cup of coffee, he shot to the phone. Trae dialed Khashia's number in a blur takin' a sip of coffee as he waited for the number to process.

"Fuck! Pussy ass hoe! Playing games, man!" Trae said, loudly, causing a few heads to look towards him. "Fuck y'all looking at niggas? Mind yo' fucking business, shit!" he mumbled as he tried Khashia's number again four more times in a row to reach her voicemail. "Kill this dumb-ass bitch, man!" Trae shook his head frustratingly. Trae gave up. He got up and walked away, muggin', before he turned back around and picked the phone back up, dialing hastily. "Fuck it, call Mom dukes. Know she up," he mumbled as he listened to the phone ring.

"Man she ain't gon' answer, nigga! You sweatin' 'er too hard! John got dick up in 'er this long, fool! Boy, you got forty-five years still trying to keep ah bitch, ah goofy!" Perc said, standing in line waitin' for the phone, still holding his hands apart, showin' how much dick Khashia had up in her. He was cracking up knowing he was getting up under his partner's skin. Everyone in earshot started laughing.

"Fuck you, Perc! Ole stupid ass nigga! You been gone so long you don't know what pussy smells like, fool! Fuck you talking about? Anyway I ain't calling no bitch goofy ass nigga," he said, smirking at Perc.

"Yeah, I know. 'Cause she ain't answer for your stalking ass the first four times, Trae. I counted 'em, nigga! I'm on point, ain't it, man?" Perc laughed, then started talking to the man next to 'em while he gave Trae his privacy.

Perc was Trae's next-door neighbor. He had been gone from the streets twenty years on eighty. Perc acted and looked like he had just left the streets, though. He was also a prison nigga too.

Perc had his cell dressed up: cell floor waxed all shiny, compound pictures plastered all on his locker, bed, and wall of the hottest Instagram models. Perc had OCD—you could catch him cleaning his cell six times a day, every day. He also had the biggest store and ticket on the compound.

Perc took a liking to Trae 'cause Trae stayed prison fly too, and had hustle 'bout himself. "Look at 'em, look," Perc pointed toward Trae's back. "Nigga ain't talking to nobody but his ol' girl! Ain't nobody fucking with his dog ass!" Perc and the dude next to him shared a small chuckle.

Yeah, we'll see, fuck nigga! I see you got jokes. Huh? Parrot-ass nigga. All you do is talk your ass off! I get up right now and fire your lame ass up. Bet you 'ont do shit, Trae said in his head as he continued to talk to his mother.

"Yes, mom, I know. I should be out in a minute," he said, as he tried to straighten his face up. Trae was hotter than a busted radiator on an old box Chevy.

"Son, don't worry 'bout me. I'm going to be okay. I've lived my life. The good old doc said I have bone cancer, giving me six mo' months to live," she said, coughing another 30 seconds before gaining control over it.

"God has the last say-so, though," he said, wiping away a small tear forming in the corner of his eye.

"You right. He knows I'm ready."

"Stop it! Don't talk like that! I need you!"

"I know, but you will be alright. I raised you to be strong, son—"

"Mom, I need you to call that agent I told you 'bout. You remember? Tell 'em I got somin' for 'em," Trae whispered as low as he could.

"I did son," she said, her words broken by a raspy cough. "But—*cough . . . cough*—they didn't want that. It has to be worth their tim—"

The phone blinked out without warning

"Fuck! Fuck! Fuck! Man . . . Damn! Stupid ass phones, dawg!" Trae got up and stormed off, mad at the world. Trae went and got his things ready and went to take a shower.

In the shower, Trae cussed everybody out who he needed but didn't need him: Khashia, his mom, his homies, his two kids, God, Satan, and his new brother—Perc. Trae thought of every way possible to seek revenge against them all but came up short as an ant dick.

"I hope she come through like she say," he said, drying off.

***

Three Hours Later—
The infirmary
Trae sat in the hall on the bench, yellow rubber gloves on, staring at the big-boned white nurse with lust in his eyes as

20

she performed her routine blood draws. Every now and then, she would glance at Trae, blushing as she coyly poked her big SpongeBob-shaped booty out at him.

Trae smiled to himself as he looked at his G-shock watch. He picked her as his target because he peeped the low self-esteem in her. She was big, fat, lonely, desperate, and super friendly. Trae had been working her for the last two months, playing it smart. She wore a wedding ring, but he knew she wasn't getting fucked at home. She told him she never had dark meat before. Trae knew he had to play this right. *You only get one shot*, he told himself. So every day for his lunch break he'd stay back, and let the other two orderlies go. The big-boned nurse would do the same in regards to her coworkers when it was time for their lunch break. Then she and Trae would take the hour to get to know one another. Trae would finger fuck her, and she would beg for the dick, but he always held out.

Today, though, was different. Trae needed to release some built-up pressure. Plus, if she did what he asked of her, Trae was going to reward her with the magic stick.

"That's it! Nurse Gilbert announced cheerfully as the inmate she'd been working with stood up, nodded at Trae in passing, and disappeared down the hall. As soon as they were alone, Nurse Gilbert let her eyes linger on Trae like he was a T-bone steak, licking her lips suggestively. Trae smirked and gave her a nod. Trae scanned the hallway to make sure the coast was clear, then mouthed, **"You gonna eat this dick up today?"** while pointing to his crotch. Nurse Gilbert's eyes widened with excitement as she nodded eagerly in agreement. *I wasn't asking you, bitch! I was demanding it*, Trae thought to himself.

The second the last nurse left the room and locked the door behind her, Trae sprang into action. He hurried back around to Ms. Gilbert's office. When he made it there, she was seated at her desk, doing some paperwork. Trae barged in, unbuttoning his prison pants and slinging out a full erection. He didn't say a word—just guided himself straight into her open mouth. Nurse Gilbert didn't resist, taking him without hesitation, her lips sliding down his shaft until her chin pressed against his scrotum sac.

"Shiiiit!" Trae hissed, unable to stop himself. He stood on his tiptoes as she worked him over, her head bobbing with skillful precision. Seven minutes later, he was exploding down her throat, his knees trembling as she drained him dry. "Damn! That's right . . . just . . . like . . . that!" Trae groaned, working her head back and forth until he was satisfied. As soon as he was ready for round two, he pulled himself out of her mouth, letting her catch her breath. "Get up . . . turn around!" he ordered.

Nurse Gilbert did as she was told, standing and turning to face the desk Trae yanked her thin pants down forcefully, exposing her bare ass. She wasn't wearing any panties—not a stitch. Nurse Gilbert tried to look back at him, but Trae was aggressive. He pressed both hands on the back of her neck, pushing her forward until her palms were flat on the desk. Then, with no warning, he rammed his ten-inch rod deep into her wet, waiting hole.

"Mmm . . . Good . . . got . . . damn!" Trae bellowed, overwhelmed by how warm and tight she felt around him.

"Ahh . . . Aw . . . Ah . . . Ah . . . Yes . . . Yes!" Nurse Gilbert moaned, throwing it back on him with surprising enthusiasm.

"Uhn . . . uhn . . . uhn!" was all he managed to get out before he hit a few last long strokes and skeeted up in Nurse Gilbert.

Quickly, Trae pulled himself together, tucking himself back into his pants as Nurse Gilbert scrambled to pull hers up. She turned 'round too fast and kissed him in the mouth before he could stop her. Trae jerked back, wiping his lips. "Okay, that's enough for today. I want this to last," he said firmly, straightening his shirt. "Did you bring what I asked for?" he said, looking at her sternly, praying she did.

Nurse Gilbert nodded, a mischievous smile spreading across her face. "Yes. It's right here," she said, reaching into her desk drawer. She handed him a small brown bag. I even added a bunch of naked pictures for you, baby," she teased.

Ugh. I bet that shit looks like a got damn roll of speed bumps under that shit, Trae thought, hiding his disgust. "A'ight, bet. We good now. Let me get to work before they come back," Trae said, tucking the bag into his pocket. He left her office, heading off to check on the suicide patients and clean out the empty cells.

Three o'clock—
B3 Unit

Trae walked into his unit, dapping harder than Pimpin' Ken. His ego was bigger than a T-Rex at that moment. He didn't acknowledge anyone as he passed by. When got to his cell, first thing he noticed was an extra mattress on the top bunk with a small plastic bag sitting on it.

"Man, what the fuck!" He looked around for the unwanted celly he knew he had. Since he saw no one, he stepped into his cell and hung his towel over the door for privacy. Trae pulled the brown bag out and took the contents out. Moving with precision, he unscrewed the light switch, stuffed the small items inside, secured the cover back in place, and stepped back like nothing happened.

"Lockdown! Lockdown!" a CO shouted from the hallway.

As Trae stepped out of his cell, a dude was standing right outside.

"What's up, homes?" the dude said, extending his hand for a dap. "I'm Conscious."

"Trae. Where you from?" he asked, dapping Conscious.

"The A', shawty. Stop what you doin'," Conscious said.

"What side, homes?"

"Zone Six, shawty. You already know!"

23

"Say no more. Come on in, shawty. You got that work, don't you?" Trae asked, referring to his court dockets.

"Yeah . . . it's on the way, shawty."

"Already." They went in the cell. Trae drilled Conscious all the way through count until they unlocked the doors.

By the end of their talk, Trae had pieced together Conscious's story: he was only doing two months for a dirty urine violation. Outside of that, Conscious had no support system—no family, no friends. Trae also learned something about himself during their conversation: everybody he'd ever loved was gone, killed in a gang war before he got locked up.

Chapter 4

2 Days Later—
Dothan, Alabama

Packing up, Freak Zeenie moved himself, Khashia, and Deshawn to a nice spacious five-bedroom custom home out in Bocage. Surrounded by more than four acres, the house sprawled over 6,409 square feet, offering plenty of room for everyone to enjoy their own privacy. Nestled at the end of a cul-de-sac, it was the perfect setup.

When Freak called Regency Management, Inc., they linked him to Aleda Holmes. Once she heard him out, Aleda told Freak Zeenie that the house was the greatest hide-n-seek house of all time. Considering Bocage was one of Dothan's most prestigious neighborhoods, Freak didn't doubt it.

Money had given Freak Zeenie time to reset, so he took only the bare minimum and left everything else behind. Khashia followed his lead, leaving her belongings too.

Yet, despite telling the officers that nothing was missing, a lot was gone. All his Cartier frames and his entire Cartier watch collection had been stolen, but Freak Zeenie wasn't about to cooperate with the police. Street niggas kept it street. That was the law! What he did do was lace up his circle to keep their ear to the ground while putting out a healthy reward for anyone who could track down his stolen belongings. Cartier Jay, Boo-Boo, Kal-Kal, Remy Red, and Pooche were all trying to pick up that healthy check plus kill whoever tried their family like that.

Meanwhile, Freak wasted no time upgrading the house's security with SafeTouch. He was already a naturally paranoid person, but the break-in had him feeling "super-noid." If you ever get the chance to meet him, Freak will probably insist he's not paranoid—just cautious. "Safety first" was one of his cardinal rules.

Today, Freak Zeenie decided to bring out his white Ferrari 812. Determined to let the streets know he wasn't hiding or scared to enjoy his life, he cruised out confidently. Khashia, however, begged him to tone it down.

"I don't see why you driving that shit for anyway! You need to put that dumb car up!" she said.

"For what? We got that legal bread. I'm Freak Zeenie! The motherfuckin' ambassador! This my city," he replied, zipping down Nottoway Boulevard before taking a left onto Highway 84, and heading east toward Ross Clark Circle.

No sooner had he merged into traffic than his phone rang. "Yeah, shoot it, son!" Freak Zeenie answered, checking his mirrors as he cut off a car and let the Ferrari's engine roar forward like a helicopter.

"You need to come to the Bottom real fast. We have a situation," Cartier Jay said, his voice urgent.

"Shit! I'm on the way to—"

"The Bottom, I hope. Hurry!" Cartier Jay interrupted, cutting him off before the line went dead.

"Damn!" Freak Zeenie bellowed, weaving through traffic like he was in a high-speed chase. His frustration boiled over. "This shit better be good too!"

***

Across Town—
The Westside
In the bottom
Cartier Jay and Boo-Boo headed to the Bottom to see what was holding up their bread. It had been more than a

week since they had served the School Yard Crips in that area, and still no payment has come through. When they pulled up, a man in tattered clothes stood atop an air condition unit holding items high above his head.

"Man, look at these goofies! Out here spending a nigga's bread and shit! Fuck they got going on?" Cartier Jay said, bringing the car to a halt and throwing it into park.

"Sh-shit, look-look li-like th-they ho-holding a-a got-got damn opt-option o-or somethin'," Boo-Boo stammered, grimacing as he clutched his Drako. Cartier Jay smirked for a split second, knowing his partner meant to say "auction".

A sea of blue flags surrounded the tattered old man as the Crips hollered out bids, shouting over each other with no shame, desperately trying to outbid one another.

"This shit crazy! Niggas is wild, man!" Cartier Jay said, stepping out of the car and weaving his way through the sea of Crips to see what all the hype was 'bout. Boo-Boo followed close behind, his Drako pointing towards the ground beside his right leg but ready for action. When they got to the front of the crowd, Cartier Jay immediately spotted something that caught his attention.

"Aye, cuz? Let me see them glasses, fool!" Cartier Jay barked, holding out his for the glasses.

"Let me see some green backs first, young blood," the raggedy man said, continuing his auction. "Seven hundred— do I hear seven fifty? Seven-fifty, going once. Sounds like eight-hundred!" Do I hear ol'—"

"G-get yo-your bit-bitch a-ass d-down o-old fu-fuck! Nigga!" Boo-Boo snapped, sweeping the Drako hard under the old man's feet. The move sent the man flipping off the air conditioning unit, landing hard on his shoulder. "Arghh! My shoulder, man! My shoulder, young blood! You fuck my shoulder up," the tattered man hollered, rolling around on the ground like it would help him escape the pain he felt. The glasses he'd been holding scattered across the lawn. The

Crip niggas rushed to get their greedy hands on at least one pair of the designer frames.

"M-man I sw-swear on cuz! N-nan nigga bet not p-pick up shit o-out th-this b-bitch c-cu!" Boo-Boo bellowed, his mug hard as stone "I-I got th-the fl-flute w-with me! And I-I'll b-blow-ah n-niggas c-candles o-out! On G-God! n-Ni m-make a-ah w-wish!" He planted his feet apart, raising the Drako to chest level, daring anyone to challenge him on his threats so he could make 'em facts.

"Damn, cuz! You trippin? That's on School Yard, fool!" one of the gang members said, but remained still. It was no secret that Boo-Boo stood on business.

The old man managed to make it to one knee, groaning in pain.

"Arghh . . . shit!" he shrieked, only to be met with a hard kick to the chin from Cartier Jay, sending him sprawling back to the ground. Picking up a pair of the glasses Cartier Jay examined them closely. Taking a deep breath, he nodded, convinced. "Aye, junky ass nigga! Where the fuck you get these glasses from, nigga, huh?" he demanded, his eyes locked on the old man, awaiting an answer.

But the question scared the man into silence. He didn't say a word. The silence aroused Cartier Jay's anger. Instantly, he launched into a brutal beating, stomping the fiend before locking him in a death grip headlock and dragging him by the neck to the back porch of the bando (abandoned house). Boo-Boo trailed behind, making one of the Crips retrieve all the glasses from off the ground and give 'em to him.

Inside the bando, Boo-Boo slammed the door shut, leaving the curious crowd of Crips outside in suspense as they waited on Freak Zeenie to pull up. Cartier Jay forced the fiend into a worn-out kitchen chair while Boo-Boo tied the man's hands behind his back using the shoelaces from his own tattered sneakers.

"Where you get the glasses from?" Cartier Jay demanded again, smacking the fuck out the old man before he could receive an answer. He'd hit the old man so hard the old man's rotten front tooth almost came out. Cartier Jay drew back again, smacking him even harder once more.

Boo-Boo had his black Drako trained on the dope fiend, itching to pull the trigger. The old man was a person of no words all a sudden though, his silence only angered them both and caused the increasing of the old man's torture and punishment.

The schoolyard Crips stood close by the windows and the back door listening to the brutal beating that they heard taking place.

"Oow . . . shit! Sounds like they cracked his motherfucking skull, cuz . . . damn!" one member said, his expression heavy with discomfort.

"Hell yeah, cuz! He a G though. Nigga ain't said shit yet, my nigga!" another member said.

"Already! Junkie Que ah real fiend, boi! You know you got to give 'em a doub' first—20 rocks—cuz! Fuck wrong with 'em? They trippin' in there!" they joked, bursting into laughter until a loud exhaust roar interrupted them, catching their attention.

Freak Zeenie pulled up in the Bottom. Cutting the engine, he stepped out of his car, scanning the scene. After being absent on his bid that long, he couldn't help but notice that the generation had changed on him. Even though he was like a god in Dothan, Alabama, he only recognized a few faces, but everyone had heard something about something from something that Freak Zeenie had once done in the hood. Only a few really had had a chance to meet him personally.

Spotting his son's car, but not seeing him, Freak Zeenie pulled out his phone out Freak Zeenie and pressed speed dial.

"Yeah, I'm out here. Where you at, boy?" Freak Zeenie said, looking towards the old chipped painted wood house.

"Oh . . . a'ight. I'm on the way in now." He stepped out of his car, locking the doors with a press of a button on the key chain. The crowd of Crips watched in awe as he passed, their gazes glued to him like he was a living legend.

"Aye what up, cuz?" one of the Crips called out, but Freak Zeenie didn't respond. He gave only a brief nod, keeping his focus on the bando.

He was witnessin' his past with a different vision for his future. Seeing all the blue flags made him think back to when he was rolling strong with his Rolling 30s Crips on the west side of Dothan with his baby blue flag. Now though he was progressing and still processing his new transition.

Same time—
Across town
Bocage
Dothan, Alabama

Khashia got off the phone with her mom, who told her that Khashia's so-called ex been blowing up her phone, asking a heap of questions about Khashia's whereabouts. That conversation sent a wave of graveyard fear washing over Khashia, because it reminded her that she'd left her second phone back at their old house in Brentwood.

"Come on De'shawn! We got to go! Now!" she shrieked, her voice cracking with panic. She hadn't meant to sound so frantic, but there was no time to care how she looked or sounded. Khashia needed to move—fast.

"Come on, D! You walk faster than that when you want something!" she barked as she practically dragged De'shawn to the car. The boy stumbled, nearly losing his balance a couple of times because he wasn't moving fast enough for her.

"Okay, Auntie, okay! Calm down!" he protested, but his words fell on deaf ears. Khashia ain't hear shit her nephew said. Her mind was laser-focused on one thing: getting that phone back in her possession before it was too late. Before

De'shawn could even fully close his door, Khashia floored the gas pedal, burning rubber as she reversed out of her mother's driveway. The sudden burst of speed caused the wind to slam De'shawn's door shut without him even touching it.

***

Back in the Bottom—
Inside the Bando

"Mann . . . Junky Que? What the hell you got goin' on, old man?" Freak Zeenie asked, his tone laced with a mix of humor and disbelief. Seeing a former legend turned fiend was bittersweet. While he was amused at the sight, he couldn't help but feel a twinge of disappointment. Freak Zeenie just stared at Junky Que with a skewed expression, waiting for some kind of explanation. But as the silence dragged on too long, an uneasy feeling crept over him. Cartier Jay seemed just as surprised. His head tilted to the side in disbelief. "You know this junked out piece of shit, Pops?" said he asked, looking at Freak Zeenie for an answer—not because it really mattered, but just to satisfy his curiosity. "Hell yeah! Man, we go way, way back! Boi this nigga taught me how to cook up," Freak Zeenie began before pausing to correct himself. "Well, fuck *taught me*, but this old coon Junky Que illustrated the underworld of the shit to me like no other, boi!" Freak Zeenie got overly excited just thinking 'bout things that his past experiences had gained him, but just as quickly, the joy faded, replaced by a grimace as the darker parts of his history weighed heavy on him.

Meanwhile, Junky Que's head had swollen to the size of a watermelon. One of his eyes was completely shut, and the other was not far behind. Straining to open his good eye, he stretched it as wide as possible and croaked out through busted lips and broken teeth, "Freak Zeenie? That's you?" The recognition brought him a flicker of hope. "Man... tell 'em to let me go, man!" Junky Que pleaded, clinging to the voice he hadn't heard in over a decade but could still recognize even in the middle of an F-5 tornado and hurricane happening at the same damn time.

Freak Zeenie nodded at Cartier Jay and Boo-Boo, signaling them to release Junky Que.

"Fuck *that*!" Cartier Jay snapped, still pointing at the designer glasses. "Where you get these glasses from, ol' smokin' ass nigga? Or I'm 'bout to make crackhead noodles up in this bitch! Y'all watch out."

"Nawl, son. Untie the old man. He good," Freak Zeenie said firmly.

"He *good*?" Cartier Jay repeated it like he was trying to comprehend the request, but Freak Zeenie nodded again in agreement. "Psst! Man, untie this raggedy-ass nigga, Boo-Boo before I—" Cartier Jay balled his fists so tight that his knuckles turned white. Boo-Boo reluctantly lowered his weapon, propping it up against the table but keeping it within reach. He then released the makeshift restraints off Junky Que.

Junky Que massaged his sore hands as if trying to warm up. Straining to see Freak Zeenie through his badly damaged eye. "Thanks, man. Long time no see. At least someone still respect their elders and OGs. These new young bloods—"

"We crippin' on this side old skool! Keep that sneak dissin' young blood shit to yourself and on that east side, nigga!" Cartier Jay snapped, frustration dripping from every word. His glare fixed on Junky Que with murderous intent.

"See what I mean, Freak?" Junky Que said, turning to Freak Zeenie for support.

"Times have truly changed, old head. You either evolve, adapt, or stay the same," Freak Zeenie replied. "See me," he pointed to himself. "I'm relevant to the present, and ahead of the curve of the future, yah hear me?" He let his words hang in the air for a moment before glancing at the glasses on the counter. "Now, the million-dollar question is," he paused, his voice turning cold, "did you break into my house and steal my shit, Junky Que? And before you answer, remember: this is *Freak Zeenie* you're talking to."Junky Que's face tensed, but he quickly shook his head. "Come on, Freak Zeenie! This me, baby!" Junky Que patted his chest. "Junky Que. Loved by many, and hated by few! You know me better than that. I'll never give up my resources, and fuck up my endorsements Freak," he said with much satisfaction. Freak Zeenie listened, letting the words sink in. He knew Junky Que was cut from the old-school cloth. and wouldn't sell out even if the price was his life. That made him hold that admiration that he always held for Junky Que in the manner that he always had, despite his addiction that had shrunk his hood fame so close that it was almost none.

Trembling, Junky Que strained to keep his one good eye open. "Just know, Freak that I'll never disrespect you knowingly, and I'm just finding out that you then made it back out here." He paused, wincing. "Now, I think that should sum it up for all y'all." Without waiting for a response, he added, "If y'all don't mind, Junky Que got shit to do, and right now I need to be where I'm gon' be before I can't see at all."

Junky Que limped out, passing them on his way out the bando, holding on to his shoulder visibly in major pain. Making it out the bando, Junky Que took off, jogging down the street.

Man, I can't believe this shit. If I knew it was Freak's house, I'd never took that job. Crooked ass bitch set us up! Wait 'til I see my brother Sam and tell him this crazy ass shit! I hope he got rid of them fucking watches, Junky Que thought as his mind raced faster than the cars on a Daytona 500 race track. Making it to the end of the street, Junky Que turned and disappeared out the hood, and out of harm's way.

Cartier Jay glanced at Freak Zeenie. "Why you let that smoking ass nigga go, Pops?"

"I owe 'em one. Plus, y'all beat him pretty good, and I got my glasses back. So let 'em make it."

"Fa' sho. Well, I still need my lil change, though. I done my part. You let the nigga get away before we could frisk that smoking ass nigga. He probably got all your watches still on him," Cartier Jay said, looking at Freak Zeenie with concern.

"Gotdammit! Son, you shole right! Man, why you let me do that? You suppose to have said something," Freak Zeenie bolted out of the bando in a rush, his glasses in one hand, looking round, hoping to spot Junky Que before he got away.

"Aye! Which way the old man go, y'all?" he called out to the Crips outside.

"He jogged down that way, cuz!" one of them said, pointing in the direction Junky Que went.

"Fuck! We got to catch Junky Que slick ass, man! Them watches cost fifty or better!"

Freak Zeenie jumped in his Ferrari, stomped the gas pedal to the floor, shaking the ground, and spun the car in a wild a donut before zipping back in the direction he had come from. Cartier Jay and Boo-Boo tried to keep up, but the sports car moved like a streak of lightning, leaving them far behind. So they did as best they could.

But it was a lost cause. Junky Que was long gone. You might catch anyone else, but a crackhead? Once they start running, it's over.

Same time—
Brentwood

Worry and fear were etched across Khashia's face once she exited her old house empty-handed. Khashia just couldn't wrap her mind around the fact that she had forgotten to check under the dresser for her phone. Now, it was gone. All she could do was shake her head, as if that would make the disappointment go away.

Checking the date on her phone, she muttered under her breath, "Shit! Still got at least a week and a fucking half before the damn thing turns off. Fuck!"

She cursed herself for not having it on a contract. If it were, she could have just called to have it tracked or shut off. But since it wasn't, time had suddenly become her worst enemy. Trying to console herself, she scoffed, "Fuck that shit! Who's gonna find out . . . God?" She brushed it off, hoping whoever broke into the house had stolen the phone and already pawned it off somewhere.

With frustration lingering in the air, Khashia and De'shawn went back home. Their minds raced with different thoughts, never realizing that they were being followed the whole time.

Chapter 5

Zacatecas, Mexico
A Day and a Half Later—
Zacatecas sent for Freak Zeenie, asking him to come and stay with him for a while. There were things he needed Freak Zeenie to fully understand. At first, Freak Zeenie tried to protest, but Zacatecas' decisions was always non-negotiable.

Freak Zeenie rode on the helicopter, squeezed between two brawny Mexican's who spoke only five or six perfect English words. *Fuck this gotdamn Migo think he is?* Zeenie fumed silently. *I ain't with all this bossing around ass TV shit either. Can't wait to see his lil short ass so I can tell 'em! Got me fucked up!* Freak Zeenie replayed in his mind how he was about to check Zacatecas on sight.

Moments Later—
The helicopter began its descent into the center of a sprawling thirty-thousand-square-foot compound. Freak Zeenie's eyes widened briefly in awe before he quickly remembered how much he despised Zacatecas. He didn't like the man—not even a little. His expression remained stoic, refusing to show any hint of wonder.

Armed Hummer trucks lined the compound, and nearly two thousand Paisa soldiers patrolled the grounds, heavily armed with assault rifles. Zacatecas was the head of the Paisas, commanding them worldwide. Despite the enormous responsibility, Zacatecas always seemed calm and in control.

Freak Zeenie was escorted off the helicopter into a waiting Hummer. A burly Mexican security guard snatched the phone, and he was frisked more times before reaching Zacatecas than he had been during his whole prison bid. They drove him deeper into the compound, passing acres of barren, woodless land.

Five Minutes Later—

If this ain't some ol' A&E Discovery Channel shit, then I don't know what is. Freak Zeenie kept his thoughts concealed in his head as the truck crept to a stop. The door was snatched open, and four strong arms grabbed Freak Zeenie roughly, pulling him out of the vehicle.

"Aye, aye, aye, man! Fall the fuck back with all that shit! Fuck wrong wit' y'all!" said he barked, snatching himself free and mugging them with death in his eyes.

Ignoring his request, the soldiers quickly rushed back in.

"English, señor!!" Zacatecas loudly said. Everything stood still except time. "Freak Zeenie . . . I hope you enjoyed the ride, sí? I requested the scenic route." He searched Freak Zeenie's eyes. He couldn't read them and started feeling a pang of jealousy but he quickly regrouped.

"Oh, we both are men of importance, is we not, sí?"

Freak Zeenie didn't respond.

"Are you not happy at my home?" Zacatecas spread his arms wide, as if embracing the compound. "Me castle, your castle, mi amigo," he chortled, amused by himself.

Still, Freak Zeenie remained silent. He glanced to his left and noticed a man, beaten, gagged, and tied up, standing against what looked like a makeshift shooting range.

"Ah . . . come walk with me, Freak. Can I call you Freak, without the Zeenie?" Zacatecas asked casually as he began leading Freak Zeenie toward the bound man.

"What is this 'bout, Zacatecas? You are on my time homes. I got shit that needs to be done," Freak Zeenie said, becoming frustrated all over again. They stopped in front of the bound man.

"See, I like you because of yo' fearlessness, amigo," Zacatecas said. Suddenly, a little boy—no older than ten—appeared out of nowhere. He ran up and snatched a rifle from one of the soldiers.

"You see that bound man right there, Freak?" He pointed towards the bound man.

"Yeah, and? What that got to do with me?"

"He no good for business. I provide plate for him. Make a way for him to eat, and the no-good bastard stole from me," he claimed. Zacatecas' face flushed red with anger.

"Why?" Freak Zeenie hunched his shoulders.

"No loyalty! That's why. He wanted to feed his family, but wanted mine to starve."

Zacatecas snapped his fingers, and a pregnant woman with two small kids suddenly appeared, lined up alongside the bound man. Soldiers ripped the blindfold off the man's face.

The ten-year-old boy was now holding the rifle to his shoulder. He looked back at Zacatecas, who nodded his approval. "That's my youngest son right there. He wants to be just like his papa."

Blistering gunshots rang out, echoing across the compound as the boy cut the woman and kids damn near in half before shooting the man over thirty times, riddling him with bullets before falling from the recoil of the massive weapon.

The boy scrambled to his feet, looking up at his father for approval. Zacatecas gave him a proud nod, and he ran off without further instructions.

Freak Zeenie clenched his jaw tightly. He loved kids—all of them. What he had just witnessed made his blood boil, but he knew better than to show emotion here. He was out of his element, and no one even knew his whereabouts.

"You are taking too long to get me my money, amigo, Zacatecas said, turning to face Freak Zeenie. "I know everyone do things differently, but time waits for no one. Bills must be paid. Your plate is also full. You need to get it moving, my amigo. Use the trucks . . . that's what they are there for. Is there a problem with the product or something?" Zacatecas looked Freak Zeenie square in the eyes.

"I heard nothing yet. I'm putting it out there, but I'm putting it out there, but I'm limited on workers," Freak Zeenie replied, throwing his hands up with a bleak expression. "Trust isn't even in my vocabulary, my man. Give it a couple of months—things should have stretched out by then. That's all I can explain to you."

Zacatecas smirked. "Nawl you will do good. You're a smart man. I know you will figure it out. I'll hate for that to be Khashia over there along with your newfound son against my son testing each other's DNA to see who's the strongest, you know?" Zacatecas said it like it was just common for these types of situations to occur all the time. "In this game, Freak Zeenie, you have to have a cold heart to win, or—" he made a gun out his point finger. "Bang! You dead! We're done."

With that, Zacatecas turned on his heels and climbed into a black armored Maybach.

Freak Zeenie didn't have a chance to speak or defend himself. He was quickly ushered back inside the Hummer and then onto the helicopter.

The whole way back to the States, the death of these innocent kids played over and over again in his mind. Freak Zeenie knew one thing for sure: if you kill the head, the tail will follow. He knew what he had to do in order to come out on top.

Freak Zeenie begun plotting his plan.

Chapter 6

The Next Day—
Dothan Police Department
Dothan, Alabama

Officer Bentley, bulky white officer, had to dip into his 401(k) to pay off the dispatcher he was having an affair with. The hush money ensured she wouldn't report the response to the breaking and entering (B&E) at the house in Brentwood. He and his partner, Officer Fortune, had been scouring the city, searching high and low for the two brothers, Sam and Junky Que.

Officer Bentley walked into the break room, looking nervous as could be. The last thing he needed was to become an overnight felon, all because of his vendetta against an alleged criminal. Right now, he was borderline alcoholic.

Meanwhile, Officer Fortune's personal life had completely unraveled. His marriage had crumbled apart, taking away his fatherhood. The courts had ruled that he was allowed only two hours of visitation with his two kids on weekends. Even though Officer Fortune was young, he was slowly falling apart. Right now, he would try anything to escape the damaging pain he endured—even crack. Letting out a nervous breath, Fortune massaged his temples with his thumbs while waiting for Bentley to speak. His head was cloudy, thanks to five shots of Cuervo he'd downed just minutes ago in his car.

Officer Bentley looked at Officer Fortune with anger in his eyes.

"How'd it go? How'd it go?" Fortune asked.

"That good-for-nothing, low-down dirty skank—Bitch charged me ten fucking grand for that shit, Fortune."

He walked towards Officer Fortune, stopping just inches away. The tension between them was thick as they spoke in hushed tones. Bentley's eyes narrowed, and disgust crept onto his face. "I thought we agreed—no drinking while on the job, Fort!" he snapped, shaking his head in disapproval.

Ignoring Fortune's sheepish expression, Bentley continued his tirade. "Man, I got slammed with penalties for pulling money out of my pension early. Five grand just for that alone. And then I had to explain to her we might need her help again. That's when the cunning bitch tacked on another five grand!" His face flushed as red as a strawberry as he ranted.

"Ten grand? You kiddin' me," Fortune shrieked, ignoring the drinking part that his partner had just chastised him about.

"Do I look like I'm fuckin' kiddin'?" Bentley shot back, his tone seething with frustration. "Which reminds me. Let's hit the streets, and find these two pipe heads. I read the reports on the Brentwood incident, and it said that nothing was missing." He snorted and gave Fortune a look dripping with skepticism. "Yeah, right. "Kiss my hairy ass if it wasn't! Somebody trying to be slick!"

Bentley rubbed the bridge of his nose in irritation. "Them two son-of-bitches got to pay—or the next job is a freebie," he muttered. With that, they both stood and walked out the breakroom.

Before they could take more than a few steps, Chief O'Neill stormed out of his office, cutting them off mid-stride.

"Officer Bentley! Officer Fortune! My office. *Now!*" Chief O'Neill shouted in their faces like they were across the room, though he was well within arm's reach. Chief O'Neill face expressed anger, anger, and more anger. Turning on the ball of his feet he beelined back towards his office in a haste. Officer Bentley and Officer Fortune both looked at each other hunching their shoulders.

Seconds Later—
Chief O'Neill's Office
Chief O'Neill stood behind his desk, his face twisted in fury, holding his hand out. "Give me your badges!"

"Huh?" Both officers responded at the same time, blinking in disbelief.

"You heard correct! Your badges—and unarm yourselves too while you at it! Come on, come on! I haven't got all day now!"

Neither Officer Bentley nor Office Fortune moved

"For what?" they both asked simultaneously, as if they were rapping the lyrics to their favorite song or something.

Same Time—
Across town
Ms. Lois had just gotten off the phone with their family lawyer, overwhelmed with joy after receiving some wonderful news. She thanked him profusely before ending the call.

"Thank you, Lord, in Jesus name!" she exclaimed, clapping her hands and spinning in celebration.

"I got to call Deacon and tell him how wonderful Jesus is!" she said to herself, picking up her phone. Turning on the TV to the news station, she dialed Deacon's number.

Meanwhile, Freak Zeenie stepped out the shower, drying himself off. Hearing his phone chime, he called out, "I'm comin' . . . I'm comin'," as he walked into the master bedroom.

"Ah, hello! Hi, Mom Dukes. How you doing? Everything okay?" he answered, sounding upbeat and jovial.

"Good morning, Deacon! Yes, yes everything's fine, son. I'm blessed and highly favored," Ms. Lois said warmly., "Well, I was calling to share the good news with you, son!" She looked at her TV. "Ooow-oow! Turn on the TV, Deacon, to the news! Hurry, hurry up, son. This it!" she shouted joyfully.

Both of them tuned in to the same news broadcast."Hi. I'm Angela Mone, and this is BREAKING NEWS," the anchor announced.

"Coming in as we speak." The camera cut to the front of the Belvedere of Dothan's Police Department, where reporters from surrounding areas crowded the entrance, microphones raised.

"Two officers have just been terminated after a civil law suit won against the Department. The suit claimed that two officers—Bentley, who was only a couple of years away from retirement, and his partner, Fortune, who had been on the force for just five years—unlawfully pulled over a civilian named Earlie D. Barber on the interstate and harassed him during the stop."

Angela continued, "Footage from their body cams, which was recovered after they intentionally turned off both their body and dash cams, revealed egregious misconduct. As word spread, cars began pulling up outside the station, and within seconds, hundreds of people flooded the streets, holding signs high in the air."

The screen showed crowds chanting in unison:

'*BLACK LIVES MATTER! BLACK LIVES MATTER!*'

The streets were covered with colored folks, demanding justice.

Angela returned to the screen, continuing her report. "Not only did these two officers embarrass the department, but they also deeply hurt the community they were sworn to protect," she said solemnly. Then, suddenly, her tone shifted. "Oh, wait! Here they come now!"

The camera panned to Bentley and Fortune stepping out of the station. Angela Mone rushed forward, microphone extended. "Officers Bentley and Fortune, how does this affect the community?" she asked as she and other reporters swarmed Officer Bentley and Fortune, peppering them with questions.

Both officers ignored the chaos, brushing off the reporters' questions as they made their way to their vehicles. "Well, silence speaks volumes, folks! There you h—"

Freak Zeenie, watching from home, smirked. "Good for their low-down as—I mean low-down selves!" He caught himself mid-sentence, refraining from using desecrating language while still on the phone with his mom.

"I told you, son! Be patient! God will always have your back when wrong hunts you for no reason! So, how do you feel?"

"Like taking everyone out for dinner on me. It's a celebration. So let's celebrate!" Freak Zeenie replied enthusiastically.

"Sounds good to me, Deacon! I'll start calling everyone getting them prepared."

"Alright, call me when it's done. And Mom Dukes?"

"Yes, Deacon?"

"Love youuu!"

Ms. Lois chuckled. "I love you more, Deacon. Later on." She disconnected.

Freak Zeenie turned back to the TV just in time to see both officers fishtail out the parking lot, almost running over the mass crowd of civilians gathered in the street to celebrate and demonstrate.

"Stupid asses! Freak Zeenie muttered, shaking his head. Then, speaking louder, as if the people on the TV could hear him, he said, "I told yah! Don't fuck with me! You'll never be nobody else in this city again! I may not be shit to you! But I'm the *shit* in this city! The ambassador! You hear me?"

Freak Zeenie chuckled, shaking his head again, and turned off the TV. He continued getting dressed before leaving the house.

Chapter 7

Same Day—
Smokey Pigs
Dothan, Alabama

The sun was halfway up as Freak Zeenie sat at a booth in *Smokey Pigs*, discussing his latest victory with his Uncle James. Freak Zeenie ate a hearty breakfast of cheese eggs, buttered Texas toast, and extra cheesy grits, washing it all down with a glass of cold, freshly squeezed orange juice. The two men laughed, enjoying each other's company, but Freak Zeenie's eyes kept darting to his wristwatch. For the third time in fifteen minutes, he checked the time.

"Gotta be somewhere, Freak? Or are you expecting someone?" Uncle James asked, sensing the impatience in his nephew.

"Uh, yeah. I'm am, Unk," Freak Zeenie said, frowning. "This late ass uncle of mines holding me up."

"Who?"

"The counterfeit pastor. Who else!" Freak Zeenie replied, and they both burst into laughter. "He's supposed to come pick up his lil bread I owe him. Should leave his crazy ass and make him wait, since he's always late."

"Oh yeah," Uncle James chuckled. "Well, you know how Pastor Barber is. Can't live with 'em, can't live without 'em."

No sooner as the words left uncle James' mouth than Pastor Barber walked into *Smokey Pigs*, swaggering in like he owned the place, dapping hard as he could. Today, he wore dark, big-frame Gucci shades, a royal purple Polo suit, and yellow quarter-cut gator boots. He threaded his way through the crowded restaurant.

"Look more like a pimp to me than a pastor now," Uncle James said, unable to hold back his comment.

"Mm-hmm," Freak Zeenie murmured in agreement as Pastor Barber took the stool next to him, placing a handful of gold and diamond rings on the counter.

"S'up, nephew?" Pastor Barber greeted him. Freak Zeenie looked to his lap.

Freak Zeenie's phone chimed, interrupting the moment. He held up a finger. "I gotta take this," he said, swiping the screen. "S'up, Uncle Duke? Been waiting on this call for some time now," he said before falling silent to listen.

"Yeah, I know. Uncle Duke began. "I had to pull some strings for that hard-headed Levi, but I got 'em pulled. You tell his nappy-headed, poor-ass I said this the last time, too!" His voice was firm. "Fuck wrong with him? Tell him: Don't cop out! Go to trial! No matter what they say—trial, trial, trial! He will win I put my casket on it, Nep."

"Alright," Freak Zeenie replied.

"Nephew?" Pastor Barber called out, snapping him from his thoughts. "Everything alright, ain't it?" Pastor Barber asked, putting a hand on Freak Zeenie's shoulder.

"Yeah, yeah. Shit's good." Freak Zeenie looked around, having second thoughts 'bout giving Pastor Barber a wad full of cash inside the place of business, because it was too crowded. Standing up abruptly, he said, "Come on, man, with your always-late ass self. Let's step outside."

"So long, Uncle James." Freak Zeenie called over his shoulder as he walked toward the door.

"Already, nephew! Stay dangerous! You hear me?" Uncle James said, trying to sound hip and trendy.

Freak Zeenie nodded, but said not another word until he was outside.

Once outside, he turned to Pastor Barber. "Here, man, you got to tighten up! Time ain't to be wasted. It's to be managed," Freak Zeenie said as he casually handed Pastor Barber a brown paper bag. It contained the remaining money he owed, plus an advance on the next shipment. "Be ready in two days. Get your old ass down here by nine in the morning, Unk," he said, climbing into his jeep.

"Okay, okay, nine in the morning," Pastor Barber said, fast-talking, his mouth dry as a desert.

"Yeah, in the *morning*! Not at night—or your ass is fired!" Freak Zeenie yelled as he drove off, his words trailing behind him as he disappeared into traffic.

Freak Zeenie was headed to Montgomery, Alabama.

Three Hours Later—
Montgomery County Jail . . .
The Federal Floor
The TV blared from its mount high on the wall as inmates bustled around B-Pod. Commissary workers had just finished their rounds, leaving the inmates to their daily routines. Some gambled on the chess board, while others had a poker table going on at another table.

Levi, housed in B-Pod, sat at another table playing Georgia Skin.

The loud intercom cackled.

"Levi Maddox— Levi Maddox! You have a visit!" a very sweet-sounding female voice announced.

"A'ight! On the way! You can pop the door!" Levi called out, already on his feet and ready to leave.

Turning to a fellow inmate, Levi said, "Aye, Mozzy? Come house this shit while I check this free world demo out right fast, mi-boi!"

"Sho—kno' what to say, when to say it," Mozzy said, wasting no time sliding into Levi's spot at the table and getting in the game.

Seconds Later—
Visiting Room

Levi sat in front of the 13-inch TV screen, picking the phone up. As soon as he did, the screen went from pitch-black to showing Freak Zeenie's face.

"What's up, bruh?" Levi said, breaking the ice. He knew he'd fucked up especially after the Feds had indicted him.

"Shit!" Freak Zeenie said, sternly holding a stoic face. "Look at you!" Freak Zeenie shook his head. "Head hard as these walls they surrounded your crazy ass with, nigga!" he said. "This where you wanna be Huh? Coulda been came and swapped places with me along time ag—"

"Man, fuck all that!" Levi bellowed, cutting Freak Zeenie off. "I ain't came out here to hear all that goofy ass shit, nigga! Fuck you talking 'bout? Shit, I coulda stayed in there playing Skin instead of listening to this dumb shit, nigga!"

The brothers stared each other down through the screen for a tense moment.

"Yeah?" Freak Zeenie asked, leaning in slightly.

"Hell yeah!" Levi's face balled up. Truth be told, he knew he couldn't change the situation now no matter what. The Feds had built a rock-solid case against him. Being that he got jammed with everything, it wouldn't be hard to convince a jury with the evidence that they had.

Looking at his younger brother, Freak Zeenie shook his head again. "Remind me to kick your ass when you get out!"

"Yeah, alright. You'll have to lift me out my wheel chair first to do it, though, old ass nigga!" Levis shot back.

"I 'ont know now! God is good," Freak Zeenie.

"All the time!"

"Yeah, I chopped it up with Uncle Duke this morning."

"And?"

"And he said, they faking! They don't have shit on you, so go to trial! Don't take no plea or you will be in that wheelchair when you get out," Freak Zeenie paused for emphasis. "Go. To. Trial."

"Yeah? They only have what? Thirty bricks! Enough to put me underground with the rest of the drug lords they already have."

"I talked to your lawyer before coming here. He should be coming through later also. I had to give him another twenty bands. We owe him forty more."

"Alright. Trial is set for next month, which is in two weeks, if I don't take the plea."

"The plea isn't an option. Oh, Uncle Duke said to tell you this is your *last* time on his end too!" He said. "No more card tricks. He ran out of magic . . . for you, anyway."

Levi plastered a cheesy smirk across his face.

"Yeah, I gotcha. Tell 'em I said I owe him one," Levi replied, holding up one finger.

"I gotcha—" The screen suddenly went blank.

"A'ight, Maddox. Visit time's up. The door is already popped!" the same sweet-voiced female officer announced over the intercom.

"Say no mo'," Levi said, walking back to his pod with his head held high with confidence of a king.

Later That Evening—
B-Pod

Levi's lawyer had left hours ago, but his message was clear: if Levi chose to go to trial, he would win. The drug lab had finally sent back the forensic results, and it turned out that the thirty-thousand plus grams weren't cocaine at all— but dry sheetrock.

Levi sat on his bunk, animatedly explaining the news to his bunky.

"I'm telling you, nigga! I'm 'bout to blow this joint, fool!" Levi said, jumping up and gesturing wildly with his hands.

"Pssht! Man, get the fuck outta here with all that lying-ass shit, fool! We both know you don't beat the Feds, nigga!" his bunky snapped, clearly annoyed. "When they get you,

you done—*until they finish!*" his celly said, getting up, frustrated, raising his voice a few octaves above normal.

"Nigga, calm down nigga! I don't want everybody knowing I'm 'bout to vamp!" Levi hissed, trying to diffuse the situation. "When I do jump through, I am opening up a jewelry store, and murder some sh—"

"Why not?" his bunky interrupted, ignoring Levi's attempts to move on.

"What?" Levi asked, confused.

"Why not? Why you don't want nobody to know, nigga? Fuck you got going on?" His bunky stared him down, mugging him hard.

"Because my lawyer is filing for a dismissal in the morning, clown-ass nigga!" Levi looked at his celly. "And I wanna be the one to show out first, Oh, I-see. You think of me as one of them counterfeit-ass niggas, huh? I'm faking?" Levi's tone grew sharper. "Look, stupid-ass nigga, you ain't got nothin' but a motherfucking pistol charge, bitch-ass nigga, that you probably was holding for somebody else with your lil dusty ass se—"

"Fuck all that slick talk, pussy! I think you ho—"

Before his bunky could finish his statement, Levi threw a jab so hard straight off the left shoulder. The punch landed clean, splitting Levi's knuckles and busting his bunky's mouth wide open.

They went at it, fighting viciously in the cell as the entire unit banged on their doors, cheering them on. It didn't take long for the COs to hear the commotion and rush the scene, alerted by the dry-snitching inmates shouting details to the guards. The COs had to drag Levi from off his celly. Levi came out the cell with one sock on and one off, and long red welp down the center of his chest. His celly came out in a wheelchair having an asthma-attack which turnt into a seizure with two black eyes to match.

The unit went crazy saying all kinds of wild remarks, teasing the loser who—unfortunately—couldn't hear none of it anyway. Levi's celly was shaking like a stripper.

Levi went straight to the hole. Only doing a night.

The Next Evening—

Once Levi's lawyer filed the motion, the prosecutor had no choice but to agree with the dismissal. If he wanted to save the government money, and himself from embarrassment. This made the prosecutor grow a strong hate for Russell County, Alabama, because they'd brought him a bogus case.

By nightfall Levi's release was the biggest news wave across country. It had been aired everywhere. His lawyer's popularity skyrocketed instantaneously.

Levi was free at last!

Chapter 8

Sunday Evening—
Father's Day & Juneteenth . . .
Montgomery, Alabama

Freak Zeenie was in his element. Momma Lois had planned a beautiful family gathering to celebrate the recent victory against Dothan's Police Department. The family was ecstatic over the outcome of the lawsuit and the termination of the two officers who had long harassed the Black community. The timing couldn't have been better—it was both Father's Day and Juneteenth, a perfect combination of celebration and freedom. Ten all-black Cadillac Escalades rolled out in a line, compliments of Freak Zeenie. His whole family was traveling in style, departing from his "Change of Heart" program building and heading to Montgomery, Alabama.

Momma Lois chose Longhorn Steakhouse as the location for their family feast. The restaurant, situated at the corner of Troy Highway and South Boulevard, was bustling as usual. But when the 10 luxury SUVs graced the restaurant's parking lot, they made a statement without a single word being spoken.

Inside LongHorn Steakhouse—

Freak Zeenie, Khashia, De'shawn, Levi, Remy Red, Poochie, Uncle Duke and his wife, Pastor Barber and his wife, and Uncle James all sat on one side of the long table that they had arranged for the occasion. Across from them sat Momma Lois, all Freak Zeenie's kids, and at the far end were his aunts from Momma Lois's side of the family.

However, the whole family couldn't quit staring at De'shawn. Their lingering gazes were making him visibly uncomfortable. Sitting next to him, Khashia could feel his unease. She assumed the family might know about De'shawn's situation and were feeling pity for him, but to both of them, the constant staring felt rude and unnecessary. De'shawn leaned closer to Khashia.

"Tee, why do these people keep looking at me like that?" he whispered, his voice low and cautious. While he was speaking to Khashia, each set of eyes he met . . . they just nodded a forward head gesture, greeting him with a soft smile.

"It's okay, De'shawn. They like you, that's all. I promise" Khashia said, touching his arm reassuringly.

"Okay, Tee, but—"

"Shh . . ." Khashia hushed him, cutting his sentence short, gently placing her hand on his arm again. Even though she tried to comfort him, she was thinking the same thing: *They are being rude with the constant staring, though.* For a moment, she thought about saying something, but when her eyes met Freak Zeenie's across the table, she dismissed the idea as quickly as it had arrived.

Pastor Barber, sweating profusely, wiped his forehead with a handkerchief before pushing his chair back and rising to his feet. Clearing his throat, he spoke:

"A'ight, family! Let's give God His glory for all these wonderful blessings first. That would be the right thing to do." His tone carried a flair of theatrics as he gestured broadly. "Now, everyone on your feet, and bow your heads, please!"

Once everyone stood and bowed their heads, Pastor Barber instructed, "Join hands."

"Oh Heavenly Father," he began, "we gather together on this most highly blessed day in honor of Your Son, Jesus Christ, to give thanks for all the strong and providing fathers here, Lord. We ask that *You* instill not just in the uncolored people, but also in the colored folks, more love and less hate for mankind."

At this point, Pastor Barber was pouring sweat, but carried on, his voice steady. "We are Your creation, Lord," he said, "and we also want to thank *You* for the return of Levi, Father God. He has been a blessing to this family in too many ways to name." Pastor Barber paused to take a long sniff, clearing the drainage from his nose. De'shawn grew increasingly irritated, finding the overly long prayer tiresome and unnecessary. As Pastor Barber droned on, completely unaware, De'shawn's thoughts turned sharp, mentally picking apart every word of the prayer.

Freak Zeenie opened one eye and glanced at his uncle, shaking his head before refocusing on the prayer.

"Now, where was I?" Pastor Barber said. "Oh, yeah. Thank *You*, Father God for Earlie, too—returning him back home to us, as we all missed him dearly!" Pastor Barber's prayer dragged on, and everyone's arms began to sag from holding hands for so long.

"Father God, thank *You* for—"

"This food that we 'bout to eat! Amen!" De'shawn bellowed, cutting Pastor Barber off mid-sentence.

Khashia squeezed his hand tightly.

"De'shawn? You apologize right now!" she hissed.

"Man, I'm hungry, Tee! He 'bout to pray us into a graveyard from starvation soon if he didn't end it," De'shawn muttered, glaring at Pastor Barber, who frowned back at him.

"Amen," Pastor Barber slowly said, patting his drenched forehead and collar with a napkin.

"Thank you, Jesus!" Momma Lois shouted, breaking the tension as everyone laughed lightly and took their seats. Freak Zeenie let out a small chortle out, looking at Levi.

Pushing back his chair, Freak Zeenie stood, holding his flute that was half full—or half empty, whichever way you look at it.

"I would like to make a toast, everyone!" he began, looking warmly at his family. "To us wonderful fathers and our outstanding kids that we are more than proud of."

He raised his glass higher. "Let's drink to the fact that, despite all the bad things that tried to tear us apart, they only brought us closer! Made us stronger!"

The family cheered lightly.

"To my freedom, of course. And to Levi's close call," he added, prompting some laughter. "To, my youngest son who is in his third year in Troy University, third year as a starter on the football team," Freak Zeenie said, nodding toward his son. "Number five, I'm proud of you, son! You're on your way to the NFL! Play hard, K'."

Freak Zeenie then turned to his daughter. "And to Dee, for finishing school on time! You did that! To all my kids— I love y'all. Keep up the good work! Y'all done all this without me here to assist you, so I know y'all gon' be great!"

Finally, he looked at the women of the family. Everyone knew Freak Zeenie could be long winded but De'shawn. "To the women that were in my corner while I was gone, helping raise my kids and putting in overtime—thank y'all!"

De'shawn, too hungry to wait any longer, had since picked his fork up and started grubbing. Freak Zeenie glanced at him but kept going.

"To Juneteenth! Let my people go!" he said with passion. "And to Houston County, for awarding us a victory by firing two well-known racist cops from our community!"

"Drink up so we can eat, 'cause some one seems to couldn't wait for us," he teased, glancing at De'shawn.

The family raised their flutes and emptied them.

Momma Lois, who had never had a drink in her 70-plus years, was already feeling saucy—borderline tipsy—by the time she set her glass down. She looked at De'shawn for a second. He was feeding his face. Then she looked at Freak Zeenie, then back at De'shawn again, studying him closely.

"Deacon," she said, her voice slurring slightly. "I might sound crazy, but you sure all your kids are on the right side of the table? Because De'shawn . . . he looks very, very similar to your son! I'm just saying!" Momma Lois stared at Freak Zeenie and De'shawn back and forth.

The entire family turned their heads toward De'shawn in unison—even Khashia. De'shawn froze mid-chew, his eyes wide with panic.

Same Time . . .
Back in Dothan, Alabama
Bocage—
Almost every house in Bocage was vacant.

"Man, hurry the hell up with your old slow ass, Junky Que," Sam said, pushing his weight forward, trying to force his older brother to move faster. "Man . . . come on, nigga! Fucking with yo' slow ass, we aren't gonna be able to see what this nice old house has to it, fool," he said. "We need to shake down a few more of these good ol' white folks' shit, fool."

Sam was trying to move his feet as fast as he could. "We can, too, if you got it moving! I bet if I put a dub roc' in front of your face, you'd find all types of speed!" Sam kept talking as they carried an 83-inch plasma TV through the kitchen and out the door that led to the four-car garage, where Sam's 2000-model Chevy pickup truck was parked.

"I'm moving 'bout as fast as my legs will allow me. Ain't nobody coming home no time soon, fool," Junky Que said. "It's Father's Day. We should be able to make a few runs," he added, backing up without looking behind him, trusting his baby brother to guide him.

"Yeah, I know what day it is, but fuck that got to do with clearing some shit out so we can get some crack money for the week?" Sam snapped. He was talking so fast spit flew out his mouth from the gap left by his missing two front teeth. By now, Sam was damn near running, holding onto his side of the TV.

As Sam rounded the corner near the kitchen island, he cut the turn too sharp, and the screen scraped the counter's edge, cracking instantly.

"I told your stupid ass to hold the hell up! Now loo—" Junky Que started, but he miscalculated the first step leading into the garage and fell hard, tumbling down the remaining two steps.

The TV followed, landing partially on Junky Que, who tried to save it from further damage. It was a lost cause. The massive screen collided with the handlebars of a motorcycle near the garage door, shattering into pieces.

"Boy, aren't you clumsy as hell! Thank you—there goes at least five hundred dollars, fool!" Sam barked before rushing back into the house to scavenge anything else of value, leaving Junky Que to crawl out from under the shattered TV on his own.

Eventually, Junky Que made it back inside. His vision still wasn't 100%—Cartier Jay and Boo-Boo had roughed him up a few days ago, leaving both his eyes badly bruised. But none of that mattered. Nothing would stop him from feeding his 30-plus-year crack addiction.

Back in Montgomery, Alabama—
LongHorn Steakhouse . . .

Momma Lois's bold accusation had set off a family feud at LongHorn. Almost everyone at the table agreed with her observation—except for Freak Zeenie, Khashia, and especially De'shawn. They were in denial.

Freak Zeenie shook his head in disbelief, irritated with his mother. Momma Lois had stirred up all kinds of speculation, getting the family to weigh in on her claim.

Meanwhile, Khashia felt anger bubbling deep in her stomach, rising like an Alka-Seltzer fizzing up to her chest. She was embarrassed and insulted by Momma Lois's boldness. Suddenly, she didn't want to be in the presence of Freak Zeenie's family at all. The table was caught up in heated debate, and she was over it.

Leaning toward Freak Zeenie, she whispered, "I'm ready to go, bae," her voice low but firm. She glanced at his face, trying to read his reaction, then leaned back in her chair with her arms crossed tightly. A mean mug was plastered across her pretty face as she rolled her eyes at Momma Lois, who continued to compare De'shawn to Freak Zeenie.

The problem was that even Khashia couldn't deny it now—once it had been pointed out, the resemblance was there. Frustrated, she pushed her chair back and rushed toward the ladies' room.

"Ma? Cut it out! Look what you started," Freak Zeenie said, watching Khashia storm away.

"Deacon, I'm your mother!" Momma Lois said. "All I said was that he favors you and my grandkids. There's no harm in that—I just made a statement. It's not like it's true or something," she added with a sly smile. "No harm done, but you know you've been around."

She turned to De'shawn with a warm smile. "I'd love to be your grandmother, handsome young man," she said, winking at him.

De'shawn squirmed in his seat, trying to avoid the attention. He stared at his half-empty plate, wishing his mom was there to rescue him.

Khashia took a Kleenex, wiping her nose from the few tears that had slid down without her permission to do so. *I can't believe Momma Lois. I mean, De'shawn does favor Freak, but okay. Everyone has a lookalike out there!*

Khashia's thoughts formed on their own. She turned the water on, running her hands under it and washing her hands. Turning off the water, she snatched a few Kleenex, drying her hands.

Denise? You watching this mess, girl? These crazy people claiming De'shawn and my boyfriend have a stone resemblance. Girl . . . now, I know we don't know who De'shawn's father was, but . . . I'm sure it's not my Freak Zeenie.

"I mean, how could it? You only been back and forth from Detroit to Atlanta for a good six years now. Freak Zeenie just done almost fifteen years. I don't even know why I'm entertaining all this mess, girl. I'm straight trippin'. Ain't I? I guess it's to protect my nephew's heart. I know he's very fragile at the moment."

Khashia took one last look in the mirror before throwing the Kleenex in the trash on her way back out to join everyone at the table, after having a conversation with her stepsister, who had been deceased for a while. So really, she'd had the convo by herself, basically.

By the time Khashia reached the table, everyone was dropping tips, preparing to leave the building and head into the parking lot. After everyone piled back into their SUVs, ready to make it back home, Freak Zeenie stopped.

"Thanks, everyone, for coming. I hope we all enjoyed one another's company as the family we are," he said. "Kids, I love you and appreciate the love y'all make your pops feel, you heard?" he added. "Again, happy Father's Day, men. Now, let's get on down this highway and back home safely," he said, before he got in the SUV, pulling the door shut, cranking up, and pulling off.

Everyone in the SUV with Freak Zeenie rode in silence. They all entertained their own thoughts.

Khashia kept shifting her gaze from the window to her nails as she played with her thoughts. *Freak, is it possible that you two crossed paths?* she wondered. *Nawl, that's it.*

She dismissed the thought after cross-examining it in her mind.

Freak Zeenie kept his eyes on the road, in a zone of his own. Man, Ma off the chain for that now. She right though. He glanced in the rearview mirror at De'shawn, who must have been waiting for him to look. They locked eyes for a microsecond, then broke the connection. *Lil nigga do favor us though. Damn . . . I can't even lie.* Shit! Freak Zeenie let the thoughts run through his mind as he floated down the highway.

I don't know why he keeps sweatin' me for. Ain't nothin'. I don't need no handouts. I need a plan so I can stand out. Know what I'm saying? De'shawn thought to himself.

An Hour and a Half Later—
Bocage . . .
Dothan, Alabama

After everyone made it back, Freak Zeenie was more than ready to take it home, knowing he had his work cut out for him the following day. Navigating his vehicle around back toward the garage, the garage door rose in slow motion, finally making it all the way up. Even in the dark, Freak Zeenie and Khashia automatically knew their crib had been violated again.

"Fuck is this?" Freak Zeenie said, leaning on the steering wheel, trying to make out the broken 83-inch TV. He put the vehicle into park, jumped out, and Khashia followed. They walked up to the TV.

"You got to be fucking kidding me!" he bellowed, his face frowning on its own. *Man, this got to be Big Man's work! Got to be! Fuck he take me for? I see through this weak-ass lame shit. A'ight, bitch-ass nigga! I'm 'bout to find you lame ass and mop yah up once and for all,* he thought as his mind fixated more and more on Big Man.

If only he knew, though, Big Man was a ghost. Deader than a motherfucker.

They went through the same procedures that they went through in Brentwood. After the police report was completed, Freak Zeenie rushed Khasia and De'shawn right back into the vehicle, driving them to the nearest hotel room for the night.

After checking in, they all took showers and laid around in their own place of thoughts until they, one by one, drifted off to sleep, agitated.

Chapter 9

Two Days Later
Yazoo FCI
Yazoo, Mississippi

Tuesday morning, the compound had just announced work call. Inmates were spilling out of the unit and into the compound. Some headed to work, some to callouts, and others were out taking advantage of the 10-minute move.

Since Trae had contracted COVID, he took off from work, claiming he had food poisoning. This way, he wouldn't have to be isolated from the population. Trae waited until the move ended to be sure his partner, Perc, wasn't coming back to stay in the unit like usual.

The CO came in, locking the door behind her. Trae watched as she went straight to the back through the middle hall where the counselors, case managers, secretary, and restroom were located. Trae stepped out into the day space, moving casually. He walked a slow lap around the whole unit, scanning cells to make sure he was on point. After coming downstairs, Trae went straight into Perc's cell.

Trae pulled the door up behind him and swiftly reached into his back pocket. He pulled out a wad of basketball tickets, placing them under Perc's blanket and a few at the foot of his bunk. Trae glanced back at the small window on the cell door to make sure he wasn't being watched. Then, he reached into the front of his pants, pulled out a shank, and slid it into the laundry bag hanging on the wall by the door.

"Yeah, bitch-ass nigga! Got to watch who you be talking to! Worrying 'bout what the next man got going on, but don't even know what the fuck going on with yourself. Mind your own business. I'll holla at ya', Perc!" Trae said, peeking out of the cell before easing out without being seen.

Trae went to his own cell and did a quick superset workout to get his heart rate up and raise his body temperature. Once satisfied with the results, he stepped out of the cell, looking very ill. Trae approached the female CO, who was in the middle of her daily cell searches. She was only two doors down from his and Perc's cells.

"Excuse me, Ms. Smith, I need a doctor, please. I'm not feeling well, I—" Trae bent over and threw up, spitting a thick white foam all over the floor.

"Errww!" Ms. Smith jumped back, disgusted. She quickly radioed the situation, and moments later, she was letting Trae out through the front door. Trae walked slowly to medical to be attended to.

Ms. Smith made the unit orderly clean up the mess Trae had caused before she resumed her five-cell daily search. When she got to Perc's cell, Ms. Smith checked under the blanket and pulled out some basketball tickets. After carefully examining them, she confirmed they were gambling tickets. Then, she moved to the foot of the bunk and found a few more.

"Oh, you running a gambling ring, huh? Okay! Not on my shift," she muttered, opening Perc's locker next. The locker was full of commissary, but after thoroughly searching it, she didn't find anything suspicious.

Finally, Ms. Smith turned her attention to the laundry bag hanging on the wall. After digging through the clothes, it didn't take long for her to pull out a 10-inch shank.

"Oh, my God! You a killer too, huh? Got me fucked up!" Ms. Smith exclaimed, immediately getting on her radio. She came out of the cell and locked the door behind her.

Minutes Later

COs flooded the unit, cameras in hand, taking pictures of the shank. Recall was announced, and all inmates returned to their units, preparing for lunch.

Perc entered the unit, and the COs rushed him faster than toilet paper rushed down a commode.

"Hey . . . Hey . . . Hey, man! Fuck going on? What the fuck!" Perc bellowed as his head was mashed to the wall as the cuffs were slapped on him. He never stood a chance. The COs dragged him off to the S.H.U (Surrogate Housing Unit) without an explanation.

"Man, what the fuck? What they got going on, Perc?" Trae yelled out as he was approaching the unit while Perc's feet weren't moving but he was because the COs carried him straight to the SHU.

"The hell if I know! Man, pack my shit, bruh!" Perc shouted, his last words echoing through the unit as he was dragged through the sally port toward the side pocket (SHU).

Trae stood there a few more seconds.

"So long, sucker! By the time you make it back, I'll be the ticket man, clown ass nigga, with your goofy ass!" Trae went into the unit.

***

Later That Night

Trae lay in his bunk with his hands behind his head, strategizing his revenge for the love of his life, Khashia. His celly was rambling, going down memory lane, but Trae wasn't listening. He already knew the perfect plan. But first, he had to get out of there to pull it off. And Trae knew just the person who could help him: his celly.

Trae casually pulled his phone out in front of his celly, setting the bait.

I knew he'd bite, Trae thought as he punched in Khashia's number, expecting it to go straight to voicemail. Instead, he heard a dial tone. Conscious, his celly, heard it too and hopped off the rack onto the floor. He looked at Trae with a sinister smirk plastered on his face.

Same Time
The Westside
Dothan, Alabama

Junkie Que sat on the passenger side of his brother Sam's truck, his mouth twisted and his mind high as hell as they rode around looking for a house to strip down to feed their addiction. Everything they'd come up on out in Bocage during Juneteenth and Father's Day was already sold.

Sam's eyes stretched wide as he brought the truck to a slow creep. "Man, I got a funny feeling 'bout this hood, bruh. Seems like all the houses are occupied for some reason—when they should be at work!" he said, agitated and confused, shaking his head.

"Yeah, Sam, that's 'cause it's summertime, fool! School's out for the sum—" Junkie Que stopped mid-sentence as his phone lit up, distracting him from the logic he was trying to explain.

"Yeah? What y'all got for us?" he answered.

"Fuck y'all at?"

"Riding 'round. What's up? You sound—"

"Pissed off! I gave y'all two pipe heads a job, and you motherfuckers ain't brought back shit incriminating yet!" the voice bellowed through the phone.

"M—"

"Man, my hairy ass! Meet us at the *Days Inn* 'round back in, say, thirty minutes—" The line went dead.

Junkie Que looked at the phone.

"Who was that?"

"You already know! Them two desperate-ass pigs in a blanket. They say meet them in thirty minutes in the back of

Days Inn a—" Before Junkie Que could finish, his phone chimed again.

"Hold on!" he said. "These motherfuckers!" he bellowed. "Yeah, man, I just told y'all we c—"

He was cut off mid-sentence.

"Who . . . the . . .fuck . . .is you, *bitch-ass nigga*? And where my bitch Khashia at, fuck *nigga*?"

"Fuck you think you talkin' to, *bitch*?" Junkie Que matched the caller's energy.

"You, fuck boy! Where my hoe at?"

"This her baby daddy, lame-ass nigga! And she can't talk right now 'cause she got my dick in her mouth!"

"Pussy a—" Before Trae could finish, the line went dead.

Sam was cracking up laughing. "That's it, bruh! You tell 'em," Sam said as he expertly hit his crack pipe while steering with his knee.

Junkie Que didn't respond. He laid the phone down and hurriedly packed his pipe. The two recent phone calls had blown his high just that quick. Junkie Que put the flame to the end of his pipe and pulled until his jaws touched each other. When he released the chalk-colored smoke, Junkie Que was higher than the atmosphere.

Sam and Junkie Que rode in a zone of silence the rest of the way to *Days Inn*.

Same Time
Back at Yazoo FCI

'Ol' pussy-ass hoe! I'm telling you—" Trae was venting, mad as hell, pacing back and forth. He got quiet for a second. Conscious wanted to ask for a call as bad as a pig wants slop, but right now, with the way Trae was ranting, he wasn't so sure.

"Man . . . I swear! *On God, boy!* This that bitch's last time! Real cap!" Trae said. "I'm 'bout to hit my dawg up right fast. I'm 'bout to put ten bands on that hoe's head! Real cap, boy!" he bellowed. "Fuck that hoe think she is? Who she think I am? Got me fucked up!" Trae stressed, punching in a number.

"Man . . . hold up! Shit, I'll take that shit up my gotdamn self, bruh! Fuck you talking 'bout, dawg?" Conscious said. He was already spending the money in his head.

"Nawl, bruh. I need this done *right now*, my nigga!"

"Yeah, but you want it done *right* too. I'm telling you, homes, this what I do! You know I'm 'bout to vamp in a second, plus I need that bread bad right now!" he said. "Shit, for ten bands, I'll do two, and one for free!" Conscious stared Trae in the eye so Trae could recognize the realness in them.

Trae ended the call he'd been trying to make. "A'ight, let me think about it, 'cause for real, I need this shit done *asap!*"

"Say no mo'," Conscious assured him.

That still didn't simmer Trae down. He was hotter than a busted radiator. Trae spent the rest of the day running down his plan to his celly, Conscious.

Trae showed Conscious a slew of pictures of him and Khashia from when he was free. Then he pulled out a few of his visitation photos too. Conscious was zoomed in.

"Man, I see why you crazy 'bout her, shawty. She tough, homes!" he said.

"Man . . . fuck that thot, shawty! She's outta here!" Trae said, his face all scrunched up.

Trae stayed up all night, imagining killing Khashia in as many different ways as he could. He couldn't wait to get retribution against Khashia, and anybody else who had ever crossed him. Trae thought about how everyone had run off on him with his money and dope while he was wasting away inside a concrete graveyard (prison).

Chapter 10

A Week and Two Days Later
Kinsey, Alabama

Since Freak Zeenie couldn't figure out who had been violating his most valued personal space for the life of him, he decided to move his family out to the country in Kinsey, Alabama. *SafeTouch* had failed him two times in a row. If you knew Freak Zeenie then you knew it was no way he'd try it a third time.

Freak Zeenie had his own choice of surveillance cameras installed all around the house and its premises. He also bought a large utility shed and placed it in the back of the home. Freak Zeenie had all the boxes of cocaine moved out of the basement and into the utility shed out back.

Going with his first mind, Freak Zeenie had begun pointing the finger at Khashia, thinking that it was Khashia's fiancé Big Man starting to come back out of hiding and wanting back all that he'd left behind. For the last few days, all Freak Zeenie and Khashia had been doing was arguing back and forth.

Freak Zeenie was positive he was fed up with Khashia. No matter how he turned the situation around and looked at the pictures, he just couldn't see it any differently—it was still the same.

Little did he know, though, Khashia wasn't feeling him the same no more either. Ever since the Father's Day/Juneteenth incident, Khashia had been on edge. That same night, when they came back to another break-in and finally made it to the hotel room, Khashia swabbed Freak Zeenie's and De'shawn's mouths while they both drifted off fast asleep.

This morning, Khashia left to go pick up the test results. The results were at the drop box she'd secretly purchased. Khashia's curiosity had damn near killed her over the last week. She hoped the test results would come back negative, but her woman's intuition radar was way too high—it told her the results were positive.

If Khashia thought she was a step ahead of Freak Zeenie, then she was sorely mistaken. Freak Zeenie had already taken out a life insurance policy for them. While Khashia was out doing what she did, Freak Zeenie transferred more than 90% of their money into a money market account and a mutual fund IRA, which only had Earlie Barber attached to it. Freak Zeenie was glad, because before he sent Levi off with Remy Red and Poochie, he had Levi make up fraudulent documents stating that the construction company and tree farm had been legally signed over to him by Khashia. His financial state was the last thing he was worried 'bout at the moment.

Freak Zeenie sent Zacatecas his share of money from out of the safe in the basement. Freak Zeenie knew that doing so would buy him some time. Now he could hit the streets knee-deep and see what was up with his bread. He was still waiting on Levi to catch up with Carlos and Lil Fred to find out what the holdup was.

Freak Zeenie came out the house with two all-black trained Bully Kuttas. They were bred as guard dogs, although they were often used for the illegal sport of dog fighting. When Freak Zeenie found out these dogs were nicknamed the *Beasts from the East*, he fell in love with them at first sight. Ever since they'd been imported four days ago from the desert of Sindh in Pakistan, he'd been getting them used to their new territory. Freak Zeenie needed them to guard his shed with their lives.

"That's right! Come on, boys. I know y'all some steppers, ain't it?" he said as they walked with a powerful stride confidently beside him. De'shawn fell in love with them too.

De'shawn was finally starting to let his guard down a little with Freak Zeenie, especially after laying eyes on the green-and-black 125 dirt bike with the matching helmet Freak Zeenie had bought for him. Before Khashia left, De'shawn told her he was staying home with Freak Zeenie today. What De'shawn didn't know was that he was staying anyway—Khashia had already set that in motion.

As soon as Freak Zeenie fed the dogs and got 'em into the shed, his phone chimed. Freak Zeenie glanced at it and saw it was an unknown number with a picture message attached to it.

"Fuck is this?" he said, opening the picture message. Freak Zeenie let out a small chortle. "Oh yeah," he said, nodding and swiping the screen to the left a few more times.

Freak Zeenie's blood began to boil instantly. "Man, this bitch paying like this?" It looked like he was gliding. The picture images were three naked pictures of Khashia and one of her and Mark (Big Man) lying in a king-size bed. Her leg was spilled across him, and she was pinching her nipples. Khashia and Big Man were smiling, enjoying the moment.

Freak Zeenie shook his head hard but couldn't shake the images away. "*Kill this slow-ass hoe, man! Fuck she playing with?*" He went into the house, grabbing his brand-new .408 rifle. It had a 100-round drum attached to it, with bullets the length and size of a number 2 pencil. Now all he had to do was pull the trigger.

"Blow this stupid bitch's candles the fuck out soon as she break the door seal and feed her dumb ass to the dogs! Watch this!" he grumbled.

Freak Zeenie went back and sat in the chair by the foyer. His phone chimed. "Not right now, lil bruh!" Freak Zeenie pushed ignore. The phone chimed again almost instantaneously.

"Yeah, man, fuck?!" he bellowed, answering his phone.

"Ho, ho, ho, my nigga! Fuck wrong with your bean-head ass, boy?"

"Man, I got shit going on right now. What you want? I ain't on all that shit, dawg!" Freak Zeenie bit his bottom lip, breathing hard.

"You too? Man, listen."

"I am, bruh. What's up?"

"I found Carlos and Lil Fred."

"A'ight, ask 'em what the fuck takin' 'em so long with my bread then," he said. "What, they can't hustle no more or something? 'Cause I need m—"

"They both dead, bruh," Levi said, cutting Freak Zeenie off.

"What?" he bellowed.

"Yeah, it's bad, man. Twelve just found them over on the south side. Niggas been gone for a minute too, bruh. This shit big," he said. "I'm talking *Fox Five News* out this bitch and all," he added. "Check it out. You need to slide through asap, my boy. Funk said tell you that." He let that linger. "I'll hit you back when I get the whole story though. I'ma tell you right now though, they already claiming it was a drug deal gone bad. I gotta go though. Love, bruh," Levi said before disconnecting.

"One," Freak Zeenie said, but Levi didn't hear him because he'd already hung up.

***

Same Time
Outside the House

De'shawn was all over the yard riding his dirt bike when Khashia pulled in. Khashia had the most dire face expression she could muster, promising herself she wouldn't cry no more after finding out that the nigga she was with back in the day was also fucking her stepsister Denise too. Like Future said: *At the same damn time*. Khashia's nerves were shot.

"I knew it! Old cheating-ass bastard!" she muttered, dabbing at the corners of her eyes with a Kleenex. Checking her presence in the rearview, Khashia made sure the test results were secure in her purse before grabbing the groceries and carrying them into the house.

No sooner than Khashia broke the front door seal, Freak Zeenie reached out and smacked the shit out of her.

"Bitch! Fuck you thought I was?"

Khashia was sprawled out across the floor in a daze—groceries, pocketbook, and all spilled across the floor. Freak Zeenie stood over her, his nose flaring, breathing fire. Right hand holding the .408 pointed toward the floor, left hand fingers spread open, Freak Zeenie looked like he wanted to give her one more.

"Huh?!" He was belligerent.

Khashia was flabbergasted and speechless, searching Freak Zeenie's eyes.

"What? What are you talking 'bout, Freak?" she finally managed to say.

"Oh, what I'm talking 'bout?" he repeated. *"What you talking 'bout, Freak?"* Freak Zeenie mimicked Khashia as he shoved the images at her—photos of her in the nude, and her in the nude with Big Man.

"You know now, right? Yeah, you know! Now, where the fuck nigga at? 'Cause he 'bout to die right along with your funky ass b—"

"Aye! Let my auntee go, nigga!" De'shawn bellowed, coming through the door, his fists curled tight.

"Let 'er go? I ain't got her yet!" Freak Zeenie snapped, but he let go of her hair and went to grab his keys.

"Freak! Freak!" Khashia called after him as Freak Zeenie stormed out the door. But Khashia didn't chase him—she decided to let him be.

Khashia pondered the pictures she'd just seen. As soon as she saw them, she remembered exactly when they were taken and knew they were from before Freak Zeenie. But what she didn't know was how Freak Zeenie had gotten hold of them. That meant one thing to her: whoever had stolen her phone knew who she and Freak Zeenie were—and knew they were together. But who? Khashia thought as she watched Freak Zeenie leave the yard with a dragon tail of dust trailing behind his vehicle.

Freak Zeenie was hotter than a furnace. He decided to head to Atlanta first to see what Levi and Funk wanted to tell him that couldn't be said over the phone. He rode in silence, thinking about how he would come out on top.

Freak Zeenie would be damned if he jeopardized his life for a bitch—especially an unfaithful one at that. He ignored Khashia's text as he continued hitting the E-way, headed to Atlanta, Georgia.

Chapter 11

Later That Evening
Dothan, Alabama

Cartier Jay and Boo-Boo had been riding around town all day, trying to pin down the location of T-Face and his gang. Not a single member of the Schoolyard Crips from the Bottom had paid Cartier Jay one iron dime, despite owing him for months. At first, Cartier Jay had been lenient because T-Face was a homie and had a small amount of street fame in the city.

Cartier Jay started by soft-pressing T-Face. That was until Freak Zeenie brought the full-court press down on Cartier Jay, leaving him with no choice but to apply the same pressure to his clientele. After consulting his step-pops about T-Face, Freak Zeenie revealed some truths that Cartier Jay never knew, didn't want to know, but absolutely needed to know. Chief among them was that while T-Face understood the grind, his heavy coke addiction always came first. Morals and principles had to fit in wherever they could, if at all.

After doing some digging of his own, Cartier Jay quickly discovered that T-Face had been avoiding him on purpose. T-Face had no intention of paying Cartier Jay—period. He'd been scheming from the jump. T-Face had used Cartier Jay to elevate himself and the Schoolyard Crips from the Bottom.

While chopping it up with his partner—Kal-Kal—and collecting his money, Cartier Jay reloaded Kal-Kal with a 20-pack (20 bricks). During their exchange, Kal-Kal admitted that he had been serving T-Face for weeks. It became crystal clear to Cartier Jay: T-Face was deliberately curving him, opting to cop from Kal-Kal instead. The revelation had Cartier Jay's blood boiling.

Kal-Kal, unaware of all Cartier Jay's clientele, hadn't intentionally stepped on his toes. He wouldn't have even known until Cartier Jay brought it up. With this new information, Cartier Jay pieced things together.

Kal-Kal didn't have T-Face's exact location but confirmed that T-Face wasn't operating in the city. According to T-Face, he'd been crossing state lines, doing business with Crip connections in Georgia and down in Marianna, Florida. Kal-Kal also mentioned that spotting the Schoolyard Crips wouldn't be hard now—they'd all gone and copped Trackhawks painted Crip blue, rolling on 32-inch gold floater dubs. The whole gang was shining.

To top it off, Kal-Kal revealed that T-Face and his crew would be at the club tonight. The event? A *"Bring It Back to the Bottom"* party, sponsored—of course—by the Schoolyard Crips. It was set to take place at the old Club 360 building.

Cartier Jay burned rubber out of the Days Inn parking lot, so caught up in his rage that it didn't even occur to him to have Kal-Kal text T-Face and set up a meet. One thing was for certain: T-Face wouldn't make it to that party tonight if Cartier Jay had anything to do with it.

Cartier Jay and Boo-Boo had been sliding on the west side all day after Kal-Kal's debrief.

"Fuck nigga think he goin' out to Webb when I slide down on him? Got to be crazy, right?" Cartier Jay said, pulling back up in the Bottom, hoping to spot T-Face or any Schoolyard Crip, for that matter.

"H-hell y-yeah, b-bruh! Y-you a-already know s-shitid!" Boo-Boo stuttered, sipping from his double cup with molly floating on top of the expensive slushy.

Same Time
Days Inn

Former police officer Fortune had convinced his partner Bentley not to destroy the phone they had taken from Junkie Que and Sam. Bentley had been hesitant because the phone could be traced back to them, linking them to the breaking and entering incident at the house in Bocage. Fortune assured him that once he finished sending the pictures to Earlie Barber's phone, he would dispose of the device. Bentley only agreed because he was in a rush—he had an appointment to look at a building he wanted to rent for his new private investigation business. He had recently acquired his LLC and was eager to get things rolling.

After Bentley left, Fortune erased all the data from the phone. Then, succumbing to his addiction, he hit his last rock of crack cocaine, straight drop. High as a tsunami wave, his body twitched, and his eyes widened with intensity. Though the phone's service was cut off, it still worked for texting. Fortune decided to use it to message his wife, pretending to be Bentley speaking on Fortune's behalf. He begged for another chance to see his kids and reconcile with her, but she dismissed him coldly. She had moved on and closed that chapter of her life.

The lack of a response sent Fortune spiraling into another bout of depression. Thoughts of suicide crept back into his mind, as they had a few times since his humiliating termination. But his crack addiction kept him clinging to life, shaky and unsteady, like a wet biscuit barely holding together.

Fortune burst into laughter, recalling the nude pictures of Khashia he had sent to Freak Zeenie's phone. He hoped the photos were causing Zeenie the same kind of trouble that

Zeenie had inflicted on him. Lust crept into Fortune's eyes as he glanced at the pictures again, and before long, he found himself massaging his manhood.

His mind was deteriorating quickly. Out of nowhere, he let out a loud braying noise and jumped up.

"Oh shit! They out there!" he yelled, rushing to the window and peeking through the curtains. The parking lot was empty, but Fortune was convinced someone was outside. "Yeah?" he shouted, though there was no one to hear him.

Paranoia gripped him. He swore he heard voices calling his name, even though the hotel room was silent except for the muted TV. Fortune tried to sit and watch, but the crack had him too jittery.

"Somebody out there! They trying to get me!" He bolted back to the window, slowly pulling the curtain back. Seeing nothing, he leaped across the room to the bed, snatched up the phone, and darted to the door, unlatching it in a blur.

"Hey, Kal-Kal! I got somethin' for you, bud!" Fortune called out, holding the phone high as he approached Kal-Kal outside.

Kal-Kal scowled at the sight of the ex-cop. Serving Fortune had been a mistake—he hated dealing with him. Even though Fortune was no longer on the force, the fact that he had once been a cop made Kal-Kal uneasy. Cutting him off wasn't an option, though; Fortune's law enforcement past made him too risky to ignore.

As Fortune moved toward him a little too quickly, Kal-Kal bristled.

"Hold up, man! The fuck is wrong with you? Don't be running up on me like that, fool. What you want?" Kal-Kal kept walking toward the parking lot, hoping to shake him off.

"Man, I got a deal of a lifetime for you!" Fortune boomed, holding out the phone. "An iPhone 12 right here, all yours for a ball." He was desperate to trade it for 3 ½ grams of straight drop crack cocaine.

Kal-Kal glanced at the phone, unimpressed. "I don't need no damn phone, bruh. I need that blue-faced white boy. Where the gwop at?"

Fortune's nerves flared. "T-this is all I got for now, buddy. Just help me out this time, and I'll come back straight next time," he stammered, his eyes darting nervously.

"I ain't your gotdamn buddy!" Kal-Kal snapped, snatching the phone from Fortune's hand. "This ain't worth no ball. I'll give you—" Kal-Kal paused dramatically— "a gram. Take it or leave it. I don't give a fuck."

Fortune seethed internally. *Lying ass nigga! This phone's worth at least a half, or nothing less than a quarter!* But instead, he swallowed his pride.

"Yeah . . . I guess you right. I'll take that," he muttered, shaking his head in disappointment.

Kal-Kal pulled a pre-bagged gram from his pocket, tossed it to Fortune, and walked off without another word. Fortune turned and bolted back to his hotel room.

Meanwhile, Kal-Kal received a text from T-Face: *Pulling in now.* Kal-Kal smirked. He wasn't about to let any opportunities slip through his fingers. He had just started seeing some real money compared to the rest of his circle, and he was ready to protect his earnings at all costs.

Kal-Kal's plan was clear. He'd serve T-Face 10 of the 20 bricks he had just picked up from Cartier Jay, sell nine more to another source, and break the last brick down into grams. He'd take those to the truck stop and hustle them at a steep markup. Anything left over would go to *Days Inn* for another quick flip.

T-Face pulled up in an all-black Impala with tinted windows, riding solo except for the G-27 with a switch resting on his lap. As soon as he stopped, Kal-Kal hopped in the passenger seat, carrying a duffel bag he had grabbed from his trunk.

T-Face eased his foot off the brake, letting the car creep forward. He scanned the rearview mirrors and rubbed his nose.

"It's the same shit, right?" T-Face asked.

"You got the right amount, right?" Kal-Kal shot back, dead serious.

"Fa' sho', yeah, yeah, yeah!" T-Face rasped.

Kal-Kal handed him the bag. T-Face hit the brakes, opened the bag, and peeked inside before handing it back.

"Put it on the floor right there," T-Face said, nodding toward the floorboard. "Then grab the money from the glove compartment."

Kal-Kal cracked the bag open, gave it a quick glance, and smiled. "A'ight, my boy. You good. Hit me up when you're ready for the next one. Let me out right here." Kal-Kal opened the door and stepped out.

As T-Face rolled down the window, he called after him. "You comin' to the club tonight, nigga?"

"Nah, it's grind time. Can't afford it yet. I'm on a million-dollar chase," Kal-Kal replied. Then he added, "Oh, and be careful. Cartier Jay's looking for you. Word is you owe him a nice piece of change. He might show up tonight, so stay on point."

T-Face scoffed. "Man, fuck Cartier Jay, Rolex Jay, and all them other designer Jays!" he shouted, his voice cracking. "I'll let that switch talk if they wanna talk, fool! My schoolyards gon' be there, and you know what it is. C-CRIP!"

With that, T-Face rolled up the window and sped off, heading back to Ozark. Though Ozark and Dothan had a subtle rivalry, the small city had taken a liking to T-Face. He brought dirt-cheap prices and accepted counterfeit money in exchange for product, which allowed him to dominate the market.

"Slow ass niggas," T-Face muttered to himself, smiling as he crossed the Ozark city limits, ready to turn up.

Meanwhile—

Kal-Kal jumped in his whip to go conduct the second sale of the day. After putting the money in the glove compartment, he locked it. He reminded himself not to forget to purchase a phone card later tonight at the truck stop. He wanted his recently purchased iPhone 12 activated ASAP.

He had almost forgotten, but Kal-Kal also made a mental note to text Freak Zeenie to see if he could get some better prices on the units (bricks). Kal-Kal wasn't feeling how Cartier Jay was taxing him for the bricks, especially since he knew Boo-Boo wasn't being charged the same rates. That fact alone started to cause ill feelings to take root inside Kal-Kal's heart.

***

Later Wednesday Night
The Club
Dothan, Alabama

The club was jam-packed! Blue Trackhawks lined up in front, their gleaming paint catching the streetlights. A *'MAKE THE BOTTOM GREAT AGAIN'* banner hung across the club's front, visible from the street and parking lot. The schoolyard Crips had brought the city out tonight.

Inside a car parked near the club's entrance, Cartier Jay and Boo-Boo sat silently, scoping the scene.

"What's up? You ready to shut this bitch down, or what, cuz?" Cartier Jay asked, his energy high from all the money T-Face was raking in from this event.

"N-naw, bruh. I'm r-ready t-to t-turn this bitch i-into a-a g-grave y-yard tonight," Boo-Boo gritted out, his tone icy as his eyes scanned the line snaking into the club.

Cartier Jay took a deep inhale. "Say no mo' then. Let's slide!"

They stepped out of the car and strode to the club's entrance. Paying $300 apiece—two hundred to get their guns in and another hundred to skip the line—they bypassed the velvet rope and entered the club. Both men pulled on their blue bandana-print COVID masks.

"There them fuck niggas right there, cuz!" Cartier Jay snarled. "If this nigga don't got my bread tonight, Boo-Boo, it's lights out." Though he was speaking to Boo-Boo, it was more like he was talking to himself.

Boo-Boo didn't reply. He was locked in, already scoping out who would be the first to go down.

The dance floor was jammed, and the atmosphere screamed money. It was obvious the world had just struck gold with PPE loans. People were flaunting wealth left and right.

Cartier Jay and Boo-Boo pushed their way through the crowd. Rough shoulders and occasional shoves cleared their path as they moved with purpose.

Meanwhile, T-Face and the rest of the Schoolyard Crips were posted up in the VIP, living it up. They were popping bottles, blowing wax, snorting coke, popping molly, smoking ice, and sipping drank. The VIP section was a sea of money, gold teeth, and blue flags. Even the women in the group were flexing hard.

Someone leaned over to whisper in T-Face's ear.

"Where?" T-Face said, sitting up lookin' around.

"Right there cuz, you see 'em!" He pointed T-Face in the direction.

"Okay, yeah, yeah, I see 'em now, bet!" T-Face got up and whispered to one of the other Crips.

The Crips quickly formed a human barricade around the VIP rope, blocking anyone from entering.

"Man, I already saw bruh! Tell 'em let me holler at 'em right fast, then I'm gone! We ain't on nuttin'!" Cartier Jay said, through clenched teeth.

Two schoolyard Crips slipped out of the VIP section and shot past them, blending in with the crowd so fast that Boo-Boo lost sight of 'em.

"What's up? I'll relay the message to 'em. He busy right now, though, cuz," one of the Crips said, using hand gestures to emphasize his words. "You see what I'm saying!" the Crip bellowed over the loud music, but Cartier Jay and Boo heard him loud and clear.

Cartier Jay's face twisted with rage. His eyes narrowed into slits.

"Don't worry 'bout it! If his soft ass ain't man enough to face ah nigga, then I—"

"C-check it o-out, l-lil nigga! I-I took that sh-shit c-cuz! Fucks th-the matter w-with you, f-fool?" T-Face yelled over the music, bursting through the middle of the Crips before he turned around, quickly disappearing behind the human Crip gate.

Boo-Boo didn't hesitate. He whipped out the Glock 33 with an extended clip, squeezing rounds at the Schoolyard Crips.

The crowd scattered like marbles spilling from a jar, the sound of gunfire echoing through the club. Boo-Boo aimed to take out as many Crips as he could. Cartier Jay followed a split second later, drawing his weapon. But just as he raised it, a bullet caught him in the shoulder. "Argh! I'm hit! I'm fuckin' hit!" He bellowed out in pure agony. His gun flew across the dance floor as he dropped to the ground.

The music stopped and the crowd stampeded out the door, and over anyone who couldn't keep up.

"I g-got you bruh!" Boo-Boo shouted, firing a few more rounds to cover them. Then he grabbed Cartier Jay around the waist, dragging him toward the door. Cartier Jay was leaking like a wounded hog.

The Schoolyard Crips managed to escape to their jeeps— except for one. Boo-Boo's shots had struck one of them in the heart, killing him instantly.

"Mo-move! G-get th-the fuck o-out th-the way!" Boo-Boo barked as he shoved people aside, dragging Cartier Jay along.

Reaching their car, Boo-Boo heaved Cartier Jay into the passenger seat, jumped into the driver's seat, and started the engine. Tires screeched as they sped out of the parking lot.

"I-i g-got o-one o-of them f-fuck n-niggas, bruh!" Boo-Boo said, gripping the wheel.

"Arghh!" Cartier Jay groaned. "I'm gonna kill all them fuck niggas, C–" His words trailed off as he passed out from blood loss.

The Next Morning
Dothan Hospital

Cartier Jay woke up handcuffed and shackled to the hospital bed. He held his head up, looking toward the door where he could hear his mom and sister on the other side, making a whole bunch of fuss about seeing him.

Cartier Jay laid back, trying to gather his thoughts about the events that took place last night. Suddenly, he thought about his main man Boo-Boo. *Where the hell Boo-Boo at? And why he brought me to the hospital for anyway?* he wondered as he laid in restraints.

Two homicide detectives entered Cartier Jay's hospital room. Cartier Jay could've won an Oscar—he acted like he was asleep. The detectives stood there making small talk for a few seconds before deciding that Cartier Jay was too drugged up and probably wouldn't be awake for a while. They left the hospital with promises to return soon.

Within those minutes, Cartier Jay found out that Boo-Boo was exactly where Cartier figured he'd be in the near future: jail! Boo-Boo had been arrested for the death of a person named Ruban. Cartier Jay knew who Ruban was but didn't give nan fuck 'bout him. Ruban was one of the local Schoolyard Crips, and he was gone die sooner or later if Cartier could've helped it.

"Fuck!" Cartier Jay whispered. He tried to fight the strong effect of the pain medicine that was mellifluously surging through his bloodstream. Cartier Jay's eyes fluttered, and he wasn't no match for the powerful meds. He wanted to think his way out of the serious situation but drifted into a calm state of sleep.

Chapter 12

Same Day
18th Street, Downtown
Atlanta, Georgia

Freak Zeenie rushed out, locking up his loft. He moved with urgency because he'd just ended a phone call with one of his baby mamas, who once had also been his wife, long before his bid. Freak Zeenie's plans to catch up with his cousin Funk and help his brother Levi at the jewelry store had been disrupted and spoiled instantly. His ex-wife-slash-baby-mama had delivered the ghastly news that their baby boy had been shot and hospitalized. All Freak Zeenie could do was listen—she wouldn't let him get a word in edgewise as she talked a mile a minute.

Hating to leave because Carlos and Lil Fred's funeral was only a few days away, Freak Zeenie was torn. He'd wanted to stay to show his last respects to both of them. During his short stay, though, he found out that Carlos and Lil Fred had been tased in the neck. The powerful electric volts caused them both to pass out, and suffocation had been listed as the cause of death in the autopsy. That detail still had Freak Zeenie puzzled, knowing firsthand that both of them were too seasoned to get caught slipping like that. But even though he couldn't understand it, the fact remained: time had called Carlos and Lil Fred's hands in.

Freak Zeenie made it onto I-85 South and floored it.

***

2 Hours and 30 Minutes Later
Dothan, Alabama

Sitting in his mother's kitchen, Freak Zeenie had a concerned, confounded, and inquisitive look plastered on his face. While listening to his ex-wife-slash-baby-mama try to explain to him and Mama Lois what had happened—and why it had happened—to Cartier Jay, Freak Zeenie's mind was constantly churning. He had a multitude of concerns at the moment: his son had been shot, and Cartier Jay was charged with conspiracy to commit murder. Those were at the forefront. Now, Freak Zeenie's confusion and curiosity came from noticing that De'shawn was at his mother's house when he arrived—but Khashia wasn't.

Mama Lois and his ex-wife-slash-baby-mama were going over so many details that Freak Zeenie couldn't wait for a chance to address his concerns. Finally, his ex-wife/baby mama paused to take a deep breath and looked at Freak Zeenie with an askance expression.

"So, Deacon. Now what?" she asked. "Where we go from here?" Concern was written all over her face and laced in her voice.

"We get him a lawyer first—"

"I have that covered already, no need to put much thought into that," she said, getting to her feet.

"Well, we have to wait until they get arraigned to see if they get a bond and how much it w—"

"I understand that much too," she interrupted again.

"So, if you know everything, then why the h—why you asking me?!" Freak Zeenie frowned, barely managing to stop himself from using profanity in front of Mama Lois twice in one sentence.

"Because that's not what I'm asking you!" she snapped, glancing at Mama Lois before her eyes landed on De'shawn and her daughter standing to the side. "Aye! Y'all two! Go in the den and get out of grown folks' mouths!"

De'shawn and her daughter turned and left the room as instructed. She waited until the kids were out of earshot before continuing.

"I'm talking 'bout what we gone do 'bout those punks who hurt my baby!" she bellowed. "You know good and doggone well what I'm talking 'bout, Deacon!" Her face twisted into a scowl, and her eyes narrowed into slits. With Cartier being hurt and in trouble, she felt a painful void in her heart.

Mama Lois didn't like where this conversation was headed.

"Now just wait a minute. God gone take care of everything. Deacon, don't you go trying to take matters into your own hands, son."

"I got it, Mom," he said in a dry, clipped tone. Freak Zeenie turned to his ex-wife-slash-baby-mama. "We gon' get to the bottom of it."

"You damn right we will! If I got to do it my motherfucking self!" she bellowed.

Freak Zeenie smirked at her statement, thinking back to their days in the projects. He knew firsthand how his ex-wife-slash-baby-mama could get down—and so did Mama Lois.

Turning his attention back to his mother, he asked, "Mom?"

"Yes, Deacon?"

"Why De'shawn over here? Where's Khashia?"

"Child, Khashia asked if he could stay here until you made it back from Atlanta. She said you'd know why and what to do once you got here," Mama Lois replied. "So, I just left it at that. Are y'all two alright, Deacon?"

Freak Zeenie's blood pressure spiked instantly. "She did what!" he barked, whipping out his phone. Freak Zeenie hit speed dial and called Khashia's number, but it went to voicemail. He tried twice more and got the same result. Frustrated, he shot her a text, only to have it rejected. "Man, I ain't got time to be playing all these games!" he bellowed.

"Calm down, Deacon, calm down," Mama Lois urged. "I can keep De'shawn if it's a problem y'all need to work on. You know I love kids," she said.

"Naw, I got 'em," Freak Zeenie replied through tight lips. "D!" he called out. Seconds later, his daughter and De'shawn came in.

Freak Zeenie hugged his daughter, kissing the top of her head. "See you later, a'ight? Keep your momma calm too," he said, handing her a handful of money, which she put into her clutch right away.

"Thanks, Dad," she said, hugging him back.

"Never thanks. That's what I'm supposed to do. Love you."

Freak Zeenie went to hug his mom, kissing her cheek. "Don't worry, Mom. I got everything under control, okay?" he said, looking at Mama Lois for a moment before backing away.

"I know, son. I'm praying for us all. I know God gone send Angel Michael to put a shield of protection around you, in Jesus' name!" Mama Lois said.

"That's right, Mama, that's right!" Freak Zeenie turned to his ex. "I'll see you in the A.M.," he said, then turned to leave. "De'shawn! Let's rock, boy!"

They left, pulling the door shut behind them. Once in the car, Freak Zeenie looked at De'shawn. "Where your auntee say she was going, D'?"

"She didn't. She just dropped me off and said not to cause Mama Lois no problems while I was here," De'shawn replied, looking at Freak Zeenie with confusion.

Freak Zeenie tried calling Khashia one more time but got voicemail again. He wasn't leaving a message—he wanted to speak to her directly. After checking his messages and finding none from Khashia, Freak Zeenie cranked up the car and pulled out of Mama Lois' driveway. Dumb bitch! he wanted to blurt out but instead turned the music up and rode in silence, deep in thought.

Twenty Minutes Later—
Kinsey, Alabama

Half expecting to see Khashia's vehicle in the driveway when they pulled in, Freak Zeenie quickly realized that wasn't the case. The house was still intact, but there was no life there. It was dead silent except for the sound of trees rustling and birds chirping.

Freak Zeenie and De'shawn exited the car.

"Here. I'm 'bout to feed the dogs and let 'em loose. I'll be in there in a minute," Freak Zeenie said, tossing De'shawn the keys to the crib. Freak Zeenie walked around the house, muttering a bunch of desecrated words under his breath.

De'shawn went inside and headed straight to the kitchen, grabbing a Simply Orange juice out the 'fridge. He noticed an envelope on the counter but didn't bother with it. De'shawn shot to his room, hopped online, and started playing the game.

Meanwhile, Freak Zeenie finished feeding the Bully Kuttas, locked the shed, and let the dogs roam the yard before heading back toward the house. His mind was lost in blissful thoughts.

Making it inside, Freak Zeenie glanced around. Everything looked the same. *Fuck this dumbass bitch at? Playing all these hoe-ass games gone get that bitch a urn just like her stepsister shitid. Like I ain't got enough shit to deal with as it is.* Freak Zeenie jogged these thoughts through his mental.

Walking into the kitchen, Freak Zeenie took a seat at the island. He glanced at his phone and noticed a missed call from Kal-Kal. *I already know what he wants. Not right now, Kal-Kal. I'll lace you up tomorrow once we have some more info*, Freak Zeenie thought, quickly dismissing Kal-Kal from his mind.

Noticing a plain white envelope on the island, Freak Zeenie snatched it up. A pregnancy test slid out onto the island. Freak Zeenie's brows furrowed as he stared at it with a stoic expression. Picking up the test, the first thing he saw was a positive sign.

"Positive," Freak Zeenie whispered. Looking back at the envelope, he slowly pulled out the contents. The first paper was a copy of a DNA test result. Reading it word for word, Freak Zeenie's eyes widened. Sitting the paper down, he couldn't stop staring at it.

Freak Zeenie rubbed his face, then picked the paper back up and read it three more times before setting it back down. His head swiveled from the pregnancy test to the test results. Man, damn! Freak Zeenie wanted to holler but remained silent. He couldn't do nothing but sit there, dumbfounded, lost in thought.

All kinds of past memories replayed vividly in Freak Zeenie's mind. Finally snapping out of it, he slapped his left hand on his forehead. *Damn! All this time. Denise, you was on point, and you too, Mom Dukes. This sneaky-ass bitch! This bitch done swabbed us. But when?* Freak Zeenie's thoughts jogged through his mind. Picking up the envelope again, he snatched out the last piece of paper. It read:

Damn Freak,

I knew you were a dog, but not a fucking low-down dirty dog! You was fucking my stepsister at the same time you were fucking me, which means you were cheating on me back then just like I figured. Now you have a child by my stepsister. Left me, got married to that thot you married back then, and she left you while they were booking you in jail.

Now my step nephew almost was my step nephew-slash-stepson! What the fuck? OH MY GOD! Umph! Umph! Umph! On top of that, now I'm pregnant. Not to worry though, by the time you read this, I will have gotten an abortion. Hopefully. President Biden's bitch ass making shit hard for a bitch! Long story short, I don't want it!

I left your son at his granny's house. She knew the whole time. They say a mother usually does. And you accused me of cheating! Which I wasn't, and that's on God.

Fuck you, FREAK! Fuck you!

Freak Zeenie had to read the letter once more.

"What you reading, Unk?" De'shawn asked as he walked in unnoticed, surprising Freak Zeenie a little.

"What?" Freak Zeenie said, quickly covering up the pregnancy test and putting everything back inside the envelope.

"I asked what you reading. Your whole face is white, looking like a ball of baking soda, Unk. Whatever it is though..." De'shawn trailed off. "What's up? Tee hit back yet for you? She ain't answering my calls either," he said. "You think she's still mad at you 'bout the other day or something, ain't it?" he asked. "I got ninety-nine problems, Unk, but a b—uh, female ain't one of 'em," De'shawn said, catching himself before cussing. Then he got up and left, leaving Freak Zeenie by himself.

That damn boy there gon' be hell now, Freak Zeenie thought before his phone chimed, interrupting him.

"What's up with it?" he answered without looking at the caller ID.

"Touch down in the A.M., Senior Si." The line went dead.

Freak Zeenie laid his head face-down on the island.

Friday Morning
Dothan, Alabama

After dropping De'shawn off at his mom's daycare center so he could help Mama Lois with some small chores, Freak Zeenie went to pay for Cartier Jay's and Boo-Boo's bond.

He didn't stick around for their release, though—Freak Zeenie was in full motion.

When he reached the construction company, it was right on time to handle business. Luckily for him, Zacatecas had agreed to send a single truckload for now, just until Freak Zeenie could build his clientele enough to meet larger orders.

Once everything at the company was in order, Freak Zeenie pulled out and headed back to Atlanta.

A Few Hours Later—
Martin Luther King Jr. Boulevard and Maple Street
Atlanta, Georgia

Freak Zeenie leaned back in Levi's new jewelry store, quietly observing transactions from the office. Levi, Remy Red, and Poochie were running the spot, selling some of the best gold, platinum, rose gold, and diamonds the city had ever seen—or at least that's what Levi claimed. Freak Zeenie couldn't help but feel proud of his little brother's success.

Levi was busy hyping up a customer, who was clearly thrilled with his new purchase.

"I'm telling you, my nigga, you 'bout to mess them up with this!" Levi said, grinning. "This the best forty bands you ever spent on yourself, my boy. Come here real quick."

The customer stepped forward, admiring his new piece: a platinum Cuban link choker with a custom, iced-out $100 bill pendant. Levi grabbed the inside of the chain and hung his full weight on it while it was still around the man's neck.

"Look at this!" Levi exclaimed. "See what I'm saying? That bitch won't break for nothing! Somebody try snatching it, they'd break your neck before they break this chain."

Levi let the chain go and tapped the diamonds with a tester. The laser jumped from red to green instantly, confirming the stones were official.

"These four-carat VVS's, homes," Levi added confidently.

"Nigga better come with a few five-point-sevens if he trying to snatch from me!" the customer joked as he put the last $10,000 on the counter.

Levi slid the cash to Remy Red, who took it to the back with Poochie locking the door behind the customer. Once the money was secured, Levi and Freak Zeenie retreated to the office, locking the door behind them.

"That's what I'm talking about, bruh!" Freak Zeenie said, beaming. "You really on your shit, boy. I need to let Cartier Jay and Boo-Boo know to come up here when they cop. Everybody keep talking about Icebox, but man, fuck that noise—might as well keep the bread in the family, you feel me?"

Levi was busy typing away on his laptop. He'd already handled the paperwork for Freak Zeenie's construction company and was now changing his brother's identity— social security number and all. Levi was transferring all of Freak Zeenie's money into accounts tied to a fictitious identity he'd created.

Freak Zeenie had stumbled across a privacy catalog called EDEN PRESS, and besides attending Carlos and Lil Fred's funerals, this was his main reason for coming to Atlanta. If anybody could pull this off, it was Levi.

Levi suddenly stopped typing.

"Nah, bruh. Let nep' them go to Icebox. This ain't for them, you know what I mean?" he said. "Their money's no good here."

"Why not?" Freak Zeenie asked, frowning.

"Because this is high-class costume jewelry, nigga!" Levi said, smirking. He knew he'd just landed a fire *jeu d'esprit*. "All that shit fugazi, my boy. I'm on a mega paper chase . . . for the . . . *free.*"

Levi couldn't hold it in any longer and burst out laughing. He knew he was finessing the game in a way nobody else was.

Freak Zeenie stared at him, letting the newfound information sink in. "Boy, you a damn fool!" he said, shaking his head in disbelief as he stood up.

"Man, you already know," Levi said, keeping his eyes glued to the screen. He was confident in his craft—whatever it was, Levi was proficient in it.

"Nigga, these folks are gonna kill you," Freak Zeenie said, coming to his senses. His head was on a swivel as paranoia set in. "Man, I need to get the fuck out of here right now! You crazy as hell!"

The more Freak Zeenie thought about Levi's scheme, the more uneasy he felt. "We could run this shit down to the country too, though," he said, thinking of the potential profits. "I'm telling you, we'd kill them boys down there."

Levi thrived on danger—it was what made life exciting for him. "Man, these folks don't even know jewelry like that. They buy whatever a rap nigga says is hot," Levi said as he pressed the print button on his laptop.

"Boy, you ain't lying," Freak Zeenie said. "I just watched you finesse a nigga out of forty bands right in my face. So all that shit out there"—Freak Zeenie pointed toward the front of the store— "you mean to tell me it's bogus?"

"Basically."

"Damn!" Freak Zeenie muttered, shaking his head in disbelief. "Even the diamonds?"

Levi smirked. "Man, the tester fake too."

Freak Zeenie was flabbergasted. This was the kind of hustle he'd always wanted to bring to Dothan and the surrounding areas, but other priorities had always gotten in the way.

"Where you find a fake diamond tester at?"

"Online," Levi replied nonchalantly.

"Why you just now doing this, though? Why you weren't on it when I touched down?" Freak Zeenie asked, narrowing his eyes. The more he thought about it, the more he suspected

Levi had swiped the idea from the plans he'd written down while staying with him after his release.

"Cos you said you didn't want me messing with the dope after the last incident," Levi said. "So I had to bring something new to the table."

"Man, don't play with me. I think you stole my idea, bruh," Freak Zeenie said, eyeing Levi suspiciously. "I had all this shit written down when I first got out!"

"What?" Levi shot back, giving him a side-eye. "Bruh, you tripping! Don't start that goofy-ass shit now."

"Nigga, you the goofy one if you think I believe you came up with this on your own!"

They argued back and forth for the rest of the day, the conversation going in circles until they finally got tired and parted ways for the night.

As Freak Zeenie walked toward his car, he shook his head, frustrated by how much of a dullard Levi could be sometimes. Sure, Levi was brilliant when it came to pulling off schemes, but his recklessness had no limits. "That fool's gonna get himself killed," Freak Zeenie muttered under his breath.

He moved through the parking lot in a solitude state of mind, his thoughts churning. The funeral was weighing heavy on him, but now he had even more on his plate— Levi's antics, the construction company, and the game he was trying to master without tipping the scales too far. Doubt lingered in the back of his mind like an unwanted guest. Could he really pull off his plans with all this chaos around him? Was Levi's hustle worth the risk, or would it all come crashing down?

Saturday Morning
Ebenezer Baptist Church
Atlanta, Georgia
Even though Freak Zeenie and Levi sat right next to each other on the same pew, not many words were exchanged

between the two. The church was packed. They were at the same historic church where Martin Luther King Jr. had preached back in the day.

The crowded sanctuary was alive with the low hum of Christian songs, audible even outside the church. Inside, fans swayed back and forth as the congregation mourned. Carlos and Lil Fred's caskets were closed, their bodies too decomposed for an open viewing. Instead, their most recent Instagram pictures rested atop the caskets as a final tribute.

After everyone paid their last respects, Carlos and Lil Fred were carried out of the church by six pallbearers. Tears streamed silently down many faces, but the wailing and weeping of mourners filled the air. It was clear—Carlos and Lil Fred were deeply loved and would truly be missed.

***

Same Time
Across the Street
Outside the Church

A black Tahoe sat idling, its engine purring steadily. Inside were four men, all intently watching for Levi to exit the church. They had followed him here but hadn't found an opportunity to strike yet.

"I'm telling you, shawty—homes think it's a game! But he got me fucked up!" one of them snarled. "'Bout to give him a halo. Watch this!"

"Nah, that nigga got all of us fucked up! What's wrong with homes?" another snapped, clutching a mini assault rifle tightly.

"I can't believe this crazy-ass nigga!" the third man chimed in, shaking his head. "This nigga got nuts the size of a hippopotamus, real talk." He tightened his grip on an automatic shotgun loaded with slugs. "Let me tell y'all—so I go to get my shit appraised, right? Tryna put insurance on my stuff, run a little insurance scam, you feel me? And this nigga gon' tell me my shit ain't worth twenty-five hundred dollars!" He bellowed, face contorted with rage. "Nigga, what? I paid fifteen racks for that shit!"

The driver let out a small chuckle. "Nah, shawty—you lying, right?"

"Shawty, I'm dead serious. Nigga hit the diamonds with a tester right there, and the shit never turned green. I couldn't believe it," he spat, shaking his head. "Man, fuck this—oh, wait. A'ight, showtime! Here this lame nigga come now!"

He let down his window, perching on the edge of the frame, shotgun in hand. The driver kept his window up—he was the only one in the car who hadn't been scammed by Levi. The other three? Victims.

Freak Zeenie emerged from the church holding one side of Carlos' casket, while Levi gripped the other. They descended the church steps carefully, one at a time. Suddenly, three masked men came into view.

"Gun!" someone screamed.

Shots rang out!

Levi was the first to drop the casket, and Freak Zeenie wasn't far behind.

"Get down! Run! Duck!" Freak Zeenie shouted as he scrambled for cover. Levi vaulted over the church rail, running down the street like a modern-day Bo Jackson.

The caskets tumbled down the steps, spilling Carlos and Lil Fred's decomposed bodies onto the pavement. The scene erupted into chaos. A woman fainted while others scattered, desperate to find safety.

Bullets ricocheted off the church building and the pavement. The Tahoe screeched into reverse, speeding back down the block.

"Come on, shawty! That nigga getting the fuck away! Go, go, go!" the front passenger shouted.

Levi darted behind the church, realizing the attack was meant for him alone.

"Fuck, shawty! Man, go, go, go!" one of the passengers yelled in frustration as Levi disappeared from view. The Tahoe left a cloud of white smoke in its wake as it sped off and vanished.

Back on the scene, an elderly woman knelt beside another older woman who lay on the ground, a crimson stain blooming on her chest.

"Somebody call an ambulance! Hurry up!" she cried, applying pressure to the wound. "It's gon' be okay, Bessie. Breathe!"

But Ms. Bessie's eyes rolled back, and she exhaled one final breath. She had been called home.

By the time the police arrived, Levi circled back to the front of the church. He spotted Ms. Bessie's lifeless body and knew she was gone.

"Freak!" Levi yelled, his head swiveling frantically. "Freak!"

Inside the church, Freak Zeenie was helping people find safety. Hearing Levi's call, he rushed outside to check on his younger brother. Together, they assisted others in placing Carlos and Lil Fred's bodies back into their damaged caskets, now riddled with bullet holes.

After answering routine questions from the police, the family had no choice but to reschedule the burial. Though Freak Zeenie and Levi had shown their respects, they decided they wouldn't return for the funeral.

Before leaving Atlanta and heading back to Dothan, Levi approached Freak Zeenie, hoping to mend fences.

"A'ight, bruh. Be safe on that highway," Levi said, still looking shaken. "Them niggas was trying to hit me, bruh! They chased me, but I couldn't recognize nobody." His face was a mix of anger and confusion.

Freak Zeenie smirked. "Shit, I know your scary ass couldn't recognize nobody, fast as you was running! Probably some niggas you ran out on 'bout they bread—with all that fake-ass jewelry you juggin'."

Levi laughed and pounded fists with his brother.

"Man, y'all be dangerous," Freak Zeenie said as he climbed into his car.

"You better say it," Levi replied.

Freak Zeenie started the engine and pulled off. *My gotdamn brother. Nigga crazy as hell*, he thought as he hit the interstate.

On the way to Dothan, Freak Zeenie checked his phone and saw a text from Cartier Jay. Cartier Jay confirmed he had the money ready. It was the only text Freak Zeenie had—nothing from Khashia.

Chapter 13

Sunday Morning
Yazoo FCI
Yazoo, Mississippi

After waiting an hour and a half, Khashia finally made it into the visitation room. The prison was still under modified visits, meaning no touching after the first hug and kiss—or the visit would be terminated, and the inmate would be sent straight to the quarantine unit for two weeks.

Before sitting down, Khashia got up and bought two big-ass rib sandwiches, two Sprites, two BBQ chips, and two Snickers bars. It had been a while since she last visited Trae, and she couldn't shake the nervousness she felt. Might as well get it over with, hell, Khashia thought as she calmly waited.

She settled into her seat, leaning back and fidgeting with her freshly manicured nails to keep her mind occupied. As she rubbed her stomach, she thought about the growing pains—both physical and emotional. After going over everything with her mom, Khashia had decided to keep the baby.

Why should I get rid of it? she reasoned. Freak Zeenie would be the one missing out, not her. Besides, she planned to put him on child support out of spite. After all, Freak Zeenie had cheated on her back in the day and even had a child with her stepsister. That betrayal still stung, and Khashia felt justified in her decision.

She'd seen all of Freak Zeenie's text messages but left every one of them on read. This was her first pregnancy in her 34 years of life, and the flood of emotions she was dealing with hit her like a tidal wave. Deep down, even though she wouldn't admit it to anyone, she was still in love with Freak Zeenie. But now, she was falling for the man she was here to see—Trae. And part of her wanted to hurt Freak Zeenie the way he had hurt her.

Trae walked into the visitation room, scanning the crowd. His eyes landed on Khashia almost immediately. Even though she looked extra sexy, Trae kept his mug on, his expression cold and unreadable.

Stopping at the CO's desk, Trae handed over his ID before approaching Khashia. She stood up, arms outstretched for a hug.

"Hey, you," she said softly.

Trae walked right past her and sat down.

Khashia's smile dropped as she frowned and quickly sat back down, folding her arms.

Trae was still heated over the phone call incident. "If I ain't had shit going on," he growled through clenched teeth, "I would've reached out and slapped the living shit out your ass, bitch!" His fists clenched as he struggled to control his anger.

"For what, Trae?" Khashia snapped. "'Cause I didn't put you here! You should've slapped your lame-ass supposed-to-be partner, not me!" She jabbed her finger at her chest.

That hit a nerve. Trae's eyes narrowed. It was a low blow, and he didn't expect her to come back at him like that.

His face softened slightly, and a smirk tugged at his lips as he thought about what he had planned for his disloyal homie. Taking a deep breath, he nodded. "You right. I should. And in due time, I will. Believe that. The streets ain't seen the last of Trae. On God!"

His voice turned sharp again. "But why the fuck you got niggas answering your phone, disrespecting a nigga and shit, huh? That's what we on now?"

Khashia looked confused. "What? When, Trae? I don't be doing no shit like that," she said with an edge in her tone. She didn't want to hear this. She'd expected Trae to compliment her—tell her how pretty she looked, how thick she'd gotten, or how much he missed her.

"I been trying to call your funky ass since the last time we talked, but yo' shit been going straight to voicemail," he spat. "Then, the other day, some nigga picked up, claiming he had his filthy dick in your mouth. Talking 'bout he yo' baby daddy." Trae's voice rose as anger boiled over. "That nigga dead once I get out! So, you got a baby daddy now? Oh, it's fuck me, huh? I'm stuck in here with forty years—it's over for me, right?" He leaned forward, speaking through clenched teeth, his glare piercing Khashia.

The more Trae thought about everything, the madder he got. Being left for dead with a 40-year sentence was eating him alive. He'd sacrificed everything for Khashia and his so-called partner. He could've snitched and walked away scot-free, but he chose to keep it solid. And where did that leave him? Bitter.

Trae replayed the events in his head. All he'd done was pick up his homie, take him four blocks over, and drop him off. He didn't know the man had just committed a home invasion robbery and murder. Next thing Trae knew, someone pointed out his car in a lineup, claiming they'd seen it leaving the scene after gunshots. Trae stood trial, only to have his own homie—the one he'd dropped off—show up as an anonymous witness for the prosecution.

His so-called friend testified that Trae had confessed to the murder. That betrayal was like a bullet to the chest. And with that, Trae became the Prince of Darkness.

His homie walked away with a $50,000 reward while Trae got a boatload of time. When Trae tried to cooperate later, pleading to tell his side of the story, it was too late. The feds didn't want to hear it.

Now, with a cell phone in hand, Trae was a different man. He had plans. Big ones. It was only a matter of time before he made his next move.

Meanwhile, his ex-homie was living large, spending reward money, selling dope, and flashing cash. Trae's house had been hit before he was even booked, and only two people knew where he lived—Khashia and his homie.

Khashia was lost in thought as Trae pieced together the puzzle she couldn't. "Naw, bae, it's not like that," she said, breaking the silence. "You still top priority, boo. This shit just takes time. Whoever you talked to? That's probably the same nigga who broke into my house a month ago." She paused. "I don't even have a phone right now, Trae. I told Momma to let you know so you wouldn't think I was dodging you," she added, her face betraying nothing.

"And no, I don't have a baby daddy," she lied. "The nigga's still in prison. But I can't wait till he gets out so we can practice," she said, laying it on thick.

Trae stared at her, unconvinced. He knew she was lying, if not about the whole ordeal, then definitely about the phone. He could almost bet his life on it. Still, he decided to let it slide. It wasn't the time to trip. He had his own plans to focus on.

"Um-hmm. So, what up? Why are you here then?" he asked, leaning back.

Khashia smiled slyly. This was her chance. She had a way out for Trae—a lick of a lifetime, if everything went according to her plan. She scooted to the edge of her chair, leaned in, and began explaining her scheme while they ate the snacks she'd brought.

Trae listened intently, knowing that Khashia might just be the key to his next move.

Right after Visitation
The Infirmary
Yazoo FCI

Trae walked down the dim corridor and tapped three times on the locked metal door. Almost immediately, Nurse Gilbert opened it for him. She was working overtime today due to the nationwide staff shortage in the BOP. Since it was the weekend, Nurse Gilbert was the only one on duty.

Trae wasted no time—and neither did Nurse Gilbert. They pressed their bodies together, feeling each other up as they slipped into the room with the medical bed. Nurse Gilbert climbed onto the bed, and Trae had her in the buck instantly.

Trae fucked Nurse Gilbert so hard she couldn't help but moan loudly from the pleasure she was feeling. Neither of them was worried about getting caught. They were completely alone in the infirmary, the only spot with no cameras, and Nurse Gilbert had turned her radio down.

Meanwhile, L.T. Wills had radioed Nurse Gilbert three times back-to-back but got no response. Wills was running behind three COs who were rushing an inmate toward the infirmary. The inmate had cut his wrist and was bleeding out fast. He was still having an episode from smoking "duce" (K-2) that he'd hit off a piece of wire and a double-A battery.

In the infirmary, Trae held Nurse Gilbert by her neck, her legs draped over his shoulders as he long-stroked her with powerful thrusts. Even though Nurse Gilbert was super obese, she had that for sho' wet wet. That pussy was tight and portly.

Trae's seed started broiling up, and he picked up the pace. "Here . . . it . . . c—"

The door burst open, and three COs stormed into the room without warning, moving fast and looking for Nurse Gilbert. Trae and Nurse Gilbert were damn near scared to death.

L.T. Wills was the last to enter.

"What the fuck?!?" L.T. Wills roared.

Embarrassed, Nurse Gilbert scrambled to her feet, snatched up her pants, and threw them on in a hurry. Her face turned red—redder than the Alabama College logo.

Two Hours Later...
The SHU, Yazzo, FCI

Trae stood at the door of his cell on the amended range, listening to all the segregation war stories. He couldn't believe his luck.

Because the SHU was overcrowded, Trae was about to make Perc's bond without even knowing it. Perc packed his few belongings, happy as fuck, and waited for the COs to come get him. But Perc found out real quick that wasn't the case at all. He'd have to wait until Monday or even Tuesday.

Perc was mad as hell when he realized the COs had played with him. He wasn't thinking straight, though, because if he had been, he'd know it was the weekend. Nobody got out of the SHU on weekends in the BOP. That was just law, period. There was nothing the COs could do for Perc until then.

"Hey, Trae?" Perc called out. "I heard you the ticket man out there now all of a sudden, boy!" Perc said, speaking on the news he'd picked up as soon as he hit the SHU.

"Yeah, man. That shit ain't 'bout nothing," Trae replied casually. "If you could do it, why can't I?" He brushed it off.

"My cell, though, for real. So you ain't heard shit 'bout that, huh? 'Cause I shole ain't."

"Nawl," Trae cut him off quickly.

"Boy, you better be glad the SMU closed, or you'd be on your way, nigga," Perc teased. The SMU (Special Management Unit) was a disciplinary prison for the BOP nationwide. It had been shut down due to all the unsolved murders COs and inmates had gotten away with.

"You a nasty-ass nigga too, homes!" Perc added, smirking.

"That's a dub!" Burn One bellowed out of nowhere. Burn One was from North Carolina, and everybody on the tier started laughing.

Trae didn't respond. He just shook his head, went to his bunk, and laid back. *Y'all think I'm going to the SMU? Bitch, I'm 'bout to evaporate out this shit. Watch me dougie!* Trae thought to himself, ignoring the laughter as the whole tier clowned him for the rest of the day. Deep down, though, Trae knew damn well any one of them would've fucked Nurse Gilbert too if they'd gotten the chance. *Niggas be killing me.*

Nurse Gilbert didn't fare as well. She got walked off the compound by two COs, officially fired. Nurse Gilbert cried all the way to the parking lot. Trae had messed up her life, but did he care? Not one bit. Nurse Gilbert was just as much at fault as he was. She played the game with one controller—and played herself.

As Trae lay in his bunk that night, he hoped his cellie, Conscious, handled the business like he claimed he would. Trae had already Zelle'd Conscious five bands, with a promise to send him the other five upon his release.

Trae had spoken to the agents earlier that morning and sent the bread to Conscious right before his visit. Now, there was no way to communicate further with the agents—Trae's phone was stashed inside his light switch.

Closing his eyes, Trae blocked out the excessive noise around him. *This time*, he thought, *time better side with me. 'Cause it sure didn't at trial.* His 40-year sentence was the proof in the pudding.

Chapter 14

Monday
The Construction Company
Dothan, Alabama

Trucks were dropping off loads and picking them up. Freak Zeenie had gotten to the spot early this morning—before work hours—getting ahead of the curve. For the first time, Pastor Barber showed up on time. Freak Zeenie had Boo-Boo load Pastor Barber's box truck with over 48 boxes, each holding 20 kilos.

The truck had a clean church wrap around it with a logo of Jesus on the cross and lettering that read First Baptist Church. Pastor Barber was overly excited about this run—his biggest one yet. He was estimated to make eighty-one thousand off it, with half already paid up front. He was running from Tallahassee, Florida, all the way to Maine. Maine was still eating off the lick from Lil Tee a month ago, right before Lil Tee went missing.

Pastor Barber had left about 45 minutes ago, high as a leer as usual. Freak Zeenie had to warn him not to rush the trip.

Cartier Jay pulled up and paid Freak Zeenie what he owed, plus half up front on his new load. Then Cartier Jay and Boo-Boo reimbursed Freak Zeenie for covering their bond. Cartier Jay sat in the driver's seat of the sprinter van with his left arm in a sling, while Boo-Boo worked on loading their package. As Boo-Boo loaded the van, Cartier

Jay broke down what happened the night he got shot—straight from the horse's mouth.

Freak Zeenie was madder than former President Trump when he found out he lost the election. He insisted on handling things himself. He didn't want to pull out his black book, but Cartier Jay stood firm, saying he had it under control. Frustrated, Freak Zeenie stormed off, cussing a string of profanities, and stashed the bread Cartier Jay had just given him.

By the time Freak Zeenie came back, Boo-Boo had finished loading the van, and Cartier Jay was buckled up, ready to hit the road. Cartier Jay had shit lined up: Kal-Kal was ready to re-up; he had the Bloods on the east side to serve; Boo-Boo, his boys out in Clayton and Clio in the country parts of Barbour County, and folks out in Troy, Alabama.

Cartier Jay wasn't even missing the Schoolyard Crips' income—he had plans to wipe them all out anyway. He had to make up for the losses they'd taken and still cover his and Boo-Boo's lawyer fees, 'cause trial costs. The best part about being out on bond in Dothan, Alabama? No ankle monitors. They could fight their case without being tracked.

Cartier Jay dropped the van into drive with his good arm.

"A'ight, pops. We out!" he said. "That shit was fucked up how they did at the funeral, though! I still can't get that out of my head. Unk up there on that BS." Cartier Jay let the van creep forward at a snail's pace, shaking his head.

"I'm trying to tell ya, boy!" Freak Zeenie said. "This shit crazy out here nowadays. Niggas ain't got shit to thank with. Did you see what that young-ass boy pulled up in North Carolina?"

Cartier Jay hit the brakes. "Nawl, what happened?"

"He just killed five motherfuckers—started with his older brother and an off-duty cop," Freak Zeenie explained. "Say they don't have a motive yet. He's in critical condition. The media claiming nobody knows if the lil boy shot his self or if the cops did it." Freak Zeenie gave Cartier Jay a knowing look. "Man, y'all be safe on the road and stay dangerous in these streets. I can bond y'all out anytime, but I can't bring y'all back from the graveyard. Feel me? That, y'all gon' have to wait on Jesus for."

"Already, pops," Cartier Jay said. "And you know the cops shot homes! We out. Later!" Cartier Jay pulled off.

Freak Zeenie watched until their van disappeared into traffic. He walked to his own van, got in, and sat there for a second, checking his phone. Now that Khashia was carrying Freak Zeenie's seed, his concern for her had heightened.

There weren't any new texts, so Freak Zeenie pulled out, headed toward the Tree Farm. *I gotta stop by her momma's crib later and check her temperature. Fuck all that,* he thought. But first, he had things to handle at the Tree Farm.

Meanwhile...
A Few Miles Outside Leon County, Florida—
Pastor Barber pulled into a gas station to fill up—he was just under a quarter tank. Draped in a money-green Polo suit with tootsie-roll brown Gucci penny loafers to accommodate his sauce, Pastor Barber paced back and forth, talking on his iPhone to his brother, Chief Duke. His wife sat inside the truck, hitting coke out the bag with a red Slushie straw—the kind with the little shovel on the end.

"I know and understand, bruh! But you need to hurry the hell up—I gots to get going!" Pastor Barber snapped, eyeing a few cars suspiciously before continuing. "Yeah, man! Down the middle!" he bellowed in rushed tones before ending the call.

Pastor Barber placed the gas pump back and climbed into the truck. His wife checked her nose in the rearview mirror, making sure no residue was left.

"What he say, Carl?" his wife asked, passing Pastor Barber the bag of coke so he could get himself right.

"He with it, but I didn't know his wife was in bad shape," Pastor Barber said, hitting the bag. "The money gon' help tremendously. Their Medicaid and health care together don't cover it."

"Awl . . . that's an issue in itself. So, how far away is he?"

"Like eight minutes. Eight minutes," he repeated impatiently, pulling the truck to the side of the gas station to wait on Chief Duke.

Meanwhile, two U.S. Marshals sat backed into a parking spot, drinking coffee after finishing surveillance in the area. It wasn't the church truck that caught their attention—it was the loud colors, gold rings, and cool-daddy strut Pastor Barber displayed.

One of the Marshals scratched his beard.

"What you think that dude got going on?" he asked his partner.

"Not sure, but he damn sure don't fit the description of any pastor I ever seen. I'll say that," his partner replied.

"Me too," the first Marshal said. "And if he is one, I wouldn't attend his service. Did you see him?"

"Hell yeah, I saw him—looking high as a flying saucer, if you ask me," Agent Simpson said, pulling out his radio. He called in the suspicious activity he and his partner were watching out of nowhere.

Moments Later—

Chief Duke pulled up next to Pastor Barber's truck in a small U-Haul truck. Chief Duke jumped out in a rush and went behind the truck, pulling the slider up.

"Come on, Carl! I ain't got all fucking day!"

Pastor Barber moved with the speed of a 19-year-old, despite being 60.

"Man if you don't shut the hell up with your late ass . . . Shit!" Pastor Barber shot back at him as he snatched a box out. Chief Duke grabbed another, and Pastor Barber grabbed one more.

"Look who's talking!" Chief Duke said, pulling the slider back down.

"Yeah, look!" Pastor Barber shot back, pulling the slider down on his own truck, and hopping back into the vehicle, spinning rocks until the truck hit the asphalt.

Neither of them noticed the two men standing on the corner of the gas station. The agents watched the whole transaction unfold.

Chief Duke pulled out headed back towards his hometown, Bakersville, Alabama. Checking his rearview, he saw the road was clear, and set the cruise control to 60 mph.

Meanwhile, Pastor Barber had his truck up to 72 mph as he crossed over into Leon County, Florida. The US Marshals trailed behind him at a safe distance. When he caught sight of a state trooper up ahead, Pastor Barber immediately slowed down to 58 mph, hoping he hadn't been noticed.

"Damn . . . Fuck!" he cursed under his breath. "Okay, okay . . . I need you right here, Father God," he bellowed, nervously checking his mirror as he saw the state trooper whip a sharp U-turn and light him up.

"We cool, we cool!" he said quickly, trying to calm himself. "Why I'm trippin', right? Ain't it, bae?" He glanced at his wife for reassurance.

"Yeah. It's nothing but a lil over the speed limit," she said quickly, staring straight ahead while shoving the coke sack down her pants. Her eyes were wide as hell.

Pastor Barber pulled over to the side of the road, and his wife passed him his license. The state trooper stepped out of his cruiser, walking toward the truck with one hand resting on his service weapon. The U.S. Marshals pulled up behind the trooper but stayed inside their unmarked Jeep.

"You know you were going at least 15 miles over the speed limit, sir?" the state trooper asked, peering into the truck window.

Before the trooper could ask for it, Pastor Barber handed him his license. The trooper studied it for a moment.

"Not really, sir. I'm still getting used to this truck," Pastor Barber replied, sneaking glances at the Jeep behind them, wondering who was inside.

"Why the rush? You hauling church supplies, right?" the trooper asked, his eyes narrowing as he studied Pastor Barber closely.

"Um, like I said, o—"

"Could you step out of the truck for me, sir?"

"Why?"

"It smells like marijuana, sir. Now, could you step out? *Now!*"

"No... it... don't!" Pastor Barber said with a prestidigitation. "Neither one of us smokes, sir! I'm a pa—"

"I'm not gonna ask you again!" The trooper glanced back at the plain Jeep. "You too, ma'am. Step out and come 'round here for me."

Reluctantly, Pastor Barber and his wife complied. The trooper frisked them both, then searched the front cabin. After finding nothing, he hopped down from the truck.

"Told you, sir. Not even an ash in the ashtray. We don't smoke—it's unhealthy," Pastor Barber said, a small wave of relief washing over him.

His wife, however, was a different story. She stood there sweating bullets behind a pair of designer frames.

"A'ight, open up the back for me real quick, and I'll write you a ticket so we can be on our way."

Pastor Barber's forehead broke out in a sweat out of nowhere. *Come on! Damn, man!* He wanted to say it out loud but bit his tongue.

"Officer, is all this necessary, sir? We're two senior citizens here now!"

The trooper nodded.

"I'll be quick for y'all then. Now come on!"

Pastor Barber took a deep breath and swallowed hard. Slowly, he walked to the back of the truck, unlocked the sliding door, and lifted it for the trooper.

The officer climbed up into the back cabin and opened the first box. Pastor Barber's stomach churned as he bit down on his bottom lip, trying to keep his composure.

The trooper dug through the newspapers in the box, then pulled out a whole kilo of coke. His eyes darted past Pastor Barber and his wife to the plain Jeep. Holding the kilo up high for the agents to see, the trooper called out, "Don't move. You two are und—"

Before he could finish, Pastor Barber's wife fainted, collapsing to the ground. She didn't hear the rest of the trooper's sentence.

The U.S. Marshals climbed out of the Jeep and walked up to the back of the truck.

"What do we have here?" one of the agents asked.

Pastor Barber squinted at the kilo in the trooper's hand.

"Man . . . what the fuck is that?"

Chapter 15

Noon Time—
Zone 6
Atlanta, Georgia

Conscious found the address Trae had given him. He'd used the five thousand dollars to put down on an apartment. Conscious had already paid a casual smoker to hit Rent-A-Center for him to furnish the place throughout. Then, he dropped fifteen hundred on a 2014 Camaro and spent $350 on a Glock 27 that came with just a standard clip. Conscious's funds quickly deteriorated.

Sitting across the street, Conscious watched the woman Trae had shown him back when they were in prison together. Even though he was a bit far from her, Conscious was certain it was the same woman he'd seen in Trae's photo album. He watched as a dude hugged all over her, squeezing on her fat, juicy ass.

Conscious gritted his teeth.

"Y'all some low-down-ass motherfuckers, ain't y'all?" he muttered to himself. "Out here fucking and carrying on like shit sweet, while y'all got my dawg doing forty years in prison!" His voice rose with anger. "*Forty years!*" Conscious bellowed. "Don't worry, my dawg gon' win that appeal, 'cause I'm 'bout to handle this business, shawty," he said, continuing to talk to himself. "You can come on with that other five too, 'cause I need it. Or, Trae, you'll be going where they 'bout to go." Conscious pulled his gloves on, muttering his plans to himself. Next, he adjusted his COVID mask.

Conscious had stalked the house all weekend and was positive the couple was alone.

The couple held hands, inching toward the backyard. Trae had told Conscious that Khashia and his ex-homie were still staying in his house, playing him for a fool. Conscious believed the dude Trae spoke to back in their cell was his ex-homie, trying to disguise his voice 'cause he was pure, raw pussy.

Trae had also told him about the extra key hidden under a flower pot on the porch. Conscious confirmed this was true—he spotted the flower pot as he moved toward the house. After a quick scan of the area, he crossed the street and crept toward the house.

Conscious made it through the gate and up the steps without drawing any attention to himself. He moved the flower pot, retrieved the key just like Trae had said, and carefully put the pot back in its place.

He checked the door first but found it locked. Conscious slid the key into the lock, turned it, and heard the door unlock. *They gotta be super stupid!* Conscious thought. Like a burglar, he crouched low, snatching the Glock 27 from the small of his back.

Pushing the door shut behind him, Conscious locked it and began checking the rooms one by one. He was looking for the perfect hiding spot to catch Trae's ops by surprise and kill them.

As soon as Conscious stepped into the kitchen, he felt the all-too-familiar pressure of a gun barrel pressing against the back of his head. His heart rate spiked, and his hand gripped the Glock tightly, ready to swing into action.

"Move, and I'll pop yo' shit like a birthday balloon, you piece of shit!"

The voice came from a female officer who quickly circled around in front of him. She was the woman Conscious had mistaken for Khashia.

"You won't be needing this where you going!" she snapped, snatching the Glock from his hand.

Conscious was confused as hell. The officer got on her walkie-talkie to call for backup. To Conscious, it felt like U.S. Marshals appeared out of thin air—some even seemed to crawl out of the kitchen cabinets.

Then the agent Conscious presumed to be Trae's ex-homie walked up to him.

"You are under arrest for murder-for-hire," the agent said nonchalantly. "You have the right to remain silent. You have the right to—"

Conscious didn't hear the rest. His brain short-circuited at the phrase murder-for-hire. It finally dawned on him—he'd been framed and set up by Trae.

Conscious dropped his head as the Marshals patted him down and slapped handcuffs on him.

3:00 PM – Yazoo FCI (The S.H.U.), Yazoo, Mississippi

Trae sat on the edge of his bunk, deep in thought.

TAP! TAP! TAP!

Trae snapped out of it and looked up to see why the CO was hitting the cell window.

"Trae Brown?"

"Yeah. What up?"

"All the way," the CO said, moving on quickly with his kick-out list. "Allen Moore! Pack it up—you're getting kicked back to the yard. You got five minutes!" the CO bellowed. "Hurry up too, so you can make it out before count!"

Perc was more than ready.

"Shit, 'bout time! Hell, I been ready!" Perc said, walking to the cell door. He looked back at his cellie. "You heard that though?" Perc pointed toward Trae's cell.

"Aye, CO! What you said now?" Trae called out, trying to catch the CO before he got too far down the range.

"I said, all the way!"

"A'ight. Where I'm going?"

"Outta here, unless you don't wanna go!" the CO shot back. "Immediate release! Now, hurry up! I gotta get y'all outta here by 3:30!"

"Oh, shit! I'm ready, nigga!" Trae said, jumping up with a smile, two-stepping around the cell.

The whole range was in an uproar. Everybody was trying to say something to Trae.

"Hey, bruh! How the fuck you got immediate release, nigga?" Perc yelled through the cell door.

"Nigga, John got me out to run a train on my whore with 'em, bitch! Say his dick wasn't big enough!" Trae joked, grinning wide. "I'm out this bitch . . . I'm out this bitch!" Trae sang as he danced.

***

Later That Night – Yazoo FCI (3B Unit)
Perc had the whole unit hyped when he finally made it back to the yard. Everyone was talking over each other at once.

"Hey, Perc, you get that scribe I sent, bruh?" one dude asked as they stood around the TV, waiting for the news to come on.

"Nawl, bruh. Who you sent it by?" Perc replied.

"Damn! I thought you got that joint! Nobody—I boomeranged it."

Boomeranging was when you put someone's info on the envelope but didn't include a stamp so it would get sent back to you.

"Nawl, homes, I never got that joint."

"I was tryna tell you 'bout that bitch-ass nigga Trae setting you up!" the dude said. "I saw him in your room that day before Ms. Smith shook you down, nigga!"

"Oh, yeah?" Perc rubbed his chin. "That nigga just got immedi—"

Perc stopped mid-sentence as the world news came on. It was 6:00 PM, and everyone tuned in.

"Breaking news!" the anchor announced. "U.S. Marshals have just arrested a man in Atlanta, Georgia, by the name of Camron Jackson on murder-for-hire charges."

A mugshot of Camron Jackson appeared on the screen.

"Aw, man, that's um . . . um—"

"Conscious, nigga!" someone blurted out. "Ah, Trae's old celly. Damn, homes just got out!"

The TV showed footage of Conscious as cameras flashed in his face, and U.S. Marshals rushed him into a blacked-out SUV.

"Man, that blurb! Trae set me the blurb up!" Conscious bellowed, but his words were censored.

The anchor came back on.

"U.S. Marshals stated that Camron Jackson confessed he'd be ten thousand dollars richer upon completing a hit on a married couple responsible for getting an unnamed criminal forty years. Jackson allegedly claimed this was how he made his living."

Another picture of Conscious appeared briefly.

"The U.S. Marshals disguised themselves as the couple and sent the real couple to safety until they made the arrest. Camron Jackson will be held at Lovejoy Federal Facility without bond. He's also being investigated for past similar crimes in Fulton County. If convicted, he could face life in prison—or even the death sentence."

"Now, out in Stockton, California, officers have finally arrested an alleged serial killer by the name of Westley Brown—"

"Ain't that just 'bout a bitch! Fuckin' super-hot-ass *fuck nigga!*" Perc bellowed, his face twisted with anger.

"Damn, that's fucked up, dawg. I'm telling you, that right there is why I don't be fuckin' with niggas now!" someone said.

"Right!" Perc replied, storming off.

***

That Same Night
Greyhound Bus Station
Atlanta, Georgia

It was 11:07 p.m. when Trae stepped off the bus and back into the city. Trae moved through the warm summer night breeze of Atlanta, Georgia, chest out.

"They done fucked around and freed a Gee. Ohh, shit!" he said with a grin. "I'm back, fuck niggas! Y'all know what it is!"

Trae took in the city he loved with his whole heart. The buildings, the lights, the energy—it all felt like home.

"I'm 'bout to go check out some of these bad-ass whores right fast," he said, hyped. "Shaking ass and titties. For a small fee!"

He crossed the street, confidence radiating with every step, and approached the entrance to Magic City. Trae showed his prison ID to the bouncer, who waved him in almost immediately, free of charge—standard policy at Magic City for fresh releases.

Trae enjoyed a free drink along with a free lap dance of his choice on his first night out.

But in the streets, the triple cross always hits harder than the double.

Chapter 16

The Next Day
Dothan, Alabama

Freak Zeenie handed Pastor Barber the other half of the money he owed him, then told him there would be a delay on the next road-running tip because something had come up. This spooked Pastor Barber tremendously. He had just been pulled over the day before and had agreed to cooperate with the northern division of Florida to protect his and his wife's freedom. Pastor Barber chose self first.

Now, all Pastor Barber had was the money Freak Zeenie had just given him, because the U.S. Marshals had split the money he had on him at the time amongst themselves. Stressed out, Pastor Barber left Freak Zeenie and headed home with just a box and a half of kilos and forty thousand, five hundred dollars to his name.

Unknown to anyone in the family, Pastor Barber was drowning in huge gambling debts that he was desperately trying to claw his way out of. Right now, Pastor Barber needed all the money he could get.

Meanwhile, Freak Zeenie got in traffic and headed to the lawyer's office to pick up the check for his lawsuit settlement. The insurance company had finally cleared it. Khashia crossed Freak Zeenie's mind for a split second, but just as quickly, he shoved the thought out.

Back at home, Mama Lois had De'shawn helping her around the house. With the house empty, Freak Zeenie was enjoying the peace and quiet he'd longed for during his time locked up.

While waiting for the light to change, his peace of mind was abruptly interrupted.

"Yeah, Uncle Duke? What you got going on?" Freak Zeenie answered his phone, asking as he began moving forward again in traffic.

Chief Duke took a long pause and let out a loud breath of air.

"Unk? What's up? You good?" Freak Zeenie asked, concerned.

"Man . . . Nephew. Not really."

"What you mean?"

"It's your auntie. Man, the doctor said she's in stage four cancer," Chief Duke said, his voice strained. "Plus, she just contracted that new Russian COVID-nineteen shit, and it's made everything worse, you know."

"Yeah, Unk, I see what you saying," Freak Zeenie said, pulling into the lawyer's parking lot.

"Naw, I'm not finished," Chief Duke continued. "This shit has broke the hell outta me. All my 401K . . . gone." He sighed deeply. "On top of that, her Medicaid ran out, and so did our health coverage. Shit, I don't know what else to do, nephew," he said weakly. "I had our daughter start up a GoFundMe and a Kickstarter page too, but it still wasn't enough."

Chief Duke went on to explain that if he didn't come up with another two hundred and fifty thousand, the hospital would kick his wife out. Chief Duke sounded depressed, stressed, and desperate all at once—if Freak Zeenie had to take a guess.

"Shit, say no more, Unk," Freak Zeenie said. "I got a cool honey bun (hundred thousand) toward that. That's the least I could do."

"A'ight, Nephew, but what the hell is a honey bun? How will that help?" Chief Duke asked, confused.

Freak Zeenie chuckled. "That's a hundred thousand, Unk, in street terms, old man."

"Oh, that would be a big help. On another note, I heard De'shawn turned out to be yo' son, Nephew!" he said. "You gon' be on so much child support in a minute, boy, you better think about getting snipped!" Chief Duke joked, sounding a little better now that Freak Zeenie could help him out.

"Man, how you heard that?" Freak Zeenie laughed at his uncle's sense of humor.

"Man, you know sis' is over-excited about her grandbaby, Nephew. Lois let all of us know about our new addition to the family," he said. "Well, let me go on inside this hospital and see how my wife coming along, Nephew."

"A'ight, Unk. Mom can't keep nothing on the low!" Freak Zeenie laughed. "I just told her this morning. Umph, umph, umph," he said. "I'll see you, say 'round six tonight. Yeah, meet me at Smokey Pigs."

"I'll be there," Chief Duke said.

"A'ight," Freak Zeenie said, ending the call before heading into the lawyer's office.

Meanwhile – Days Inn, Dothan, Alabama

Kal-Kal was on an all-around come-up, but he was blowing more bread than he wanted to for the Fourth of July. Kal-Kal had been grinding like never before. He was overjoyed because he'd just picked up his whip from the paint shop that morning.

Last year for the car show, Kal-Kal had been a passenger—fresh out the joint. But this year was totally different. He couldn't wait to show out. He'd already copped a nice gold Cuban link and stashed it away like a Band-Aid.

Earlier that morning, Kal-Kal had run into ex-cop Fortune. Unfortunately, Fortune was short on cash again, like always, ever since he started his crack binge. Kal-Kal wasn't in the mood for crackhead games today.

As Kal-Kal turned to walk away, Fortune pulled out a bust-down skeleton Cartier watch. Kal-Kal's eyes grew wide as silver dollars—he knew exactly what the timepiece was worth.

Fortune had gotten the watch from Junkie Que and Sam, who were back at the hotel room waiting for him to return, hoping he'd bring back that straight-drop crack cocaine they were fiending for.

Kal-Kal inspected the watch closely.

"What you trying to do with that?" Kal-Kal asked, knowing he had to have it no matter what.

Fortune thought about his asking price for a minute. "Since it's you..." He paused. "Give me a big eight." He repeated what Junkie Que and Sam had coached him to say.

"Man . . . I ain't got no big eight for real," Kal-Kal lied through his teeth. A big eight is 4.5 ounces.

"Come on, Kal-Kal. Not this time, buddy," Fortune said. "Don't miss out on this nice watch now." Fortune pressed on—he wanted and needed a good amount of dope, especially since three of them were smoking today.

Kal-Kal thought quickly. "Look, man, here's what I can do—and will do," he said. "I got you two and a half ounces, and I got fifty of these." Kal-Kal held up a Ziploc bag of Percocets.

Kal-Kal had come across a deal he couldn't pass up at a truck stop a few days ago. These days, Percocets went for $30 a pill street value and were considered downers when misused.

Fortune knew all too well about pain pills—his grandfather had used them after surviving a car crash. Fortune hesitated, wondering what Junkie Que and Sam would think. But in the end, he decided to take the deal so he could trade the pills for crack later.

"A'ight, buddy, I'll do that this time, but n—"

"How many times I gotta tell you, motherfucker—I ain't yo' goddamn buddy!" Kal-Kal snapped, snatching the watch from Fortune mid-sentence.

Kal-Kal handed Fortune the 50-pack of pills, then reached into his boxer briefs and pulled out a Ziploc bag full of crack. He counted out two ounces and passed them to Fortune.

"Hey, you said two and a half—" Fortune caught himself.

"Well, that's all I got. This shit already sold, my guy. You can take it or leave it. Look around," Kal-Kal said, gesturing at their surroundings. "We out in the fucking open. You used to be a cop—you know better than that."

Kal-Kal stuffed the Ziploc bag back into his boxer briefs and dropped the watch into his front pocket.

Wasting no time, Fortune beelined back to his hotel room, where Junkie Que and Sam were waiting impatiently. Fortune showed them what he'd settled for, and a small argument broke out before they split the pills down the middle.

"Molly . . . Percocet . . . Molly . . . Percocet!" Junkie Que chanted, Bankhead-bouncing to the lyrics from Future's album.

Junkie Que popped a Perc' before loading his crack pipe. Sam mimicked him, popping a pill right after his brother, and the two of them started laughing when Fortune joined in. Fortune's attempt at rapping the lyrics made him sound like a redneck.

"What?" Fortune asked, confused.

"Man, you sound just like a dawg gone hillbilly, Fort!" Junkie Que said, putting fire to the end of his pipe and taking a hit.

Fortune shrugged, threw a pill back, and grabbed his pipe. They were as happy as a crackhead could be, having a full-blown crackhead party in the hotel room.

35 Minutes Later ...
The Lawyers Office
Dothan, Alabama

Freak Zeenie stepped out of the lawyer's office after signing all the paperwork agreeing not to sue or bring any more claims against the police department for the same reason. Checking the time on his phone, Freak Zeenie decided to swing by Khashia's mom's house to check on her. He figured he'd let Khashia make her own decisions about whether to come back, just like she'd made the decision to leave in the first place.

As Freak Zeenie drove past the Days Inn, he noticed it was swarming with cops, ambulances, and a crowd of bystanders. A white sheet covered what looked like a body, and he wondered what the hell was going on.

Still, Freak Zeenie wasn't curious enough to stop and pull over, so he kept it moving.

Same Time – Days Inn, Dothan, Alabama

Kal-Kal pulled out two cars behind Freak Zeenie, unaware of his presence. Moments earlier, he'd watched the ex-cop scream his name like he'd lost his damn mind before Fortune ran straight into the railing and flipped over it from the second floor. Fortune fell to his death right in front of Kal-Kal.

Shaken, Kal-Kal grabbed everything he had and left, vowing never to return to that hotel again.

Once in the car, Kal-Kal called T-Face and postponed their weekly meeting until further notice. T-Face wasn't happy about it, but since he'd just copped a solid amount of product from Chief Duke at a good price, he could stretch it out and feed his family for a while.

Pulling into his grandmother's driveway, Kal-Kal felt a brief sense of relief. His grandmother was in her early seventies, and she loved her grandson dearly. The two of them were the last of their family, survivors in a harsh world.

Kal-Kal's grandmother had raised him since he was a toddler and had stood by him through his entire prison bid. Unbeknownst to her—or so Kal-Kal thought—he stashed all his drugs and profits at her house.

Hearing his car pull into the driveway, his grandmother came to the door.

"Kal-Kal, that's you?" she called, her scratchy voice sounding frail as she peered through her glasses, bracing herself on a cane.

Kal-Kal glanced at her and smiled. "Yeah, Grannie, it's me. I'm on the way in. Gimme a second."

"Oh, alright," she said, turning and slowly making her way back inside the house.

Kal-Kal grabbed his duffle bag and headed into the house to stash what he needed.

***

Miles Away – Khashia's Mom's Residence
Dothan, Alabama

Freak Zeenie left Khashia's mom's house with deep wrinkles across his forehead. Her mom claimed she had no idea that he and Khashia weren't together anymore and said she couldn't even remember the last time she'd physically seen her daughter. From the concerned look on her face, Freak Zeenie could tell she was just as confused as he was.

"Shit! Where the fuck she at then?" Freak Zeenie muttered to himself, finishing a text to Khashia's phone.

As soon as he hit send, his phone lit up with an incoming call.

"Yeah, what's good?" he answered. "I know when you call, it's dollar signs multiplying! Talk to me," Freak Zeenie said, navigating his Ferrari muscle car toward his bank to deposit the check from his lawsuit.

He became silent as his financial advisor spoke on the other end.

"What?" Freak Zeenie bellowed. "Ain't . . . no . . . way! Fuck you mean?"

The car's autopilot braking system stopped him just short of rear-ending a car at a red light.

The financial advisor sighed before continuing.

"Yeah, man. I'm sorry, but in this game, this is how it goes sometimes," the advisor explained. "I'm afraid the market's gonna be like this for a while. Right now, with the war in full swing, everything's inflated. And President Biden pulling barrels of oil from the reserves ain't making it any better," he added. "Mr. Calhoun, you really need to come in so we can rebuild a stronger portfolio for you, you know?"

The financial advisor referred to Freak Zeenie by the alias Levi had created for him: Kevin Calhoun.

Freak Zeenie's breathing grew shallow. He was hyperventilating as the realization hit him—every last dime he'd transferred out of Khashia's account had evaporated into thin air. Just like that.

Clenching his jaw, Freak Zeenie shook his head in disbelief. His anger bubbled over as he gripped the steering wheel tighter. He had half a mind to wring his financial advisor's neck for convincing him to make those investments in the first place.

"I'll be over there," Freak Zeenie said before abruptly hanging up.

Slamming his foot on the gas, Freak Zeenie weaved through traffic. Picking up his phone, he hit Levi's number on speed dial.

Chapter 17

A Few Days Later, a Couple Hours After . . .
Khashia's Mom's Residence
Dothan, Alabama

Khashia stood in the middle of her old bedroom, her older sister standing in front of her and their mother lingering in the doorway.

"Girl, are you sure about this?" Khashia's sister asked, clearly hesitant to go through with what her younger sister was asking of her.

"Yeah, Khashia. You just having mood swings, baby. Just think about this for a minute, girl!" her mom chimed in. "What about the baby? The m—"

"I've already thought about it," Khashia cut in. "Trust me," she said. "Long and hard! Fuck him! Freak got me fucked up! I know he fucked with my money or got something to do with it!" Her voice was rising with every word. "I ain't stupid, Mom. So I'm 'bout to show him how much of a bitch I can really be! Since he wanna play!"

"This the second time—hell, for real, it's the third time if we count my missing bread!" Khashia snapped, shifting her gaze back to her sister. "Now come on, 'cause my mind is fucking made up!" Khashia put her hands behind her back, bracing herself for what was coming.

A few days ago, Khashia had gone house shopping, only to find out her money wasn't right. She'd gone to her mom's house and learned Freak Zeenie had just left. Later, at the bank—where she barely missed Freak Zeenie again—she discovered her whole account was damn near empty.

Khashia hadn't dealt with any of these problems before she left Freak Zeenie's house. Just as she was considering going back to see if they could untangle their twisted fate, Freak Zeenie kept doing things to piss her off, bringing Khashia's promise to Trae back into play. In her mind, Freak Zeenie had crossed the line into the unforgivable.

The missing money was the final straw. It gave her all the conviction she needed.

Khashia had it all planned out. She wanted her sister to blacken both her eyes so she could call Dothan's police department and report a domestic violence incident. The story she'd tell was simple: her deranged boyfriend had snapped when she told him she was keeping the baby.

In her version, Freak Zeenie—frustrated with his drug business not going as planned—didn't want any more kids and took his anger out on her.

The crazy part? Khashia had convinced herself this would work. She needed it to work. If it did, she could use Freak Zeenie's drug stash to free Trae, her true love. She knew exactly where Freak Zeenie kept all the kilos, even though he thought she was clueless.

Stupid-ass nigga! she thought to herself. *Must forget— this why the world in sin now. Because of a woman! Eve— short for evil! If Adam paid his bitch more attention, she wouldn't've thought about biting no damn apple, let alone handing it to him with his short-ass attention span.*

"Come on! Shit, I a—"

Before Khashia could finish, her sister drew back and hit her square in the left eye, cutting her words short.

"Argh—"

Khashia couldn't even complete her cry of pain before her sister followed up with a two-piece jab straight from the hip and shoulder. Blood sprayed across the room as Khashia's eye swelled instantly.

Their mom covered her mouth to stop herself from screaming, looking like she was the one who got hit.

"Again," Khashia mumbled, standing back upright and bracing herself for more. Her sister punched her again.

"Umph, umph, umph," Khashia moaned.

"That good, sis'?" her sister asked, breathing hard and clearly not wanting to hurt her any more than she already had.

"Hell naw! This shit gotta look real, girl!"

Khashia's eyes were already swelling and turning a bluish-purple against her high-yellow complexion. Her sister threw a flurry of lefts and rights, busting her own knuckles in the process. Khashia's left eye was now swollen completely shut, and her lip was split wide open.

Khashia's older sister stood there heaving, exhausted from the damage she'd just done to her baby sister.

"Okay, fuck that, sis', I'm through," her sister said. "It looks real now. You got it from here." She turned and stormed out of the room, furious at Khashia for her insanity—for what she saw as a desperate cry for love from a man.

Khashia turned to the mirror, examining her reflection. Nodding in approval, she grabbed her phone from the dresser. She pressed 9-1 and was about to hit the last number when her mom's voice screamed her name from down the hall, frantic like it was a matter of life or death.

"What?" Khashia hollered, stepping into the hallway to see what the commotion was about.

As her vision cleared, she froze.

"Trae!" she screamed. "How you g—"

"Fuck happened to you?" Trae bellowed, pushing past Khashia's mom and sister to get to her. He stared at her swollen face, his mouth dropping in disbelief.

"Who did this to you, Khashia? Huh?" Trae demanded, his face twisting into a grimace.

131

Khashia's lip quivered. She didn't know what to think, let alone what to say. Trae had decided to visit the last address she'd written him from years ago, unable to find anything about her on social media.

Before showing up here, Trae had already dealt with his ex-homie who'd set him up. He'd left him in the same house he'd found him in—dead.

Now, Khashia was his second task to handle.

"Say what?" Khashia finally managed to stammer.

"Huh?" Trae shot back. "Who the fuck did this to your face?"

His voice boomed through the house, shaking the walls. Khashia's mom and sister stood frozen, terrified of what Trae might do.

Khashia burst into tears.

"Fr—Freak Zeenie, h-he did th-this t-to m-me," she stuttered.

"Who? Man . . . Where this bitch-ass nigga at?" Spit flew from Trae's mouth as his face contorted into something satanic.

"Come on! You 'bout to take me to him right now!" Trae grabbed Khashia by the elbow, forcing her toward the front door.

"Okay, I will," she muttered, stumbling along. She didn't dare resist.

"We'll be back, y'all, alright," Khashia called over her shoulder to her mom and sister—who were still frozen in shock—as Trae and Khashia passed by.

Thirty Minutes Later – Kinsey, Alabama
As the sun set, the first shadows of night fell over the horizon. Khashia sat silently, thinking about the danger she was about to put her nephew De'shawn in. But even that didn't stop her.

When they pulled up, the house was dark, and no cars were visible in the driveway.

"This the house, but that fuck nigga ain't here," she said, thankful for her nephew's sake that Freak Zeenie wasn't home.

Trae kept his foot on the brake, scanning the house like a predator sizing up prey.

"So, this where he lay his head, though?"

"For sure," Khashia said, her voice slurring slightly from the effects of the exotic weed and her busted lips.

"You sure?"

"Mm-hmm, Trae. Positive."

"A'ight. I'ma handle him ASAP," Trae said, logging the address into his GPS.

Slamming the gas pedal, the car spun into a donut, tires screeching until it faced the direction they came from. Trae sped back up the highway, the darkness swallowing the muscle car whole.

Thirty Minutes Later
Khashia's Mom's House
Dothan, Alabama

Khashia's mom opened the door, studying Khashia and Trae with a disapproving eye. Khashia walked past her, but Trae turned around and headed back to the car.

"I'll be in there in just a sec'," he called over his shoulder.

Trae opened the glove compartment, pulling out a cheap-looking taser that packed 5,000 volts of electricity. He tucked it into the small of his back and grabbed a pair of rubber medical gloves, sliding them onto his hands.

"Bitch think I'm stupid. Told her, I'm motherfucking Satan himself," Trae muttered, indignation thick in his voice. "Hoe trying to set me up. I see through that super green-ass shit," he continued, talking to himself.

Satisfied, Trae got out of the car and headed back to the house. The front door was ajar when he got there. Trae paused, peeking inside and listening for any sounds. Hearing nothing suspicious, he eased his way in.

Khashia's mom was in the kitchen, her back to the door as she rinsed the last of the dishes and prepared them for the dishwasher. Trae looked around but didn't see or hear Khashia or her sister. He crept up behind her silently.

Quickly, Trae snatched the taser from the small of his back. Khashia's mom glanced up at her reflection in the window and saw him moving fast. But it was too late— before she could turn or react, Trae pressed the taser to the side of her neck and pulled the trigger.

The 5,000 volts surged through her body, knocking her out cold. The shock was so powerful that it caused her to lose control of her bladder, urine running down her legs. Trae caught her limp body before she hit the ground.

Dragging her over to the pantry, Trae pulled her inside and quickly shut the door behind them. Wrapping his gloved hands around her frail neck, he applied pressure for three straight minutes.

Once he was sure there was no pulse, an evil grin spread across his face. Trae stepped out of the pantry, closing the door behind him and leaving Khashia's mom lifeless inside.

Meanwhile – Khashia's Sister in the Den

Khashia soaked in the tub upstairs, while her sister sat in the den watching the news. The TV volume was louder than usual. She sat Indian-style on the couch but sat up straight when a report about the *Days Inn* flashed across the screen.

Her mind raced. She had been at the *Days Inn* just the other day, selling pussy.

"Whattt . . ." she dragged the word out as she continued to listen.

"Breaking news," the anchor announced. "At the press release earlier today, Chief O'Neil stated that—"

Trae rounded the corner, walking slowly with both hands behind his back to conceal his gloved hands and the taser.

Khashia's sister broke her attention away from the TV.

"Oh, Trae," she said, startled, placing a hand on her chest. "I almost forgot you were here, boy. Khashia said she'll be out in a minute. To be honest, I like to forget," she said, turning back to the news.

"Oh. Bet," Trae replied, taking slow steps toward her, closing the distance.

Same Time – Kal-Kal's Grandmother's House
Dothan, Alabama

Kal-Kal sat in his grandmother's den, feeling himself. He had $175,000 in pure profit stashed away. Kal-Kal had already paid Cartier Jay in full and served T-Face the morning after the Days Inn incident. He'd added the money from T-Face to his profits, pushing him just $25,000 shy of two hundred bands.

With his chest out, Kal-Kal finished polishing his Cuban link and placed it down on a jewelry cloth. He reached for the jar of jewelry cleaner and pulled out his recently purchased bust-down Cartier watch.

As he admired the watch, something on the TV caught his eye. The Days Inn was in the background behind the reporter.

Kal-Kal grabbed the remote and took the TV off mute.

"Ex-police officer Fortune, who was terminated from the force not long ago, was found dead in the Days Inn parking lot. It appears he fell from the second floor of the hotel," the news anchor reported.

The anchor shook her head, her tone heavy with sadness.

"High amounts of fentanyl and crack cocaine were found in his system. There were also two more male individuals found dead in room 217 on the second floor."

Tears began rolling down the news anchor's face as she continued.

"These two gentlemen were my father and uncle," she said, pausing to compose herself. She took a deep breath and pushed forward.

"Samuel Jackson and Quincy Jackson were also found with fentanyl and crack cocaine in their systems. One of them died in the bathtub, and the other was sitting up in a chair facing the TV with a whole bag of Percocets and an undisclosed amount of crack cocaine sitting in his lap—along with a crack pipe still hanging from his lips."

Her voice cracked, and she dropped the mic, running off set in hysterics.

"Oh shit! Damn! What the fuck!" Kal-Kal blurted out, his mouth hanging open. "I'm glad I got rid of them damn shits, man!"

Same Time – Across Town

Ex-police officer Bentley sat at his desk in shock, rewinding the DVR three times to replay the news about his former partner, Fortune.

"Fortune done lost his damn mind," Bentley muttered, shaking his head.

He didn't give a damn about Junkie Que and Sam, though.

"Say what, sir?"

Bentley looked up, startled. "Huh?" he said. "Oh, nothing. Just watching the news about all the shit going on out here in Houston County."

Bentley was talking to his new fine-ass secretary, whom he'd recently hired for his private investigation business.

Bentley muted the TV as his secretary glanced up at the screen.

"Isn't that your old partner, Mr. Bentley?" she asked innocently.

"Yes, my dear, I'm afraid it is. Only the strong survive, you know?" Bentley said, focusing back on his first case as a P.I.

"True dat," she replied, sounding all hip before heading back to her desk.

Bentley turned his attention back to his work, though his thoughts lingered on the karma that had been making the rounds lately. He just hoped it wouldn't come barging in unannounced at his door.

Meanwhile
Back at Khashia's Mom's House
Dothan, Alabama
Trae had Khashia in a death headlock, and a pen and piece of paper sat in front of her.

"Pick it up and write it!" Trae snarled through clenched teeth.

Khashia's feet dangled, barely touching the floor. She desperately tried to pull air into her lungs, but it was no use. Her vision began to cloud.

"Bitch . . . I . . . said, pick up the . . . pen . . . and write it!"

Trae tightened his biceps even more, nearly collapsing Khashia's esophagus. The pressure caused her hearing to fade for a moment. Panicked, Khashia tapped Trae's arm rapidly. Trae loosened his grip slightly.

"Do it!" he barked.

Khashia picked up the pen with trembling fingers and scribbled something onto the paper before the pen slipped from her grasp. Trae glanced at the paper and nodded in satisfaction.

When he released her, Khashia crumpled to the floor, bent over, coughing and heaving as she fought to catch her breath. Before she could recover, Trae hit her with a hard right hook directly to her temple, knocking her out cold.

Three Minutes Later—
Khashia stirred back to life. It took her a moment for her vision to clear. The first thing she saw was Trae, his mouth moving. At first, she couldn't make out what he was saying, but then his words became clear.

She realized there was a sheet around her neck, and her feet barely had any leverage on the surface of a kitchen chair.

"If you thought Trae was stupid, bitch, then you must really be on that dope," he whispered. "Hoe, you was just gonna leave me for dead in that hellhole, huh?"

Trae's face twisted with rage. "Well, Khashia, you'll get to hell before I will! Oh yeah," he sneered, stepping back. "Tell my co-dee I said life's a bitch . . . then you die."

Trae kicked the chair from under her feet, making it look like she had done it herself.

Elsewhere in the house, Khashia's mom and sister lay in separate rooms, their necks sliced wide open. Trae left the butcher knife in plain sight, its handle smudged with Khashia's fingerprints.

Khashia squirmed and kicked desperately, trying to resist death, but her struggle wasn't enough this time. Trae stood still, watching her with a grim expression as if he were the reaper himself.

Minutes passed. Finally, Khashia's body went limp, her last breath escaping her lips. Her corpse swung gently from the ceiling fan, her head tilted to the side, mouth ajar, and lifeless eyes landing where Trae still stood.

A few moments later, her bowels released—the final confirmation Trae had been waiting for.

Without wasting another second, Trae sprinted out of the house, pulling the door shut behind him. He didn't stop to look around or check if anyone was watching. He just got the hell away from Khashia's mom's house in a hurry.

Seven Minutes Later—Dothan, Alabama

Trae headed back toward Kinsey, Alabama, to the house Khashia had told him was full of money and drugs. Smoke from the blunt he was puffing filled the cabin of the car, leaving him good and high.

Suddenly, blue lights flashed in his rearview mirror.

"Damn, man!" he muttered, frustrated as he quickly ducked the roach and kept his eyes on the rearview.

Cracking the window, he lit a cigarette to mask the lingering weed smell.

***

A Few Seconds Later—

The police officer tapped on Trae's window. Trae rolled it down slowly, the officer's hand resting on the grip of his service weapon.

"Do you know why I pulled you over, sir?" the officer asked. The sweet aroma of marijuana hit his nostrils immediately.

"No, sir. What seems to be the problem, Mr. Officer? I know I wasn't speeding or nothing," Trae replied calmly on the outside, though his insides churned with tension.

Trae knew the murder weapon—used on his ex-homie—was still hidden somewhere in the vehicle. Even worse, just possessing a pistol was enough for an ex-felon like him to face an indictment under 922(g). He wasn't going back to prison after all he'd done to regain his freedom.

"Well, you've got a taillight out, and now I smell reefer too, sir. Where are your license and registration?" the officer asked.

"Um, right here," Trae said, pointing toward the glove compartment.

"Go ahead and grab them for me, and after that, please step out of the car," the officer said, already calling for backup on his walkie-talkie.

Trae froze at the request, his thoughts racing. The officer's eyes locked onto Trae's blue latex gloves.

"Do you always wear gloves while driving, sir?" the officer asked. Then, his gaze shifted to the butt of a pistol sticking out from Trae's console.

"You know what? Just step out of the vehicle for me, please," the officer said firmly, his tone leaving no room for negotiation.

"A'ight, be cool. I'm just grabbing my—"

"Get the fuck out the goddamn car! *Now!*" the officer bellowed, his grip tightening on his pistol.

Trae didn't listen. He leaned toward the glove compartment.

"Don't! Don't go—"

Boom! Boom! Boom!

The officer fired three shots, all hitting Trae's body.

One pierced his left lung, another shattered his intestines, and the last deflated his heart.

"Goddammit! I told you not to go for it!" the officer yelled.

Trae slumped motionless in the driver's seat.

Minutes Later—

Backup and an ambulance arrived at the scene. The initial officer pulled on a pair of latex gloves and reached over Trae's corpse to retrieve the gun he'd spotted in the console.

As soon as he pulled it out, his face twisted in disbelief.

"Ah . . . motherfucking taser?" he muttered, shaking his head.

The senior officer stepped closer, putting a hand on his shoulder.

"It's dark out. Don't worry. The way the handle was sticking out, it could've easily looked like a pistol," the senior officer said, trying to reassure him.

"Yeah. Tell me 'bout it," the first officer mumbled, still shaking his head.

Moments later, EMS confirmed what everyone already knew—Trae was dead.

They removed his body from the vehicle and searched it thoroughly for more weapons, hoping to justify the officer's actions.

But they didn't find anything.

If only they'd popped the hood and checked under the battery, they might've saved the officer and the department from disgrace.

But karma, being bisexual, had dealt its hand. Trae faced death as his payment to the universe, and the officer faced the embarrassment and potential termination that came with his actions.

Karma went both ways.

Chapter 18

The Next Morning
18th Street Downtown
Atlanta, Georgia

Freak Zeenie sat in his loft, deep in thought. For the past few days, he'd been in the A' fucking off with his first cousin, Funk, and his brother, Levi. They hit a few well-known spots like the *Flame Thang*, The Fifty Yard Line, and *The Gold Rush*. Freak Zeenie had finally caught up on his sex game, and right now, he was completely fucked out.

After laying all his problems on the table for Funk, Freak Zeenie listened as Funk and Levi gave it to him raw. Funk suggested, even insisted, that Freak Zeenie move back to the A' and focus more on the rap scene, like they'd planned months ago. Levi, though, was on a whole different vibe. Levi went ape shit when he found out Freak Zeenie had been slanging bricks like a brick mansion, especially since Levi had run him out of Dothan the first time he got jammed up for bricks. Levi couldn't believe Freak Zeenie had the nerve to preach to him and Cartier Jay with that long prison speech, only to turn around and put truckloads of dope in his son's hands.

The argument got so heated that it turned into a full-on tussle, with Funk stepping in to break them apart.

Now, Freak Zeenie was sitting alone, reflecting on how right both Funk and Levi had been. He blew a cloud of thick, rich smoke from a blunt full of moon roc'. The aggressive coughing fit that followed left his eyes watery. Everything Funk and Levi said was making perfect sense now. Freak Zeenie was ready to finally get things done—things he'd been planning ever since he'd gained his freedom back.

One thing was fo'sho: Freak Zeenie was doing shit his way.

Fuck I'm out here trying to save a bitch who don't wanna be saved for anyway? he thought. She chose her route, so I'm on top of mine too—shit.

He stood up, walking toward the windows to take in the prestigious view of the city skyline.

As he stared out in a daze, his phone chimed, snapping him back. He grabbed it from the coffee table.

"Oh now. Make it make dollars," Freak Zeenie said confidently into his phone.

"Si, si si! That's what I'm trying to say, Freak." Zacatecas said in a thick voice.

Freak Zeenie's face twisted like he swallowed sour milk. "Aye, check it out, wet-back-ass fuck boy! Chalk that! Ain't shit going! I took t—"

Freak Zeenie kept ranting, not realizing Zacatecas had hung up the moment he heard the slur. When Freak Zeenie noticed he was talking to the screensaver, he hit his blunt again. Another coughing fit followed.

"Good . . . got . . . damn!" he managed to say, as drool slipped from his lip.

Freak Zeenie didn't give a fuck 'bout no Zacatecas or what money or dope that Zacateca thought he owed him. Even though Freak Zeenie took a lot of financial losses recently, he still had enough money to move and get loopy to get some major things in motion if he wanted to and didn't need the help of anyone.

Minutes later, Freak Zeenie locked up the loft and headed out to Ten on Northside Drive to grab something to eat. Afterward, he linked back up with Funk, Levi, Remy Red, and Poochie for one last night out before heading back down to Dothan, Alabama.

Back at The Flame Thang, Freak Zeenie was back in his zone, popping bottles and throwing bandz. The club scene was just what he needed to take his mind off the drama that had been messing with his livelihood. The deaths of his partner Carlos and his cousin Lil Fred weighed heavy on his heart. And on top of that, he still hadn't found the right words to say to his baby boy, De'shawn. Everything seemed to be trying to jade Freak Zeenie.

Later That Night
McDowell Street/The Old Bankhead
Atlanta, Georgia

Blue Flame's parking lot was jam-packed like a can of sardines. Everybody who was anybody was there, flaunting their money, cars, jewelry, and clothes, all to splurge on some hoes.

Lil Baby came out, showing love for the city before heading out on tour. Lil Durk and OTF were in the building too. Gucci Mane, Big Walk Dog, and Glow Rilla—along with her squad—had their own sections.

Inside, the club was lit. The diamonds sparkled so brightly under the lights, the room looked like the static from a busted TV screen. Between the glistening jewelry and the sparkling gold bottles, it was like the liquor and diamonds were in a contest to outshine each other.

Freak Zeenie and his family had their section front and center by the stage. He wasn't one to be starstruck, though. Freak Zeenie didn't care who was in the club. He'd been famous and ghetto fabulous his whole life.

A platter stacked with one-dollar bills, still wrapped in plastic, sat behind Freak Zeenie. He tossed armfuls of ones onto the stage, ordering so much money that it had to be wheeled out on a dolly.

"Y'all shoulda used a forklift!" Freak Zeenie shouted.

Even with all the known celebrities in the house, Freak Zeenie and his crew managed to grab everyone's attention. Bottles were coming their way from Gucci Mane, Lil Baby, and Lil Durk. Freak Zeenie accepted them all and sent them back with platters of ones to show his gratitude.

Freak Zeenie leaned over. "And you trying to go back down to 'Bama! For what?" he said. "This where it's at, cuz—you know that!" Funk leaned in close, speaking into Freak Zeenie's ear.

That brought a grin to Freak Zeenie's face.

"I can't lie, cuz. This shit feels good, bringing back old memories. Plus, times done changed out here! I know I'll soak up at least eighty percent of it with what I got in the cut," Funk said, glancing around at all the potential bread he was missing on the legal side of things. Freak Zeenie glanced askance behind him for a split second, his eyes landing on a group of about seven Mexicans. A timid feeling crept over him, but he shook it off, turning back to the fine, dark-skinned stallion who had his attention—and his money.

So many *George Washingtons* were sailing through the air that Levi, Remy Red, and Poochie looked invincible at their side of the table, keeping the cash flying. Levi caught more than a few mean mugs, but he brushed them off as nothing more than hate. He was used to the resentment of those who wanted to swap places with him and the lifestyle he lived.

Levi reached for a plastic sleeve of ones, tore it open, and doubled down for his group of haters. He'd been making a killing online selling costume jewelry and still managed to serve around the city. Even his last incident hadn't slowed him down. All Levi had done was reinvest—this time in a few high-end, real pieces. He'd been selling to cats like *21 Savage*, *Lil Uzi Vert*, and *Lotto*. Once the celebs posted Levi's pieces on the Gram, business exploded again. It was a gift and a curse, though, because some of his clientele felt some type of way. Levi didn't give two fucks, though. The game was sold, not told—that was his creed.

Freak Zeenie reached for more ones but kept glancing back. He made eye contact with one of the Mexicans in the group. They held each other's glare longer than Freak Zeenie liked. Meanwhile, the Mexicans were busy enjoying lap dances.

Funk noticed how his cousin was glued to the back of the club and turned around to see what had Freak Zeenie's attention. "Damn. When they start letting Mexicans in this joint?" Funk yelled over the music.

"Oh, yeah. Shit done changed out here, cuz. You know the Flame Thang went nationwide. That's just the Paisas, though," Freak Zeenie replied.

"They always be up in here, buying black pussy. A dollar is a dollar, you know. Shit spend the same way worldwide, cuz," Funk said, turning his attention back to the strippers.

What Funk had clearly forgotten was that Freak Zeenie worked for Zacatecas—the same man who headed up the Paisas. The mention of the name made Freak Zeenie's ears perk up like a deer's and his eyes dart around like flies. Suddenly, he noticed everything. What he hadn't told Funk, though, was that earlier that day, he'd told Zacatecas to chalk that shit—more or less. Even though Funk and Levi had warned him how to handle the cartel, Freak Zeenie hadn't exactly followed their advice.

The money was finally running low. Levi looked over at Freak Zeenie and the others.

"Shiid . . . I gotta piss like a racehorse! Be right back," Levi said, grabbing a half-full bottle of Ace of Spades off the table as he headed to the restroom.

"Yeah, you gotta know that!" Freak Zeenie slurred. "I done blew enough tonight to pay a couple of these hoes' college tuition." But when he looked again for the Mexicans, they were already gone, and a small pang of concern crept into his chest.

Levi took a swig of champagne just before entering the filthy restroom. He made it to the stall quickly and started pissing hard.

"Man, you shoulda been took that fake-ass shit off, homes. You embarrassing us in here!" Levi heard someone say as he finished. He looked around and saw two brawny African dudes entering the restroom. "Man, where you get that shit from anyway? I told you to shop up in New York. Now you down here gettin' played by a bunch of country bumpkins, nigga!"

"Man, I copped this shit off Old Nat!" one of the men said. "I think I saw the nigga here tonight—" Levi turned and locked eyes with the two men.

Levi's neck glowed like a disco ball. Around it hung a bust-down platinum Cuban link chain that weighed a whole kilo.

"This that fake-ass nigga?" one of the men asked.

"Yeah! Fuck nigga, run them pockets for that fake-ass—" The brawny African rushed Levi with lightning speed, swinging a hard right hook at his head. His brother charged in from the opposite side to get in on the action.

Even though Levi was drunk, he slipped the wild punch and spun around, crashing the Ace of Spades bottle into the side of the first man's face. The hit temporarily blinded the man, but his brother kept throwing jabs at Levi. The slippery floor, soaked with piss and champagne, made it hard for him to land a solid blow.

Levi ducked and bolted for the restroom door, making it back into the club. The two Africans gave chase, running full tilt toward Levi. He grabbed a beer bottle off an empty table, hurling it at one of them. The bottle shattered against his head, but it barely slowed them down. They tackled Levi, taking him through the table.

"Argh—shit, bitch-ass nigga!" Levi yelled as he crashed onto his back.

"Let me get this chain, bitch!" one of the men snarled, trying to snatch the Cuban link from Levi's neck. The force nearly ripped Levi's head clean off his shoulders.

Screams erupted as the bouncers rushed toward the commotion. Out of nowhere, Freak Zeenie appeared, slamming a bucket of ice and Ace of Spades onto the head of one of the Africans.

"Well, damn!" Gucci Mane said, jumping out of the way to let them work.

Funk was stomping the same man's head with his red bottoms while he lay dazed on the ground. Moments later, the bouncers arrived, snatching, pulling, and dragging everyone toward the exit of the *Flame Thang*.

Remy Red and Poochie were riding the bouncers' backs, clawing at their faces and scratching at their heads. That was until one of the bouncers pulled out a fire-extinguisher-sized can of mace and sprayed it toward them all. Everyone started coughing violently, scattering to their vehicles.

Levi and Freak Zeenie jumped into the front seats of the electric blue Lambo truck while Remy Red and Poochie clambered into the back. Levi had the spot truck fishtailing out of the parking lot, tires squealing as they tore away. Funk slid into the driver's seat of his seashell-white 600 Maybach and drove off without further incident, heading straight home. Meanwhile, Levi headed toward the garage where Freak Zeenie had parked his car.

Freak Zeenie was still coughing and struggling to breathe from the mace, his chest heaving as he tried to calm down. Finally, he looked over at Levi.

"Man, b-bruh—what the fuck happened?" he asked, momentarily forgetting all about the Paisa situation.

"Shit, bruh—all I know is when I got done pissing and turnt around, two niggas tried to snatch my chain off my fucking neck!" Levi lied. There was no way he was about to admit the African had caught him slipping after buying bogus jewelry. He knew he'd never hear the end of that.

"Man, we shoulda killed them bitch-ass niggas!" Freak Zeenie said, his face balled up tighter than a dope fiend's fist clutching a twenty roc'.

Blakka!

"I te—" Poochie started to say before her words were cut short by the sound of rapid gunfire. Bullets tore through the truck, shattering Poochie's window and riddling the passenger side.

"Go, go, go, bruh!" Freak Zeenie shouted, trying to duck the hail of bullets. But there was so much fire coming their way that all he could do was hope—hope that Levi could get them out alive.

Poochie slumped over into Remy Red's lap, her head limp. The side of her face had been blown open, leaving a hole the size of a grapefruit.

"Nooo!" Remy Red shrieked, tears welling up in her eyes. She reached under the driver's seat, pulled out a Glock 27, and climbed onto her knees. Bracing the gun with both hands, she squeezed the trigger as fast as she could, aiming for the driver of the high-end sports car chasing them.

"Hold on!" Levi bellowed, ramming the Lambo truck into the side of the other car. The two vehicles raced up the interstate at breakneck speeds, weaving through traffic. Freak Zeenie just knew they were going to die tonight.

Finally, Remy Red's bullet hit the driver in the neck. The man slumped to the side, his foot still pressed on the gas, and the car began swerving wildly. The passenger, wearing a ski mask, leaned halfway out of the window, trying to grab the wheel and regain control. But the car veered across lanes, slammed hard into the divider, and flipped into oncoming traffic. It collided with a propane big rig, and the explosion was immediate and catastrophic. Flames erupted, illuminating the interstate for miles.

Remy Red dropped the Glock to the floor, her hands trembling as tears streamed down her cheeks, falling onto Poochie's lifeless body.

"She dead! She dead! They fucking killed 'er!" she sobbed.

"What?" Levi shouted, glancing at the rearview mirror to get a look at the damage. He finally made it back to the garage where Freak Zeenie's car was parked.

When Freak Zeenie turned around in his seat to assess the situation, he caught sight of Poochie's face—or what was left of it. The right side was 85% gone.

"Damn!" he exclaimed, gagging at the horrific sight. He turned back toward the front window and vomited out the side of the truck.

Once he finished retching, he gasped out, "Shit! Let me out right here!"

Levi slammed on the brakes, bringing the truck to a screeching halt. Freak Zeenie stumbled out, barely keeping his balance. He glanced down at his feet and muttered, "Aw, shit!" His voice was shaky. "Bitch-ass motherfuckers almost got me."

The heel of his Prada boot was completely gone, leaving him limping toward his car. He climbed in, cranked it up, and sped off, leaving the city—and the state—immediately. He'd been saved by the boot.

Levi pulled off too, speeding toward the beltway of 285. Freak Zeenie hit 85 South and disappeared into the night. But as Freak Zeenie drove, Poochie's mangled face flashed in his mind. He gagged again, almost vomiting for a second time.

Levi had to slap some sense into Remy Red to convince her they had to leave Poochie behind. At first, Remy Red flat-out refused to abandon her BFF. She couldn't believe Levi would stoop so low as to do Poochie like that. But after Levi calmed her down and explained what their fate would be if they stayed, she finally gave in, storming off to sit in the car while Levi handled what needed to be done.

Levi poured gasoline all over the Lambo truck, then lit it on fire. He stood there for a moment, watching the flames consume the vehicle. The truck was chopped and registered in Poochie's name, so he didn't care about losing it—especially when his own life was on the line. Still, Levi felt sick. Poochie had been his baby, and no matter what, she'd always have a place in his heart.

"Come on, bae!" Remy Red yelled, leaning out the Bentley truck's window. Levi snapped out of it, jumped into the Bentley, and they took one last look at the burning Lambo before pulling off.

Levi drove up the street, scanning the area for any nosy-ass witnesses. He parked the Bentley, jumped out, and sprinted toward a jewelry store. Without hesitation, he hurled three Molotov cocktails through the windows and stepped back to watch the fire take hold. Satisfied, Levi slowly backed away, slipping into the truck.

As they sped down 85 South en route back to Dothan, Levi's mind wandered to the insurance money he'd collect on his store. Atlanta needed a break from him anyway, at least until things cooled down.

Hours Later
Khashia's Mom's House
Dothan, Alabama

The sun was overpowering the darkness, painting the sky with smoky shades of black and orange. Freak Zeenie pulled into Khashia's mom's driveway, his mind racing. I'm 'bout to see who lying 'round this bitch! The thought crossed his mind but went no further.

"Somebody ass up," he muttered to himself, killing the engine. He noticed lights shining throughout the house. Freak Zeenie got out of the car and walked up to the door, ringing the bell. He waited a few seconds, then rang it again.

Freak Zeenie wasn't worried about waking anybody up or pissing them off. He was tired of playing games with Khashia, and he also needed to warn her about the Mexican ordeal. At the very least, she deserved a heads-up. Either

151

way, Freak Zeenie was done selling for Zacatecas. Whether Khashia came back or stayed didn't matter to him; that was her choice. He just didn't want her ending up like her stepsister, Denise.

When no one answered the doorbell, Freak Zeenie started knocking. Knocking turned to banging. Now they playing. I know damn well somebody in there heard me. He stood there, trying to decide what to do next. He couldn't see through the windows. Fuck it, I ain't with all that hoe shit. Fuck 'round and slap the shit out that bitch! the thought flashed through his mind.

As he turned to leave, something told him to try the door. It was unlocked.

"Ms. Kerry? Oh now, Ms. Kerry?" he called out as he stepped inside. "Good morning, it's—"

A foul odor hit him like a brick wall, cutting his words short.

"Damn! Fuck is that?" he whispered. "Aye…this early? Is everything okay, y'all?" Freak Zeenie called, scanning the spacious living room. Everything looked normal. But as he moved deeper into the house, the smell grew stronger.

By the time he reached the kitchen, Freak Zeenie nearly threw up.

"Oh shit! What the fuck? What the fuck?"

Khashia's lifeless body hung from the ceiling, swollen and discolored. Her skin had turned a bluish-purple shade. Just a few inches away on the kitchen floor lay Khashia's mom, her throat slit wide open. When Freak Zeenie saw her, his eyes damn near popped out of his head.

Panic set in. Freak Zeenie's paranoia kicked into overdrive, and he started scanning the floor, checking for any tracks he might've left. His mind raced. Carefully, he backtracked through the house, retracing his steps until he reached the front door. Freak Zeenie pulled the door shut, yanked off his shirt, and wiped down the doorknob to clear his prints.

He bolted for his car, jumping in and throwing it into reverse, backing into the street. Then he floored it, speeding off and putting as much distance between himself and the crime scene as possible. All he could think about was his last conversation with Zacatecas.

Just as Freak Zeenie disappeared from sight, a patrol car pulled into Khashia's mom's driveway for a wellness check.

Chapter 19

Later That Day
Webb Road
Webb, Alabama

CLANG! CLANG! CLANG!

"Argh! Argh! Hrgh! Man, please! Stop!" That's all Boo-Boo kept hearing as he drove the van down the country road, en route to the hog farm.

"Shut your bitch ass up, fuck nigga! You—saying—the—wrong—SHIT!" Cartier Jay growled, punctuating every word by slamming the heavy chain wherever it landed on Crip Ruben's swollen, bloody body. "Where—the—fuck—is—T-Face—bitch-ass nigga, huh?" Cartier Jay loomed over Crip Ruben, waiting for an answer. Catching Crip Ruben slipping had been pure luck.

Ever since the shooting at the club, T-Face and the gang had gone ghost. Despite strict orders to stay out of Dothan until further notice, Crip Ruben had disobeyed. All he wanted was to grab some exclusive threads. Even though inflation was high as hell, the mall still stayed packed.

Cartier Jay couldn't believe it when he spotted Crip Ruben in the food court, macking on a short, fine-ass redbone with a sprinkle of freckles across her face. After looking around to make sure it wasn't an ambush, Cartier Jay and Boo-Boo followed them from a safe distance.

Crip Ruben had led them down a back road, trying to sneak in a quick shot of pussy, but ended up snatched at gunpoint by Boo-Boo. Boo-Boo forced Crip Ruben and the innocent, cute redbone into the back of the van, hogtying both of them. As soon as they pulled off, Cartier Jay shot the redbone in the head. She'd be used as extra hog food.

Cartier Jay wiped sweat from his brow with the back of his hand. "Huh?" he bellowed impatiently, raising the chain to beat Crip Ruben again.

"M-man, I told you—I don't know where T-F—" Crip Ruben muttered weakly before passing out from his injuries. Cartier Jay snapped, bringing the chain down on Crip Ruben's head and body in a fit of rage.

"Ole weak bitch!" Cartier Jay yelled, wincing in pain as his still-healing shoulder, wrapped in a sling, throbbed from the strain.

Boo-Boo slowed the van as they neared the hog farm, keeping a close eye on a black Honda that had been tailing them the whole time. The car stayed far enough back that Boo-Boo couldn't tell if the driver was male or female—the dark tint on the windows didn't help either.

When Boo-Boo turned into the hog farm, the black Honda kept going, coasting past with its tinted windows. Boo-Boo watched until the taillights disappeared, finally feeling more at ease. He knew Cartier Jay was taking a huge risk being out here in the daytime, but Boo-Boo was all in for the sake of loyalty.

Meanwhile, Kal-Kal sat behind the wheel of the black Honda. He'd happened to be right behind Cartier Jay's van at a traffic light in Dothan and decided to follow them out of curiosity. He was hoping they'd lead him to a stash spot he could double back and hit later without being a suspect. The ongoing beef Cartier Jay had with others only made Kal-Kal more eager.

"Fuck he got going on? Ole slick-ass nigga. Probably hiding his shit out here on somebody else's property," Kal-Kal muttered. "Nobody'll ever suspect that."

Kal-Kal pulled off into a fork in the road, hiding his car in grass so tall it damn near swallowed it. Once the car was concealed, Kal-Kal jogged down the road toward the hog farm, cutting into the woods. He stuck to the woodline, creeping closer in hopes of catching Cartier Jay slipping and scoring a sweet come-up.

Back at the farm, Cartier Jay couldn't physically help Boo-Boo break the bodies down due to his injured arm.

"Man . . . fuck it. Cut they heads off. We'll get rid of that shit somewhere else, bruh," Cartier Jay said. "We ain't 'bout to be out here 'til no damn tomorrow, bruh." He handed Boo-Boo the chainsaw.

Boo-Boo cranked the chainsaw on the first pull. The motor roared to life, and he revved it a few times before raising it over Crip Ruben's neck. Crip Ruben stirred awake, blinking a few times before realizing what was happening.

"Wait! Nooo—"

Kal-Kal's eyes grew wide as buckshot shells while he crouched in the woods, recording everything on his phone. Crip Ruben's head rolled off his shoulders, bouncing three times before coming to a stop.

"Got-damn! What—the—fuck?" Kal-Kal whispered, still recording. He didn't even know why he'd started filming, but his hands kept steady as Cartier Jay walked over, picked up Crip Ruben's head, and placed it inside a gas station cooler. When Boo-Boo severed the redbone's head, Cartier Jay tossed hers in the cooler too.

The hogs smelled blood, snorting loudly and fighting to get to the front of the pen.

***

4 ½ Hours Later...

Drenched in sweat, Boo-Boo swung a 30-pound sledgehammer to break the remaining bones in the bodies. His breaths came in shallow gasps.

156

"M-man, t-this s-shit a-a r-real j-job, b-boy!" Boo-Boo panted, flipping the last body over into the hog pen. The hogs attacked the remains instantly, devouring them with horrifying speed.

"Ain't it, man?" Cartier Jay said, laughing at his ace. Suddenly, his laughter stopped, and his head snapped toward the woods. He thought he'd heard tree branches snapping.

Snatching his pistol from his waistband, Cartier Jay fired a few shots in the direction of the noise. "Probably just a damn bobcat or some shit," he muttered. He and Boo-Boo stood still, listening.

Kal-Kal, low to the ground, nearly got himself killed from stepping on a twig. Heart pounding, he whispered to himself, "Shit real! Niggas got-damn crazy as hell, got-damn!" He crawled away as quietly as he could, eventually making it back to his car.

Minutes later, Kal-Kal jumped in his Honda and took the long way back to the city, shaking his head in disbelief. He couldn't believe what he'd witnessed—but the video on his phone confirmed it all.

Cartier Jay was ready to leave. "Come on, bruh, let's hit it," he said, climbing into the passenger seat of the van.

"W-we a-ain't g-gone wait t-till they finish, bruh?" Boo-Boo asked, giving Cartier Jay a doubtful look. He was thinking of all the wrong possibilities that could happen.

"Nah. They gone do what it do, trust me, bruh," Cartier Jay said. Boo-Boo didn't look convinced. "Trust me!" Cartier Jay reassured him, pulling the van door shut.

Boo-Boo shrugged and climbed into the driver's seat. He cranked the van, and they pulled out slowly, leaving the hogs to finish the evidence.

Chapter 20

The Next Weekend
First Baptist
Dothan, Alabama

Freak Zeenie sat in the third row from the front of First Baptist. Bags sagged under his eyes, a reflection of the exhaustion brought on by relentless police questioning. Even after the autopsy ruled Khashia's death as a self-inflicted strangulation, Freak Zeenie wasn't convinced. Suicide just wasn't Khashia's style. Not even the note she left behind—claiming responsibility for the brutal murders of her mom and sister—could sway him.

What kept gnawing at Freak Zeenie was the timing. The same day he found Khashia's body, he had told Zacatecas that he was running off on him. The whole situation smelled foul, and Freak Zeenie's gut told him it wasn't suicide.

De'shawn sat in the second row, tears brimming in his eyes—not from sadness, but from anger. Death had shown up too early and too often in his life. First, it took his mom, and now, months later, his favorite aunt was gone too. At just 12 years old, De'shawn felt completely alone in a cruel and complex world.

Outside, across the street, two Mexicans sat quietly in a new-model Dodge Durango, watching the small church through a tiny camera installed on Khashia's casket. Zacatecas had paid a hefty amount to have it done, ensuring he could see everything that unfolded inside. The men sat behind the heavily tinted windows, waiting patiently for the perfect time to handle what they were paid so well to do.

Inside the church, the first row of mourners returned to their seats after paying their final respects to Khashia, her mom, and her sister. Freak Zeenie sat with tears streaming down his face, not caring who saw. Those who noticed assumed they were tears of heartbreak for the love of his life. And they were partially right—but only partially. Freak Zeenie's tears were also for the ten-million-dollar life insurance policy he had just lost. The policy was null and void because of Khashia's suicide, but Freak Zeenie couldn't shake the question running laps in his mind: Why the fuck was she smoking while pregnant? The only answer that made sense to him pointed straight to Zacatecas.

De'shawn was the last to leave the second-row pews, and Freak Zeenie fell in line behind him. De'shawn moved slowly toward the casket but froze. He couldn't bear to see his Aunt Khashia lying dead in a church. Suddenly, he turned and bolted, running full speed toward the church doors.

"De'shawn! Son, wait!" Freak Zeenie called out, running after him to console his last-born child.

"Here goes!" the Mexican in the passenger seat said. He was the alpha male in charge between the two. The alpha Mexican swiped his finger across the tablet screen, bringing Freak Zeenie into view. "Bye-bye, puta. Maricón," he sneered, raising his finger to jab the blinking red dot on the screen. As soon as Freak Zeenie got close to the casket, the alpha Mexican slammed his finger down on the button.

"¡Gooo!" the alpha bellowed as a deafening explosion rocked First Baptist Church. A massive hole tore through the roof.

The Mexicans in the Durango high-fived, proud of their work. They began chatting in Spanish until the alpha's phone chimed, breaking up their celebration. He calmed himself before answering.

"Sí, sí, sí. Yes. We got that puta," the alpha Mexican said into the phone, listening for a moment. "Okay." He looked at his partner. "Boss says, 'Well done.' Now get us back to Atlanta, asap!" The alpha leaned back in his seat, grinning from ear to ear.

As they sped out of Dothan, they believed they had succeeded, unaware that a glitch in the laptop caused the device to malfunction briefly. What they saw on the screen had already happened in real time. Freak Zeenie wasn't dead. The alpha Mexican rolled his window down and tossed the laptop out onto the interstate, where it shattered on impact.

Inside the church, Freak Zeenie found De'shawn balled up on the ground, holding his ears and squeezing his eyes shut.

"D' . . . D', you alright, son?" Freak Zeenie asked, rolling him onto his back to check for injuries.

Dothan police swarmed the scene within seconds, questioning survivors while fire marshals worked to contain the blaze. Paramedics ran around frantically, tending to the injured. There were too many dead bodies to count. Some survivors were missing limbs—or multiple limbs. It was a horrific scene.

2 ½ Hours Later—
Federal marshals combed through the rubble of First Baptist Church, demanding answers. They turned Houston County into a ghost town in mere hours.

After the paramedics patched up Freak Zeenie and De'shawn, the two were finally allowed to leave. Both were shaken but grateful to still have their souls connected to their bodies.

1 Hour Later—
Mama Lois' House
Dothan, Alabama
Freak Zeenie sat silently in the den of his mother's home, joined by his brother Levi and Remy Red. De'shawn was in

the kitchen, staring at a plate of untouched food. The house was quiet, the air thick with shock as they tried to push through Sunday dinner.

Freak Zeenie was convinced now—this was Zacatecas. The explosion had to be his attempt at making a statement, a punishment for Freak Zeenie reneging on their deal.

Mama Lois had cooked baked barbecue chicken, mac and cheese, butter-steamed cabbage, homemade buttermilk corn muffins, slow-simmered butter beans, and fresh sweet tea. Levi wasn't playing with his plate. He had cleaned it so fast you'd think he hadn't eaten in weeks.

"Now, Mama Lois, that food was deee-licious!" Levi exclaimed, wiping his hands. "It'll make you slap your momma and knock your daddy straight out!"

Mama Lois smiled, accepting the compliment. "Thank you, son, but you better not ever raise your hand at me in this life or the next! Understand?" She began gathering plates to take to the kitchen.

"Aww, naw, Mama. You know what I mean," Levi said, glancing at the TV. "Aye, bruh, turn it up real quick!"

All eyes shifted to the screen. Channel 9 News was broadcasting footage of the now-burnt First Baptist Church.

Freak Zeenie turned up the volume. The anchor was already speaking.

"We've learned from fire marshals and U.S. Marshals that today's events at First Baptist Church were not accidental. Authorities are calling this an act of terrorism—a horrific crime that claimed numerous innocent lives," the anchor said. "This is one of the worst crimes in Houston County history to date." She went on to report that the FBI and DEA were working together to track down whoever was responsible for planting the bomb in one of the caskets.

Mama Lois paused mid-stride. "What in the worlddd . . . is the world coming to these days, Lord?" she said.

"I'm lost," Levi added, shaking his head. "Why would somebody wanna blow up sis' them caskets, though?"

Freak Zeenie stayed silent, deep in thought. He knew in his gut exactly who was behind it. If he wanted to protect his family, he'd have to put an end to Zacatecas once and for all.

Walking into the kitchen, Freak Zeenie saw De'shawn still sitting at the table, his plate untouched. "What's up, champ? How you holding up?" he asked, holding out his fist for a pound. De'shawn ignored it, keeping his eyes down.

Freak Zeenie didn't take it personally. He could only imagine the pain De'shawn was in, having lost his mom and his aunt within months of each other.

"Don't worry, my boy. In due time . . . in due time," Freak Zeenie said, ruffling De'shawn's finger-length dreads.

He walked over to Mama Lois and planted a kiss on her cheek. "Mom, you think you'll be able to keep an eye on De'shawn for me for a while? School starts in a few weeks, and I gotta get things straight."

"Deacon, you know you don't have to ask me that," she replied, her hands never pausing from cleaning.

Freak Zeenie hugged her tightly.

"A'ight, D'. I'll be back for you soon. Till then, you're the man of the house, okay? Protect this woman with your life," he said firmly.

De'shawn nodded but didn't look up.

"Levi! Let's do it!" Freak Zeenie called out, heading for the door.

Later that Night
The *Change of Heart* Building
Dothan, Alabama

Freak Zeenie was on the phone with his cousin, explaining the events that had gone down earlier. Levi was furious after hearing his older brother's theory.

"Yeah, Funk, fuck a rap right now, cuz!" Levi barked. "I gotta handle this first. Man, they killing rappers every other month or so, nigga!" His tone sharpened. "You saw what just happened to PnB Rock, right?"

Freak Zeenie paused, letting Levi's words sink in.

"Now, this weekend they done took that boy Takeoff. Umph, umph, umph! RIP to them boys, man. This shit crazy!" Levi said, his voice heavy. "I ain't tryna go out like that, cuz. Now, I need that info on those Paisas we saw at the Flame Thang that night," Freak Zeenie bellowed, his voice cutting through the tension.

After finishing his conversation with Funk, Freak Zeenie, Levi, and Remy Red sat together, going through a chain of possibilities and different strategies to apply. Freak Zeenie didn't want to involve his brother or Remy Red in his personal affairs again, but neither of them was taking no for an answer.

The only way to explain the fire burning in Freak Zeenie over what he believed Zacatecas had caused would be two words: *relentless again.*

Chapter 21

A Day Later—
Georgia

Zacatecas sat in the back of a smoke-gray Maybach, sipping tequila with the partition raised, feeling oddly tepid after seeing his youngest son. His son had recently run away after killing an entire family at the shooting range—the same day Zacatecas had flown Freak Zeenie in. The boy had been staying with Zacatecas' mother, the woman who was not only his mama but also the reason his heart beat.

Zacatecas' mother lived in a beautiful home in Gwinnett County, a house Zacatecas had purchased for her many years ago. His son was surprised when his father came for him but flatly refused the offer to return to the small town of Zacatecas, Mexico. Zacatecas just smiled to himself as the tequila burned its way down his throat, remembering his own rebellious days as an adolescent. Instead of forcing the issue, he let his son be, content to let the U.S. act as a pacifier. Back in Mexico, there were no such luxuries—the pacifier was snatched away as soon as the doctor handed the baby to its mother.

Zacatecas had already sent his Paisas to Dothan, Alabama, to handle Freak Zeenie, confirming that his "expiration date had expired expeditiously." With that matter handled, Zacatecas had no further interest in lingering in the United States. The country had become a mere trivia question in his empire since his Paisas held a death grip on the drug trade.

Greed and power had driven Zacatecas to force Freak Zeenie to do his bidding. But truth be told, Zacatecas didn't need Freak Zeenie to move his product. When Zacatecas first learned about Freak Zeenie, he saw potential—a higher caliber dealer than most. But after crunching the numbers, Zacatecas realized that the diesel fuel spent trafficking drugs across the border to Dothan cost him more than Freak Zeenie ever earned for him. As of now, he'd only broken even. He couldn't help but wonder if dealing with Freak Zeenie was ever worth the risk.

Pulling up to the airport in College Park, Zacatecas threw back the last of his tequila and prepared to board his private jet.

Si, Freak Zeenie. You could've been a billionaire, my amigo, but your deceitful ways made you live in the sky, my friend. Soo long. Like they say . . . RIP, Zacatecas drunkenly thought as the car came to a halt outside the jet.

Zacatecas treated Freak Zeenie like he treated all his Paisas: if they became incapable of doing their jobs or too deciduous— "seasonal" as Zacatecas liked to call them — they were finished. Their season was over.

The back door of the Maybach swung open, and Zacatecas stepped out, staggering slightly from the liquor he'd consumed. He was ready to get back to Mexico and focus on his campaign to become governor. By now, Zacatecas was as powerful as the Incredible Hulk, and when it came to the drug trade, he had surpassed El Chapo in viciousness.

Zacatecas flicked Freak Zeenie off like a flea and made plans to send his most prestigious Paisas to take over the southeast region of Alabama, just as he'd done across the eastern U.S.—one city at a time, like Akon once sang about. As he boarded the jet and buckled himself in, Zacatecas was already planning his next move.

***

Same Time—
Gwinnett County, Georgia

Freak Zeenie and Levi sat parked outside a Mexican tire shop. Funk had told them the shop belonged to the Mexicans they'd seen at The Flame Thang the night Poochie was murdered. Judging by the constant flow of traffic, it was clear that more than just tire changing was going on at the spot.

"They got this bitch jumpin', ain't it, bruh?" Levi said, his eyes scanning the busy operation, his energy building for what was to come. "So, what's the plan?" he asked, looking at Freak Zeenie.

"We need to find out who the manager is," Freak Zeenie replied. "He's gotta be the one who can help us get to Zacatecas."

Levi rubbed a hand down his face, barely hiding his disbelief. "That's the plan, bruh?" he muttered under his breath. Man, I ain't 'bout to let this nigga get me killed up here lackin' and shit. Fuck 'round and end up in a burrito somewhere, Levi thought, already formulating his own plan.

"Yeah, nigga! I go for the head—" Freak Zeenie started, but Levi was already out of the car.

"Fuck this stupid nigga doing? I knew I shouldn't have brought his wild ass, man!" Freak Zeenie bellowed, reluctantly jumping out to follow Levi.

Levi walked straight into the shop. "Sí, sí, sí! Commode say!" he said loudly, calling himself speaking Spanish but knowing almost none.

A large Mexican man stepped out from behind the desk. "May I help you, señor—"

Levi shoved a Glock 27 into the man's mouth, chipping two teeth in the process.

"Yeah, you chalupa-eating motherfucker! Where's the manager at 'round here?" Levi growled, his eyes scanning the shop. "Take me to your boss, my amigo," he said mockingly, shoving the man's head back like he was forcing him to do the limbo.

Freak Zeenie stepped in, quickly locking the front door and flipping the "Open" sign to "Closed."

"Who else in here?" Levi barked, his finger hovering dangerously close to the trigger.

The large Mexican, bleeding from the mouth, tried to speak. Levi eased the gun out slightly to let him talk.

"J-just me and my brother, Tito, man! What—"

"Take us to Tito," Freak Zeenie calmly demanded, shoving the man forward.

In the back office, Tito sat behind a desk, feeding bills through a money counter. A safe sat ajar, stuffed with neatly stacked cash on three shelves. If Tito had been watching the security cameras, he'd have seen them coming. But he wasn't, and Freak Zeenie burst into the room, leading with his silenced pistol aimed chest-high.

Tito jumped, reaching for his gun, but Freak Zeenie shot him in the upper shoulder.

"Argh!" Tito's weapon hit the floor. He tried to grab it again, but Freak Zeenie stomped his hand hard, then kicked the pistol across the room.

"What you was gonna do with that? Shoot me?" Freak Zeenie taunted, pointing at himself. "Now, you're gonna take me to Zacatecas. He needs to know I'm back from the dead."

Tito froze, his eyes widening. He thought Freak Zeenie had been killed in the church bombing.

"Hey, hey, man! He made me do it, I swear! Sí, sí, I don't even know you!" Tito stammered, his perfect English betraying his attempt to play dumb.

Levi and Freak Zeenie exchanged a glance.

BLOCKA!

The sound of Levi's pistol echoed as he shot the large Mexican in the temple. Blood and brain matter splattered across the floor as the body crumpled.

Tito's face twisted in rage. This was his brother, and he vowed silently to kill both of them if he made it out alive.

Freak Zeenie responded by slamming a steel-toe boot into Tito's head, holding onto the desk for leverage. Tito's face swelled grotesquely.

"Ho', ho', bruh! You gonna kill him!" Levi warned.

"That's the object, nigga!" Freak Zeenie gritted, stomping Tito's teeth in. "You're gonna take us to Zacatecas, bitch!"

Freak Zeenie stopped only when he noticed cars pulling up outside the shop and quickly leaving.

Levi lifted Tito's head, now swollen and bleeding profusely. "We need answers, Tito, if you wanna keep your life, homes," Levi said, but Tito barely mumbled.

"What he say?" Freak Zeenie asked.

Levi stood up, grabbed a gas can, and drenched the room—and Tito—in gasoline. "Last chance, Tito. You hear me?" Tito remained silent.

"He'd rather die than rat," Levi said, pouring a trail of gas to the door.

Enraged, Freak Zeenie drew his pistol.

BLOCKA! BLOCKA! BLOCKA!

Three shots to the skull ended Tito.

After cleaning out the safe, they waited for the streets to clear before leaving. Freak Zeenie struck a match and dropped it, watching the fire consume everything.

"Burn in hell, bitch-ass motherfucker," Freak Zeenie spat, slamming the door shut. Sprinting to the car, they pulled off into the night, leaving no trace behind. By the time they turned the corner, the tire shop was ablaze, burning like a Phoenix in the dark.

Chapter 22

The W
Atlanta, Georgia

Since Levi didn't want to go to the *Flame Thang* with Freak Zeenie, Freak Zeenie went alone. Levi went to the 10th on 18th Street downtown to put the money and drugs away. Then he got some much needed rest for the remainder of the night.

Freak Zeenie, meanwhile, was taking out his frustration on a short, petite Mexican female with a phat voluptuous ass. Her long, silky, curly jet-black hair all the way down her back. Freak Zeenie worked out on her backside, holding tightly to her hair, pulling her back aggressively.

"Um-hum, puta! This some gas!" he mumbled between powerful strokes, ramming into her hot tunnel. Her soft ass jiggled, sending waves rippling through her ass cheeks.

The Spanish chick loved it.

"Fuck me harder nigga!" she cried. "Yes, yes, yes, harder! Just like that—um-hum!" She moaned in pure pleasure, enjoying the aggressive sex Freak Zeenie demonstrated as he demolished her tiny pussy. "Ah-ah-ah y-yesss!" Her convulsive orgasm the left her sprawled out across the bed, breathing hard as cum seeped down her inner thighs.

Smiling Freak Zeenie admired his work. He had buss to good nuts for less than $200, so he was feeling his self. "I'm getting my freak on!" he sang, quoting the lyrics from an underground rapper by the name of PAPER BOI RARI.

All of sudden an uncertainty appeared in Freak Zeenie's expression. He stared at the massive tattoo scrawled in bold letters across her lower back. The Spanish belle glanced back, noticing that he was still watching her. Smiling, she made her ass cheeks vibrate for Freak Zeenie, showing off her exotic dancer skills to a beat in her mind that only she could hear.

Sweat beaded on Freak Zeenie's forehead as he noticed how succulent her pussy seemed to become all over again. Shaking off the lust, he tried to figure out how he'd missed something so small yet so big to him. "PAISA," he mouthed.

Trying to figure out if he'd been followed to the upscale hotel, Freak Zeenie's sharp, suspicious gaze scanned the room. His uneasy demeanor was clear as day when he scratched his arm like he'd caught eczema out of nowhere, instantly catching the attention of the Spanish belle.

"What's wrong?" she asked, abruptly stopping her performance. She turned over and sat up, her face suddenly laced with concern.

Freak Zeenie didn't answer. He just shook his head dismissively before striding toward the dresser beside the king-size bed. Yanking the drawer open, he wrapped his palm around the cold grip of a Glock 27, powering it up immediately. In one fluid motion, he turned back toward her, the pistol now locked and loaded, ready to send her soul skyward.

"Bitch! Fuck you thinkin' 'bout? Tryna put Freak Zeenie in the blender, hoe?" he growled, jabbing the pistol at her while speaking about himself in the third person.

The Spanish belle's expression was frozen in a mix of confusion and fear as Freak Zeenie's menacing tone and gun in her face did all the damage necessary to her psyche.

"Bitch ... you bet not fucking move!" he barked.

Backing up, Freak Zeenie reached the door, unlocking it. He yanked the door open and held the Glock chest-high in front of him, his head swiveling sharply down the hall, expecting Zacatecas or his goons to be lurking, ready to pounce. But when he saw no one, he slammed the door shut and locked it before speeding back toward the Spanish belle.

"How many of yo' people supposed to be out there?" he snarled, grabbing a fistful of her hair and yanking her head back hard.

"Lie, bitch, and I'm gon' send you . . . way up there!" he added, pointing the gun toward the ceiling for emphasis.

The Spanish belle's face twisted with confusion as she struggled to maintain her innocence. Her mother's warnings about the dangers of night dancing echoed in her mind. She wished she could reach her mace without losing her life.

"Umm . . . I-I don't understand what you mean or what you're talkin' 'bout, Freak," she stammered, her voice trembling as she fought to keep her fear hidden.

"A'ight. You don't understand shit all of a sudden, huh?" Freak Zeenie growled. He glared at her, his rage seething through clenched teeth. "Well, understand this then—"

He brought the muzzle of the Glock down hard, raking it across the bridge of her nose. The impact split her skin, and blood gushed out instantly.

"*Bitch!* You a gotdamn Paisa! You think I'm stupid?"

"Aah, shit!" she shrieked, clutching her face. "You fucking crazy, puta! My fuckin' nose, puta!" She shouted, her hands now stained burgundy from the blood pouring out.

"Fuck are you talkin' 'bout, you stupid motherfucker!" she babbled, her tears blurring her vision as pain radiated from her broken nose.

If the Spanish belle thought her emotional outburst would soften Freak Zeenie, she was fooling herself. To him, her dramatics only made her guilt more obvious.

"I ain't asking again after this . . . are you a Paisa?"

"What? I mean, no!" she protested. "On God—I'm not no motherfuckin' Paisa, man, damn!" Her tone was high-pitched, almost pleading, but her eyes squeezed shut, preparing for the worst. She didn't want to witness her death.

The thought of her three-year-old daughter growing up without a mother crushed her, and she began sobbing uncontrollably.

Her words didn't sway Freak Zeenie. To him, "on God" sounded hollow. Most Mexicans he'd known in prison worshipped shrines and saints, not the Christian God. What made her different? He was sure she was lying.

"Oh, so now you a Mexican Christian?" Freak Zeenie scoffed.

"Huh? What?" she stammered. "I mean . . . hell yeah, man!" she managed through bloody fingers, trying to slow the bleeding.

Freak Zeenie took a deep breath, his nerves on high alert. Any second now, he expected the door to burst open with Zacatecas and his crew storming in. Keeping the gun trained on her, he demanded, "Why you got 'Paisa' in big bold letters tattooed across your back then, if you ain't one?"

"Because . . . my baby daddy's a Paisa, man! What the fuck you trippin' on?" she snapped, inadvertently snitching.

"Oh yeah? What's his name?"

"Why?"

"*Bitch, what's his name?*" he roared, spit flying from his mouth as his voice shook the room.

"Flocko! My baby daddy's name is Flocko!" she blurted out. *And he gon' kill your fuck ass once he finds out you hurt me, puta!* she thought to herself.

"Where he be at? Like hang out, work, hustle—shit like that?"

"Gwinnett! He owns a meat market out in Gwinnett County!" she snitched again, hoping he'd take the bait. If Freak Zeenie went to Gwinnett, she was sure Zacatecas' crew would turn him into Taco Bell meat and scatter his remains across the sewage system.

"A'ight, call 'em then," Freak Zeenie ordered.

The Spanish belle wiped her bloody hands on the soiled bedspread before grabbing her phone.

Early the Next Morning
Gwinnett County

It was 20 degrees below in the back of the meat truck, but it still wasn't colder than Freak Zeenie's heart. He didn't feel a damn thing as he brutally pounded Flocko's thin torso with a crowbar, each swing landing with bone-crushing impact. Levi kept his focus on driving, steadying the truck as Flocko swung side to side, helpless against the blows and the sway of the vehicle. Freak Zeenie had Flocko's wrists bound, hanging him from a meat hook like just another slab of frozen beef. Flocko couldn't believe it—his own baby mother had sold him out.

His eyes were swollen shut, bruised to a bluish-purple, and four of his teeth were scattered somewhere on the truck's bloody floor. Blood dripped from his mouth, pooling on his battered chest as he struggled to cling to life. Each ragged breath sounded like it could be his last.

The Spanish belle lay hogtied in the corner, forced to witness the horror. Her face was soaked in tears, her spirit sinking further into despair with every sickening thud of the crowbar. She cursed the decisions that had brought her here. This wasn't how she imagined things going—not for her, not for Flocko, and not for the child they shared. Her misguided plan had blown up in her face, and now she and her baby's father were on the verge of death. The thought of her mother jumping in to search for her brought a flicker of hope, but it was quickly snuffed out when she remembered her line of work. Still, all she had left was her faith—and even that felt shaky now.

Last night, the Spanish belle had called Flocko with deceit dripping from her words, telling him their daughter needed to go to the emergency room. She claimed the child might have contracted COVID and swore she couldn't take her because of her own doctor's appointment. That was enough to convince Flocko to meet her in Gwinnett early that morning. Posted up beside his truck, smoking a blunt laced with K-2, Flocko had no idea what hit him. Freak Zeenie had crept up behind him and knocked him out cold with a single blow to the back of the head.

Now, as she watched Freak Zeenie beating Flocko to death in the frozen hell of the meat truck, the Spanish belle wished she'd never made that call. But wishes couldn't undo the damage. The reality was blood, pain, and desperation.

"You gonna tell me something, bitch!" Freak Zeenie barked, gripping the crowbar tighter. "How do I get to Zacatecas, huh?" His voice was venomous, each word punctuated by the sickening crack of steel against flesh.

"Argh! No comprende!" Flocko gasped, his words strained and dripping with agony.

Freak Zeenie shot a look back at the crying belle, his face a mask of rage. "Tell his fuck ass what I wanna know," he snapped. "Tell him I need to know when Zacatecas is coming back to the States—or how I get to him in Mexico." He paused, tilting his head as if in thought. "If he helps me, I'll spare both y'all lives. If not…" He gestured to a frozen cow carcass swinging from a nearby hook. "I promise to serve death on a cold dish." A twisted laugh escaped his lips, but the menace in his tone left no doubt he meant it.

The Spanish belle, trembling, spoke rapidly to Flocko in Spanish, her voice rising and falling with urgency.

Thirty Minutes Later—

Levi pulled the truck over and left it running as he stepped out, his hat pulled low to shield his face. He glanced around the truck stop, the lot bustling with big rigs, before unlatching the lock and swinging open the back door. Freak Zeenie jumped out without a word, still gripping the crowbar, his knuckles pale from the cold. Levi locked the door behind him, but Freak Zeenie jammed the crowbar into the latch and broke it clean off with one forceful twist.

The two of them walked casually through the gas station parking lot, blending into the chaos of truckers and travelers. As they reached the far side of the lot, Freak Zeenie wiped the crowbar clean on his black tee before discreetly tossing it under a random semi-truck.

"You find out anything useful or what?" Levi asked, his tone low and guarded.

"I think so," Freak Zeenie muttered, his eyes scanning their surroundings as they approached the Uber Levi had prearranged. They climbed in without a word, leaving Flocko and the Spanish belle to freeze to death in the back of the truck. Tears had frozen into icy trails on her cheeks, and Flocko's shallow breaths were growing slower, each one closer to his last.

Several Minutes Later—
18th Street, Downtown Atlanta, Georgia
The Uber pulled to the curb on 18th Street as a car sped past, whipping into a reckless three-point turn. Levi stepped out into the street, and Freak Zeenie climbed out on the sidewalk side, slamming the door behind him. The Uber peeled off, leaving the two standing there as the car that had turned around came screeching to a halt in front of them.

"Aye! What up, Levi?" a voice called out from the car, but the tone was anything but friendly. Both Levi and Freak Zeenie turned to face the vehicle, tension crackling in the air.

Blocka! Blocka!

Gunshots erupted, shattering the night.

Tires screeched as the car sped off, disappearing into the shadows just as quickly as it had appeared.

Chapter 23

The Next Day
Federal Building, Northern Division
Tallahassee, Florida

Pastor Barber sat in the chair, listening and thinking at the same time, all while Agent Simpson tore into him. Pastor Barber was facing the very real possibility of federal charges—serious ones that carried lengthy sentences in the F.B.O.P. (Federal Bureau of Prisons).

"I'll put your old, rusty, fake-preaching ass in prison for the rest of your life—and your kids' grandkids too!" Agent Simpson bellowed. "You better get me something on Freak Zeenie like you promised me!" he hollered, veins bulging, jabbing his stubby finger aggressively at Pastor Barber.

Prison didn't sound so bad anymore as Pastor Barber dwelled on it. For the life of him, he just couldn't understand his misfortunes. Less than a month ago, Pastor Barber had truly fucked up a check—40 bands (forty thousand dollars), gone. And along with it, all the untraceable kilos he'd run through. His wife had told him repeatedly that he needed therapy for his gambling addiction. At first, Pastor Barber couldn't see it. But now? After gambling away the house mortgage at different casinos, losing the 1.9 billion Powerball lottery by just two numbers—money he'd secretly pulled from their joint savings account without telling her—he finally saw the truth. She was right.

Now, therapy felt like the least of his problems. Pastor Barber was almost ready to try prison out.

He came out of his train of thought just in time to hear Agent Simpson's voice rise even louder. "Yeah, but if he won't put nothing in my hands," Pastor Barber stammered, his voice heavy with defeat. "I mean, what can I do?

Agent Simpson stormed toward him, closing the gap between them until their noses were mere centimeters apart. "You better plant a kilo or something—I don't give a fuck—or . . ." Agent Simpson leaned in, kissed Pastor Barber's cheek mockingly, and sneered, "Kiss your old ass good fucking bye!" He jabbed a finger toward the door. "Now. You're dismissed! Get the fuck OUT!"

Without another word, Pastor Barber left, his heart sinking deeper with every step.

Minutes Later—

Sitting in his car, Pastor Barber fumbled around in his glove compartment until he found what he was looking for: an 8-ball of cocaine. He glanced up at the building, half wondering if Agent Simpson could see him. He expertly unknotted the plastic bag, took his key, dug in, and fed his craving. He did a quick 3-on-3 (three bumps up each nostril).

Leaning his head back against the seat, he waited for that bitter taste to slide down his throat and rush into his system. His phone chimed, but he ignored it, eyes closed, savoring the drip. Taking a good sniff to help the drain, he finally sat up, started his car, and pulled out of the parking lot.

As he drove, his phone began to ring again. This time, he glanced at the screen. The number wasn't familiar, but he answered anyway.

"You have a collect call from . . ." The automated voice paused.

"Duke," a raspy voice said.

"Press zero if you accept or nine if you wish to decline . . ."

Pastor Barber didn't let the service finish. He pressed zero immediately, sniffling as the last of the cocaine drained down his throat.

"Bruh, why you calling me from a jail phone?" Pastor Barber rushed out, his words quick and slurred. "What's going on?"

"Man, Carl . . . She gone. She gone, bruh," Chief Duke's voice cracked on the other end.

"Who gone, Duke? What that got to do with you being in jail?"

"My wife!" Chief Duke yelled. "She fucking passed! I tried to help her, bruh. Everything was going to pay for her treatment," he said, his voice heavy with emotion. "Everything was going good until the feds showed up at the police department." His voice dripped with hate.

"For what, Duke?"

"They got me on counterfeit charges!"

"What!" Pastor Barber shouted, swerving just in time to avoid an oncoming car. His heart raced as he straightened out the wheel. "How the fuck did that happen?"

"This nigga gave me a hundred grand to help pay for her treatment, but the shit must've been *fake!*" Duke trembled with rage.

"What? Who?"

"Nephew! You know who!" Chief Duke's voice dropped, filled with bitterness. "I been in here four days. Got a bullshit sleezy lawyer already talkin' 'bout six to ten months. I'm trying to get out on a leg monitor, know what I mean?"

The call disconnected before Pastor Barber could respond.

"Duke?" he shouted into the phone, stunned. Before he could process the conversation, his phone lit up again.

"Hello, talk to me, bae," he answered, trying to sound normal, even cheerful.

"Carl?" His wife's voice screamed so loud he had to pull the phone away from his ear. "Tell me why I come home to an eviction notice on our fucking door? Huh? Why?" Her voice shook with fury. "I could've sworn this house was paid for over fifteen fucking years ago!"

"Are you serious?" was all Pastor Barber could muster.

"Am I serious? Am I serious? Carl . . . If I find out this eviction has your name anywhere near it—" she took a breath, her words slow and deliberate, each one laced with venom—"I will file for a divorce first, then turn around and sue your hypocrite ass second, you old bastard!" She slammed the phone down, disconnecting the call.

Usually loquacious, Pastor Barber was rendered speechless. Her words hit him like a gut punch. His stomach churned, a queasy feeling rising inside him. If only he hadn't tried to straddle the fence between God and the devil, his life might have turned out differently.

Desperate, he began calling Freak Zeenie's number back to back. He needed a sacrifice—badly. His gambling addiction, his debts, and the federal threats hanging over him were pushing him to make reckless decisions.

Later That Day—Mama Lois' House
Dothan, Alabama

Before heading back to Dothan, Freak Zeenie had left Remy Red the key cards so she could visit Levi at Grady Hospital. Levi, who was still in the ICU, clung to life after suffering multiple gunshot wounds. The doctors couldn't explain how Levi was still breathing on his own, given the amount of blood he'd lost. Freak Zeenie knew one thing for sure—Levi was fighting to stay on earth.

Freak Zeenie had just arrived at his mother's house when he saw Pastor Barber sitting in the kitchen. Fifteen missed calls from his uncle lit up his phone. Freak Zeenie already had a strong hunch about what Pastor Barber wanted, so he hadn't returned any of them.

Now, sitting across from him, Freak Zeenie could feel the weight of his uncle's desperation. Sweat glistened on Pastor Barber's brow as he spoke.

"Come on now. I need you, baby!" Pastor Barber pleaded. "Man . . . The house is gone, my wife is gone, and the congregation is disappointed." He dropped his head. "I'm begging you, nephew. I got to get my face back. If anybody can do it, you can!" he said, but pessimistic thoughts invaded Pastor Barber's mind from the culprit actions that he knew he was responsible for.

Even though Freak Zeenie sat there, sharp-eyed and fully aware, listening to Pastor Barber bickering about all his petty complaints, his mind had no room left to deal with the kind of nonsense his uncle was presenting. Freak Zeenie knew exactly how much money he had helped Pastor Barber raise for running loads, so he didn't feel the slightest bit guilty about his uncle's poor decisions and mismanagement.

Since coming home, all Freak Zeenie wanted to do was focus on building up his business endeavors. When you're the breadwinner, everyone expects you to hand out slices, but when the loaf runs out, nobody's around to help bake a new one so everyone can keep eating. Family included. And remember: even Jesus' own family nailed Him to the cross.

As Freak Zeenie carefully weighed his words before responding, Pastor Barber grew even more persistent. The cocaine coursing through his veins had his thoughts speeding ahead of him, twisting his intentions into something desperate and dangerous.

"Unk, look," Freak Zeenie finally began, rubbing his hands slowly down his face. He was clearly stressed, life dumping more problems on him than he could handle. "If I could help you, I would have by now," he said. "I ain't about to sit here and give you a big lecture on what, why, or how you choose to use your money." He paused, letting the words sink in. "What I will say, though, is this: you're a preacher of a well-established church," he continued. "That makes you a public role model, Unk. In no form or fashion should you be sitting here telling me how you're in a bind."

Freak Zeenie leaned forward. "Me and you both know there's rules to this shit. What you did was mismanage your securities," he said bluntly. "You gotta pray, Unk."

Freak Zeenie saw a shift in his uncle's face but didn't realize just how far off his perception was from what Pastor Barber was truly revealing inside. "For real, Unk," Freak Zeenie added. "God disciplines and punishes those He truly loves. That's the way it is."

"Right now, Unk, it just ain't the time," Freak Zeenie said with finality. "I don't even want to talk about how much bread I've lost, man. My hands are tied."

Just as Freak Zeenie finished his thought, De'shawn walked in, drenched in sweat and carrying his basketball. He had a confident bop in his walk that made Freak Zeenie smile. That tiny distraction, that moment of pride, caused Freak Zeenie to miss the lurking schemes forming in Pastor Barber's mind.

As De'shawn passed by the table, he stopped. "What's up, y'all? I just skunked a couple of lames 'round the corner and won a quick hundred," he said, grinning. "Testing my left wrist like it ain't deadly! That's why I killed 'em. Swish!" He held his hand up like he was shooting a jumper. "I'm going to the league!" De'shawn declared as he headed off to take a shower.

"That's right, boy!" Freak Zeenie hollered after him, proud to see someone feeling good for a change.

But just that fast, dark and desperate thoughts swarmed Pastor Barber's mind. When Freak Zeenie turned his focus back to his uncle, making eye contact, the malicious intent brewing in Pastor Barber went completely unnoticed.

"I do have a way we can raise some bread, though," Freak Zeenie said after a pause. "You in the water, but I ain't gonna let you drown."

"Oh yeah? And how's that?" Pastor Barber asked dryly, more out of obligation than interest. He was already ready to leave, disappointed he hadn't made any progress with Freak Zeenie. Before arriving at his sister's house with hopes of catching his nephew, Pastor Barber had briefly considered not cooperating with the Feds to help lock Freak Zeenie back up. But after how Freak Zeenie had just dismissed him, the thought of sabotage crept back to the surface. If his boat was sinking, why not shoot a hole in Freak Zeenie's first?

"We do a few fundraisers at the Change of Heart program!" Freak Zeenie suggested enthusiastically, like it would spark something in Pastor Barber. "We get Unk to bring out the smoker, hook up some food, and speak to the youth. That type of scene, Unk. That's where we gonna get our blessings at, you feel me?"

Even though Freak Zeenie had a valid point, that was the last thing on Pastor Barber's rogue mental Rolodex. *This nigga done bumped his gotdamn head!* Pastor Barber thought to himself. *Now he wanna help the community all of a sudden, after poisoning it for years? Just like the rest of 'em—go to prison, catch an identity crisis, then come home on some righteous shit. Who you think you foolin', Freak Zeenie?* His thoughts trampled over each other, his bitterness growing by the second.

"Nawl, I'mma let you have that there, nephew," Pastor Barber said, rising to his feet. "I gotta get my own life back on track before I can help anyone else get theirs right."

For once, that was the truth. But even as Pastor Barber judged his nephew for wanting to change, he conveniently exempted himself from the same scrutiny. If he'd bothered to look in the mirror, he would've seen the log in his own eye while obsessing over the speck he saw in Freak Zeenie's.

Pastor Barber left without acknowledging his sister or anyone else on his way out. He headed straight for Montgomery City Jail, where his brother Duke was still in federal custody in the annex.

Known as a disreputable pastor in the community, Pastor Barber was already in a predatory mindset. The Feds had him in a precarious position, his livelihood hanging by a thread. He was determined to keep what little he had left, even if it meant throwing common sense and morality out the window. Driving to Montgomery, he cursed loudly, his language desecrated and frantic. He was running out of powder to snort, and the panic set in. He'd banked on Freak Zeenie to come through for him. Now, he had to figure out his next move—fast—if he wanted to keep riding that rich-man high.

Meanwhile, Freak Zeenie enjoyed dinner with his mom and son before heading out to Kinsey, Alabama, to feed his dogs. Before leaving, he promised to take De'shawn school shopping soon. On his way home, he received a text from Kal-Kal about linking up. *What this lil' nigga want?* he thought. Freak Zeenie made a mental note to holler back later. Right now, his mind was focused on the betterment of his and his youngest son's lives.

Later That Night—I-95

Cartier Jay and Boo-Boo were going back and forth, arguing as Cartier Jay kept the car steady, driving at the speed limit toward the Alabama state line. They'd made a trip to Florida to play a few numbers and pick up some rolls of scratch-offs. Everything had gone smoothly—until just before they pulled out of the gas station parking lot.

A crip blue Trackhawk rolled in, catching their attention immediately. They decided to sit tight and see who it was. Time didn't disappoint. Two of their most hated opps stepped out and walked into the gas station, completely oblivious to their surroundings.

That turned out to be a fatal mistake.

Now, those two same opps were professionally wrapped up in what looked like giant vacuum-sealed plastic, lying lifeless in the backseat. Matching .40mm bullet holes marked the center of each of their foreheads. Boo-Boo stood over the bodies, still catching his breath, beads of sweat dripping down his face from the quick work they'd just put in.

"Man, w-we c-can't r-ride al-al th-the w-way b-back t-to W-Webb w-with t-two d-dead b-bodies, c-cuz!" Boo-Boo stammered, his voice shaky from both adrenaline and exhaustion.

"Shit, I'm thinking the same thing," Cartier Jay replied, trying to come up with a plan. His uncle's words echoed in his head—Never leave evidence behind. The dead tell their own stories. But this situation wasn't leaving them much of a choice.

"Sh-shit, I-I don't k-know, b-but th-they ne-need t-to g-get th-th fuck o-out th-this r-ride, c-cuz. Th-that's a-a f-fact!" Boo-Boo said firmly. "W-we c-can l-leave 'em o-on th-the s-side of th-the highway, f-for r-real sh-shit!" He was dead serious as the words spilled out.

Cartier Jay glanced at his rearview mirror. No headlights. He checked the opposite lane. Nothing there either. They had luck on their side—for now. Quickly, Cartier Jay pulled over to the side of the interstate, his paranoia kicking in.

"A'ight, bruh, hurry up and drag them bitch-ass niggas out! Push 'em down the ditch! Hurry the fuck up!" Cartier Jay hollered, the edge in his voice betraying his growing anxiety.

Without hesitation, Boo-Boo hopped out, opened the side doors, and dragged the corpses out one by one. He rolled each of them down the embankment as far as he could, their plastic-wrapped forms disappearing into the shadows.

"A-a'ight, c-cuz, h-hit i-it!" Boo-Boo called out as he slammed the door shut, jumping back into the passenger seat.

Cartier Jay stomped on the gas, the car roaring to life as they sped off, putting as much distance as possible between themselves and the ditch.

He couldn't stop replaying his uncle's lessons in his head—*Never leave a dead body behind unless you want someone else to explain what went down.* This was the first time Cartier Jay had gone against the grain of those rules, and it didn't sit right with him.

I had to this time though, he reasoned with himself, gripping the steering wheel tightly. He told himself it was the only option. Still, the regret weighed on him as the remainder of the drive stretched on, the eerie silence in the car broken only by the sound of tires against the pavement.

Chapter 24

Four Days Later
Veracruz, Mexico

The Paisas had left a massacre in Veracruz, wiping out as many members of the Martinez Cartel as they could. The drug wars between the two factions dated back as far as the early 1900s. Back then, the Martinez Cartel held the crown, but in the past decade, the tides had shifted. Zacatecas had built the Paisas into a massive force. Hailing from the small city of Zacatecas, Mexico, his deep love and support for his community earned him so much admiration that they honored him with the city's name. Zacatecas had inherited his position of power from his father and vowed to carry the torch even further. For over 15 years, he had served as mayor, solidifying his influence. Now, Zacatecas was running for governor. This step wasn't just about power—it was a prerequisite for his ultimate goal: the presidency. Though far from a law-abiding figure, Zacatecas understood that to rule, dissimulation was key. Over the years, he'd tried time and again to negotiate with the Martinez Cartel, offering deals and proposing alliances. But they refused to meet him halfway. The Martinez Cartel wanted it all or nothing, which cemented their roles as sworn enemies.

Since the Martinez Cartel refused to cooperate, Zacatecas devised a bulletproof plan for a mass takeover. Becoming governor would give him unprecedented control over drug distribution. With the Colombians already in his pocket, the only thing holding him back were the constant disruptions caused by the Martinez Cartel's control of the Rio Grande following El-Chapo's departure. These delays were costing Zacatecas millions, a price he was no longer willing to pay. To him, the Martinez Cartel wasn't just competition—it was a destitution to his country.

Determined not to falter, Zacatecas sent a small army to Veracruz to end Rico Martinez's life once and for all. Rico, the head honcho of the Martinez Cartel, was having a special lunch meeting when Zacatecas' men bombed the restaurant. The explosion killed Rico, several key cartel members, and a number of innocent bystanders. Zacatecas, ever the despot, didn't lose a wink of sleep over the carnage. War was never pretty, and he had no regrets. With Rico gone, Zacatecas was poised to elevate Mexico to a magnitude it had never seen before. Neither the Gosman Cartel, Gormez, nor any other syndicate could rival the heights Zacatecas intended to reach.

Same Time—

Zacatecas lounged on his lavish balcony, getting topped off (head) from his wife who on her knees and tipsy off too many Mai Tais. His head tilted back, eyes closed, as he enjoyed the sensation she was providing him. It didn't take long before he erupted down her throat. She swallowed all his bitter seed without hesitation. After cleaning Zacatecas up, she tucked his member, then got up and staggered back inside their lavish compound, leaving Zacatecas to tend to his thoughts.

A sly smile crept across his face as he fantasized about the billions he would soon make. The thought alone almost brought him to a second climax. Zacatecas glanced at the flat-screen television mounted on the wall outside. His campaign ad for governor was playing. He laughed out loud, imagining Rico's expression right before the explosion. Rico had been running against him for the governor's seat—a rivalry now buried in rubble and ashes.

Zacatecas was always thinking ahead. His next move? A thousand of his Paisas would undergo plastic surgery to look exactly like him. It was a foolproof security measure—if someone was gunning for him, they'd never know which "Zacatecas" was the real one. He understood the game: kill the head, and the body dies. So, he ensured that getting to him would be nearly impossible.

Zacatecas prided himself on mastering deception. As he climbed higher on the political ladder, he would hide behind masks, manipulating the system while securing his position as Mexico's most powerful figure. His phone chimed, and he glanced at the screen. It was his Colombian associate. He took the call with haste, letting out a welching chuckle as the man on the other end explained a plan to inflict suffering on the masses without them ever realizing it.

Later That Day
Atlanta, Georgia
Remy Red sat vigilantly by Levi's bedside in the ICU at Grady Hospital. She whispered soft prayers, pleading with him to pull through. "You hear me, nigga? I need you. You got to make it," she murmured, her voice filled with both love and desperation.

Seeing Levi hooked up to IVs, his head completely bandaged, tore at her. The pain she felt watching the man she loved like this was unbearable. But if Levi pulled through— and she believed he would—Remy Red would be there for him no matter how long it took. Their loyalty and love for one another ran deep, *ad infinitum*. Nothing and no one could change that.

A nurse entered the room, breaking the silence.

"Visiting hours are now up, ma'am," the nurse said gently.

Remy Red leaned down close to Levi, her lips trembling. "I love you," she whispered. "You hear me, nigga! I love you!" A single tear rolled down her cheek as she kissed his bandaged forehead before reluctantly leaving.

Walking out of Grady Hospital, Remy Red's heart was heavy, but her mind was filled with malice. Whoever was responsible for this would meet death head-on. She'd been hunting since day one without luck, but she wasn't about to stop now. Remy Red was pertinacious when it came to the people she loved. Without Levi, she felt a deep, unfillable void—an unbearable lacuna in her soul.

An Hour and a Half Later
Tower Liquor Store
Westside of Atlanta
Riding around, hoping to catch a victim but coming up empty, had Remy Red feeling slightly disappointed. She pulled into Tower Liquor Store, needing some liquid courage to help level her out. Jumping out of her Benz, Remy strutted inside, her heels clicking with attitude. After grabbing her preferred bottle, she paid and headed back out.

As she reversed her car to leave, her eyes landed on a familiar face. *Game time, motherfucker! You think my nigga sweet or something, don't you, bitch-ass nigga?* she thought to herself, silently letting her rage simmer. She watched one of Levi's recent customers bop into the liquor store, moving carelessly, as if life couldn't touch him. Remy Red noted that he wasn't wearing the big-boy Cuban link he had bought from Levi either. She shook her head, already knowing how this was about to go down.

Minutes Later—
He came back out, laughing and talking loudly on FaceTime without a care in the world, and oblivious to his surroundings. *Probably high as hell,* Remy Red guessed, but

didn't give two shits. She watched him back his car out and start driving.

Remy tailed him, keeping a safe distance while holding her Glock 27 in her lap. Her blood boiled with vengeance as she followed him all the way to Dogwood Apartments. Parking four spaces down, she got out, her movements calm but deliberate. She scanned the area, crouching low as she made sure there weren't any witnesses.

The dude got out of his car, still chatting away on FaceTime, a black duffel bag in hand. He didn't notice her as he rummaged through his trunk. Before he could even close it, Remy was on him, the space between them closed in an instant.

"Um . . . excuse me? Do you know where—" Remy Red started sweetly.

The dude spun around, startled by her sudden presence.

"—Levi at, stupid motherfucker!" she snarled, cutting him off mid-thought.

Pop! Pop! Pop! Pop! Four quick, deadly shots ripped through his torso, sending him halfway into the trunk. His lifeless body slumped over as blood seeped into the duffel bag. The person on FaceTime, still watching through the phone, froze with their mouth wide open, witnessing the cold-blooded murder in real-time.

Remy ignored the phone, flipped the dude's legs into the trunk, and slammed it shut. His car had just become his graveyard. Before leaving, she stomped on the phone three times, shattering the screen to ensure no one could trace it. Grabbing the duffel bag but leaving the phone behind, Remy sprinted back to her Benz and drove off slowly, blending into the night.

A While Later –
18th Street, Downtown Atlanta, Georgia
Remy Red used the keycard to let herself into the loft. She felt a little better, but not by much. Taking out one of Levi's

lames had helped, even if he wasn't directly responsible for what happened to him. *Fuck it. He shouldn't have shopped with us in the first place. Anybody who did was fair game now,* she thought.

As soon as she stepped in, a figure startled her.

"Oh shit! Nigga, you about to get yourself shot the fuck up in this bitch! What the hell wrong with you?" Remy Red yelled, pulling her pistol from under her arm and aiming it at Freak Zeenie.

Freak Zeenie didn't flinch. He stayed silent, lost in his thoughts.

Seeing his calm, Remy Red locked the door behind her, dropped the duffel bag off her shoulder, and headed to the kitchen. She placed her pistol on the counter and pulled her liquor bottle from the waistband of her pants, setting it beside the gun.

"How long you been back up here?" she asked, flopping down on the couch next to Freak Zeenie.

"'Bout two hours or so," he said, exhaling a thick cloud of kush smoke. "How's bruh coming along?"

Remy sighed deeply. "Still the same, Freak. Still the fuckin' same," she said, her voice steady but heavy with emotion. "The doctor said Levi could wake up tomorrow . . .or maybe never. It's up to how strong he is. They told me to keep praying for him and talking to him, that it might help."

Freak Zeenie shook his head, frustrated. "I'm going to see him tomorrow. I got there late today," he said, flipping through the channels.

Remy Red got up and grabbed the duffel bag she had taken from her victim earlier. When she sat back down and unzipped it, Freak Zeenie's eyes widened.

"Zacatecas!" he blurted out, half-speaking to himself.

"Yeah, Mexico?" Remy said casually, pulling stacks of neatly bundled cash out of the bag.

"Huh?"

"You said Zacatecas, right?" she asked, her face lighting up as the bundles of money spilled onto the coffee table.

"Yeah . . . how you know him?" Freak Zeenie asked, his attention torn between the stacks of blue hundreds and the TV. The news anchor on CNN was talking about Mexico's political scene, mentioning a bombing that had killed Rico Martinez, one of the candidates running for governor against William Zacatecas.

"Damn, girl!" Freak Zeenie said, eyeing the money. "You ran up a bag, didn't you?"

Remy Red's smile faded as she thought about the reason she'd come across the cash.

"Yeah, something light," she said, her tone shifting. "But I didn't know Zacatecas was a person too. I thought it was just a city in Mexico. Our teacher used to use it in spelling bees when I was in middle school."

"You lyin'?" Freak Zeenie asked, more as a question than an accusation.

"What?" Remy Red looked at him, confused. "Hell naw! Here, let me show you." She took his phone and pulled up a map of Mexico, zooming in on the small city of Zacatecas. "Now do you believe me?" she said, showing him the screen.

"Hell yeah," Freak Zeenie said, scrolling through the search results. He immediately began researching the city and its connections.

Remy watched his sudden intensity. "What's so important about Zacatecas, Mexico, that got you all in your phone like that, Freak Zeenie?" she asked, curious.

Freak Zeenie's mind was already scheming. "I got a man to go see about a dog," he said cryptically, grabbing bundles of money and helping her count the grand total.

"A dog? A *gotdamn* dog?" Remy said, raising an eyebrow. "You 'bout to go all the way to another country for a damn dog, Freak? What kind of dog is this?"

"Yeah, something like that. But I'm gon' need your help when it's time. You down to ride?"

"Yeah, I guess so, shit," she said, shrugging.

They continued counting the money in silence. Freak Zeenie didn't share his full plan with her yet. He needed more time to research and get everything lined up.

Chapter 25

A Month Later—
Gwinnett County
Georgia

Zacatecas had just received word that one of his top lieutenants, Tito, had been found burned and murdered at his tire shop in Gwinnett. Zacatecas was lugubrious for no more than four hours tops. He quickly arranged to cover the costs of Tito's and his brother's funerals. On top of that, Zacatecas set Tito's family up with a generous retirement plan to ensure they would be well taken care of.

Wasting no time, Zacatecas promoted his Paisa, Chucky, to lieutenant and assigned him to run their detail shop in Gwinnett. The shop was more than a front—it moved more pills than the Sackler brothers ever dreamed of. Chucky's promotion was well-earned; he was instrumental in driving and assisting with the bombing of First Baptist Church in Dothan. On top of that, Tito had been Chucky's first cousin, and Chucky took his death personally. Chucky wanted to carve through anyone who crossed his path while questioning them about Tito's murder. But no matter how hard he pressed, he couldn't dig up anything useful.

Chucky's newfound glory didn't last long, though. He couldn't provide Zacatecas with any information about the whereabouts of Flocko—Zacatecas's baby brother and trusted overseer. Flocko's prolonged absence had their mother in a state of hysteria. She knew her youngest son would never go this long without checking in on her. The pressure she put on Zacatecas trickled down to his Paisas, and Zacatecas even sweetened the deal with a handsome reward for anyone who could locate Flocko.

When Zacatecas finally got the call from Chucky revealing the unthinkable truth about Flocko, everything stopped. The campaign became ephemeral—temporarily paused. Zacatecas thought Chucky must have been mistaken, but Chucky couldn't avoid the hard questions from his boss. Standing in the morgue, staring at his baby brother's frozen, lifeless body, Zacatecas's heart shattered into a million pieces. Flocko's corpse was frozen solid, frost covering him and the Spanish belle entirely. They looked so brittle that if they fell to the ground, they might shatter like glass.

Even through the ice, Zacatecas could still recognize his brother. He identified the body as Flocko, and the mortician explained that it might take months for the corpses to thaw, meaning an autopsy couldn't be performed anytime soon. Zacatecas left the morgue with a storm brewing inside him, consumed with deadly thoughts about who could have committed such a heinous act against his family. He couldn't believe anyone would have the audacity to pull something like this. On the drive to his mother's house, he agonized over how to break the news.

After Zacatecas told their mother about Flocko's fate, she lashed out, slapping him viciously across the face multiple times for letting her son die. It took some time, but Zacatecas finally managed to calm her down. He then sat his own son down to talk about the importance of protecting family and the responsibility that came with it, especially since his son had chosen to live with his grandmother.

"You better not hesitate when the time comes. You hear me, son?" Zacatecas said.

"Sí," his son replied.

"Alright, I must get going. Here." Zacatecas handed his son an early 19th-century Colt chrome .45 with a pearl handle. The gun also had a Spanish signature engraved on the side. His son smiled and thanked him, clutching the weapon, as Zacatecas turned and left the house without another word.

Later that night, Zacatecas climbed into the waiting gray Maybach beside Chucky. Chucky, eager to please, was waiting for his boss's orders on how to proceed. As the car pulled away, Zacatecas instructed Chucky to ship his money to Mexico immediately. He also ordered Chucky to keep his ear to the ground and, when he found out who was responsible for Flocko's death, to save their lives so Zacatecas could personally take them.

That same night, as Zacatecas boarded his private jet to leave the States, Remy Red was boarding a first-class Delta Airlines flight, also preparing to flee the country. Both of them were en route to Zacatecas, Mexico.

Chapter 26

Labor Day Weekend
The Fair Grounds
Dothan, Alabama

The end of summer had finally arrived, and the whole city came out to party. Dreamer had managed to pull it off again. The 4th of July car show had been canceled and postponed until now due to Dreamer running into a few legal issues, but he made sure to make up for it in a big way.

Dreamer had been promoting the festivities non-stop on Hot 105.7. He even had his own commercial running six times a day. Clearly, the strategy worked because the Fairgrounds were jam-packed. This was how Dreamer did things if you hadn't been keeping up with the facts from the year before.

Dreamer brought down the City Girls to perform their latest hit with Usher. Nicki even agreed at the last minute to come party down South and perform *Super Freaky Girl*. Dreamer also had Finesse2tymes, Young Bleu, and, after a personal call with Big Gucci Mane, he managed to get him to pull up as well.

This year was going to be one for the books. Dreamer had everything lined up: a wet T-shirt contest, a car show that, by the looks of it, was about to be lit, and every kind of tricked-out vehicle you could imagine. He even had a thousand-dollar prize for a two-on-two little league basketball tournament, which De'shawn had already claimed he was going to win. You already know there was big money side-betting going on. Freak Zeenie put up ten bands on De'shawn. And if that wasn't enough, anybody who wanted to bet more just had to, as Drake says, 'Say Sumin Baby', and Freak Zeenie would call it.

Freak Zeenie stood not too far from his uncle James, who had the grill fired up and a line so long you couldn't even see where it ended. Uncle James was showing out, proudly displaying his six-foot-tall trophy he'd recently won to make sure everyone knew his BBQ was nationally recognized as the best—no debate.

Across the Fairgrounds—

Cartier Jay and Boo-Boo had the Lambo truck rocking side to side as they took turns running a train on T-Face's baby mama in the back seat. One was getting some fire head while the other smutted her out from the back, then they swapped. T-Face's BM was in full boss mode, getting her freak on. She was already pissed that T-Face didn't take her to the Fairgrounds in the first place, so this was her way of getting revenge.

Boo-Boo wanted to kidnap her, while Cartier Jay was trying to use sex to make her give up T-Face's location. Neither of them got what they wanted, though, because T-Face's BM swore she didn't even know where her BD stayed. So, they just enjoyed the pleasure while it lasted.

"Umh hum!" she moaned as Cartier Jay hit her with powerful strokes, his thumb buried deep in her ass at the same time. Boo-Boo had to step back because the force of Cartier Jay's thrusts made it impossible for her to keep sucking his dick.

"This bitch tight as hell, boi!" Cartier Jay blurted out as her hot, wet pussy clamped down on his dick like a vice. He couldn't hold it anymore and busted off in the condom. Funny thing was, Cartier Jay didn't even want to hit her at first because he thought she was a clown for choosing T-Face as her baby daddy. But her slutty strut changed his mind quick. Now, he was glad he didn't miss out on the grade-A pussy she was carrying around.

Snatching the condom off, Cartier Jay threw it out the window, nearly hitting a bystander. "Suck me up one more time before I bounce," he said, not waiting for her to answer. Grabbing her head, he pushed her lips back down onto his manhood. She took him in greedily, her jaw locking like she'd been waiting for it. After a few bobs, Cartier Jay pulled out. All he really wanted was to get the latex taste off his dick.

"Gut this bitch out, Boo-Boo, then get her the fuck out my truck," Cartier Jay said, fully disrespecting T-Face's BM to her face without a second thought. "I'm 'bout to see what's poppin' out here," he added, grabbing his Glock before hopping out of the truck.

Boo-Boo kept going, fucking her until he got his nut. Then, just for the hell of it, he pie-faced her out of the back of the Lambo. Boo-Boo had been mo' and mo' cranky lately—probably from withdrawals from the syrup. Scratching his neck like a fiend, he got himself together while she stumbled, trying to pull her skirt down.

"Hey, motherfuckers!" she bellowed, staggering to cover her exposed ass cheeks since she wasn't wearing any panties. Snatching her mini-skirt down as far as it would go, she drunkenly walked off, cussing about the unappreciated mistreatment she just went through.

A crowd of people who had seen the whole thing whispered among themselves, talking shit about her. But she didn't give a fuck about none of that. She was grown and her own lady.

Across the Fairgrounds—
On the Stage
"Hands on yo' knees hands on yo' knees / If that nigga broke, make that ass freeze, we ain't—" JT was popping her

thick, chocolate, voluptuous ass while she rapped. JT and Yung Miami performed 3 tracks from their latest album. They had the females shaking their money makers all 'cross the Fairgrounds. The crowd was having a phenomenal time.

Nicki came right behind them with her super-freak smash hit, stepping onto the stage like a goddess of chaos. Draped in her Chanel line, every piece she wore was see-through, leaving little to the imagination. When Nicki squatted down and started twerking that thick, yellow ass, the crowd lost it. You could vividly see her shaved pussy, her labia on full display—super succulent and impossible to ignore. Phones were out, niggas recording like TMZ while throwing money on the stage and hollering obscenities, their voices a blend of lust and admiration.

Nicki kept flowing, unfazed, then turned her back to the crowd and started popping, her phat booty commanding attention, making it seem like it was everywhere at once. The crowd was lit. *"Sleepin' on me, now a crook in your neck – "* Finesse2tymes jumped on stage, bringing a gangsta energy that had heads bobbing and grills glinting in the lights. After hitting the crowd with two short but addictive tracks, Young Bleu took the stage, feeling the love from his Alabama roots.

As soon as Young Bleu wrapped up, Glorilla, Lotto, JT, and Young Miami hit the stage like a bombshell, surprising everyone with a track from Glorilla's album. They killed it, setting the bar high before the final act. Then came the closer—Big Gucci Mane himself. Drenched in three million dollars' worth of flawless diamonds, he reminded everyone why he was the boss of Big So Icy Gang. Ain't nobody dumb enough to try him; the streets knew what it was.

When the performances wrapped, the wet T-shirt contest took over. Nicki, GloRilla, Lotto, Young Miami, JT, and even some locals jumped on stage, bouncing their big ol' titties like they were omnipresent. Them hoes were twerking to an old classic, *Scrub the Ground*, and trust and believe, they made it happen.

Now, I hate to be the one to break it to my Alabama homies and homegirls, but man, if y'all didn't catch this shit on YouTube or any social media sites, you missed out. JT took the crown, dawg. Her black ass lifted her T-shirt, showing her quarter-sized nipples, then dropped into a split, bouncing up and down, scrubbing the ground. The crowd lost their damn minds. The road team took the win this year.

Freak Zeenie, Cartier Jay, and Boo-Boo were throwing 20s on stage like it was Monopoly money. Even Gucci Mane joined in. Kal-Kal was there too, though he kept his distance. No one even realized he was there the whole time.

Then came the basketball game. Lil' De'shawn drained the final three-pointer, winning a thousand-dollar prize for him and his partner. Freak Zeenie, hyped up, was talking his ten bands' worth of shit while splitting the winnings with De'shawn, who was riding high on his God-given talent but staying mostly humble.

After the game, it was time for the car show. Kal-Kal had planned to enter until Cartier Jay pulled up, easing his brand-new Urus Lambo truck into the spotlight. The truck, sitting on all-gold 30-inch Forgies, flipped seven shades of blue in the sunlight, killing all Kal-Kal's hopes on sight. Even Freak Zeenie was stunned.

"That's how we do it in these bushes, now! Bag talk, baby! Do it, son!" Freak Zeenie hollered, throwing in a playful jab as he and Gucci Mane negotiated over the Dodge Durango with its 700 horsepower under the hood.

Blaza, last year's car show winner, rolled up in his Aston Martin truck sitting on 34-inch Forgies. Blaza had a low flip tropical color paint job sprayed on the new truck. Last year, the hypothermal paint of Blaza's whip turned prime gray when wet, then faded back to tropical colors after his four hoes sprayed it down with Super Soakers. Now, everyone waited to see if he could outdo himself.

After cashing Gucci Mane out for his souped-up Durango, Freak Zeenie locked eyes with Kal-Kal and gave him a wave to come over. Kal-Kal swallowed his pride, knowing Freak Zeenie held the key to putting him where he needed to be.

"What's up, boy?" Freak Zeenie greeted. "Man, I been meaning to get back at you, but shit been happenin' that I just couldn't control. Shit, what's up wit' it though?" he added, pocketing the keys to his new truck, speaking his truth.

"Shit, sorry 'bout your loss first, bruh. That shit was crazy," Kal-Kal said, his tone laced with genuine sympathy. "Man, you know shit was super-hot after that church bombing—FEDs everywhere and all that shit."

"Already," Freak Zeenie nodded.

"Man, I'm trying to cop a lil' somethin'-somethin', you feel me?" Kal-Kal smirked, trying to make his request work.

"Why you ain't holler at Jay 'em, shit?" Freak Zeenie asked, quickly catching the subtle shift in Kal-Kal's expression.

"Man, bruh got the inflation too high on a nigga, dawg. Fuck with me, bruh," Kal-Kal replied, lowering his voice as Boo-Boo started making his way toward them. Freak Zeenie noticed too. Not wanting to step on anyone's toes, especially not his son's, Freak Zeenie made a mental note to talk to Cartier Jay about it later.

"Shit, I gotta see what I got going on, my nigga. Fuck with me in a few days, and I'll let you know," Freak Zeenie replied.

"Say no mo'. I'ma call or text, one of the two, so be on point," Kal-Kal said, acknowledging Boo-Boo with a nod before making up an excuse to exit their presence.

Cartier Jay wasn't playing. Amped up and geeked up on whatever concoction was fueling him, he wasted no time, not even letting Dreamer introduce the rules.

"Oh now! Oh now! Check out my new toy, cuz!" Cartier Jay hollered, swiping his tablet. The Urus came to life. With a few more swipes, doors opened, music blasted, shaking the ground, and the SUV crept forward like a ghost, driverless, its doors ascending like wings. Then it started bouncing, its big-ass rims lifting off the ground.

The crowd went wild. Boo-Boo was stunned. He hadn't known Cartier Jay's ride had those features.

"W-what th-the f-fuck? H-hell n-nawl!" Boo-Boo stuttered, the percs he'd been secretly popping finally hitting.

"You killed 'em, boy! You just fucked 'em up!" Freak Zeenie shouted, running up to Cartier Jay.

A kid jumped up and down, clapping. "Mom! I want one of those! Please, Mom! Please!" he yelled.

Cartier Jay's truck swerved side to side, bouncing on its rims like it was alive. As the crowd roared, Cartier Jay jumped onto the hood, while Freak Zeenie climbed into the passenger seat. They backed the truck into its spot as women rushed over, twerking on the headlights. Even Glorilla joined in, hyped by her song blaring through Cartier Jay's speakers.

The judges, unable to resist, threw up straight 10s across the board, and the crowd was lit. Even Blaza—right before he cranked up and dipped out—nodded in respect, acknowledging Cartier Jay, knowing Cartier Jay had taken the crown this year. Cartier Jay returned the nod, grinning.

"Big Bama, nigga! I'm the Black Nick Sab'! Boy, I can't lose twice at home, you hear me?" Cartier Jay roared, beating his chest. The crowd echoed his hype. Freak Zeenie chuckled.

Suddenly, a big commotion caught everyone's attention. When Freak Zeenie looked back, it was a gang fight taking place near the back of the parking lot. Freak Zeenie spotted 10 niggas stomping the fuck out of someone on the ground while people screamed for it to stop. He went looking for

De'shawn, hoping to keep him out of the mess, as chaos unfolded in the humid Alabama air.

BLOCKA! BLOCKA!

Gunshots rang out, sending the crowd into a stampede. People scrambled for the safety of their vehicles. Freak Zeenie tossed his keys to Boo-Boo.

"Take my car, lil' bruh, I got my truck!" After making it to the Dodge Durango, Freak Zeenie and De'shawn jumped inside the vehicle and sped off from the Fairgrounds, the sound of gunfire still echoing behind them.

Three people were killed, and forty more were injured—either from the bullets or caught in the panic of the stampede. Freak Zeenie, Boo-Boo, Cartier Jay, and Kal-Kal all made it home safely, without harm or causing harm, marking the last day of summer for the year.

Chapter 27

Three Weeks Later—
Brentwood
Dothan, Alabama

"Yeah, yeah, yeah, grab that too, cuz!" T-Face commanded. He and his gang ransacked the luxury stash house tucked away in the suburbs.

For the past month, T-Face had been searching for three of his schoolyard Crip homies but couldn't locate them. Two of them eventually turned up—but they'd been shot in the head and wrapped in plastic, dumped alongside Interstate 95 North. The other member's car was finally located, but no one had seen or heard from the dude himself.

After chopping it up with Kal-Kal—who was mostly giving maybes, throwing hints, and beating around the bush—T-Face decided to take matters into his own hands. He started piecing together that Cartier Jay might've been torching them or pulling some deranged shit based on how Kal-Kal was skirting the subject.

T-Face had come a long way since he'd been out in Ozark, Alabama. Between the bricks he scored from Chief Duke and the counterfeit money he was pushing, T-Face was just $300,000 away from becoming a low-budget millionaire. To the hood, though, T-Face was already living that life. You know how it is—a hundred grand in the hood feels like a million, and a million is like ten million. T-Face was hood rich.

To tighten his grip on the situation, T-Face hired P.I. Bentley to dig up Cartier Jay's location. After three months of surveillance, Bentley had tracked Cartier Jay to a stash house—not his main crib, which was only three blocks away and hadn't been touched in 90 days. To T-Face, this was even better.

When they hit the stash house, it didn't take long to figure out what it was. Inside, they found 20 kilos and all of Cartier Jay's cash. They cleared out everything—drugs, money, and any trace they'd been there—then vanished in broad daylight without a single neighbor noticing.

Turns out, upscale neighborhoods weren't much different from the hood. You could still get got, and your enemies could still get away—neighborhood watch or not.

Same Time
Across Town
The Doctor's Office, Dothan, Alabama

Cartier Jay stepped out of the doctor's office, stretching his arm up and down to loosen it after months confined in an arm sling. He felt good to have his mobility back—he was tired of that handicap life.

Cartier Jay threw a couple of quick left-right jabs, testing his strength.

"Shit, bruh! I'm back like good crack!" he bellowed, satisfied with the results.

He and Boo-Boo hopped into the Urus. "A'ight, bruh. We got that handled. Now it's time to go cash these crooked-ass lawyers out real quick," Cartier Jay said. "We gotta get these court dates pushed back so far that by the time we hit trial, the case'll be weaker than tap water. You feel me? We gon' beat that shit like an egg beater beat eggs, my boy!"

Cartier Jay backed out of the parking lot and eased into traffic. Boo-Boo had been quiet all day, which didn't sit right with Cartier Jay. He shot a side glance at his partner. "You good, bruh?" he asked. "You ain't back on that act', is it?

Man, I told you, I need you, my boy. We gotta stay focused so we can handle this business. You already know—we gotta get this bitch-ass nigga."

"Y-yeah, I-I'm g-good, b-bruh. J-just c-coolin', y-you know?" Boo-Boo stammered. "I-I'm a-already f-focused. W-we g-gotta m-make i-it h-happen. C-can't w-wait. N-nah, I-I a-ain't s-sippin' n-no mo', b-bruh. I-I already t-told y-you t-that."

Boo-Boo leaned back, resting his head against the expensive headrest, and closed his eyes. He wasn't sipping lean anymore, so technically he wasn't lying to Cartier Jay. What he hadn't shared, though, was that he'd started popping Percocets. With all the bodies piling up on his resume, Boo-Boo needed something to help numb his mind. Truth be told, Boo-Boo hated being sober—just like Chief Keef said.

Cartier Jay heard him out but wasn't entirely convinced. "Mmm-hmm. I'm just saying, nigga—you look high to me. Fuck all that!" Cartier Jay snapped, never one to sugarcoat how he felt.

"Yeah, a'ight, nigga," Boo-Boo replied, brushing off the comment. He grabbed the remote and cranked up the volume on the sound system as Cartier Jay navigated through the city toward their lawyers' office.

Same time—On the other side of town
Kal-Kal's Grandmother's house—Dothan, Alabama . . .
"Grandmom, if anything ever happens to me, I want you to send this video to my Facebook account," Kal-Kal explained, his tone unusually serious. "Here, let me show you how to do it, so you know what to do."

Kal-Kal handed her his phone and shared his password—it was his real name so she wouldn't forget it. He patiently walked her through the steps to upload the video footage he needed posted.

To his surprise, Kal-Kal's grandmother caught on like a pro. She even got Kal-Kal to set up her own Facebook page so she could reconnect with old school friends. "Now, Kal-Kal," she asked, her voice heavy with concern, "is something wrong, grandson? You're not in any trouble, are you?"

Her question made sense—Kal-Kal had never spoken to her like this before in all his life.

"Naw, Granny," he replied, brushing off her concern. "I just like to stay on point. You know, insured. Leave a legacy behind if I ever go." He paused, the weight of his words lingering in the air. "Ain't nobody know when it's their time. So, if mine comes before yours, these are my only wishes."

Kal-Kal carefully placed the phone in her top dresser drawer. "It's gon' be right here, Granny. Don't forget!" he said.

"I won't, grandson. I'm old in age, not in mind," she replied sharply. "I know everything that goes on 'round here, especially under my roof." Her words carried a double meaning, letting Kal-Kal know she was aware of the drugs, guns, and cash he stashed in her house. She was old, but she wasn't senile.

Kal-Kal didn't respond. Instead, he bolted to the bathroom, overwhelmed by the vivid memories of what he'd witnessed out in Webb, Alabama. He vomited violently, as if trying to purge the images from his mind.

When he returned, Kal-Kal's thoughts had shifted entirely. He was thinking about making major bread. Everyone around him seemed to be eating, and even though he had more money than ever, it still wasn't enough. No matter how much he stacked, he wasn't satisfied.

But what really ate at him was Cartier Jay and Boo-Boo. Kal-Kal felt like they were forgetting about him.

The truth was, though, it wasn't them—it was Kal-Kal himself. He'd been distancing himself from them, building false narratives in his mind about betrayals that never happened. The reality was they had nothing but love for him, but Kal-Kal couldn't accept that. Instead, he chose his own selfish thoughts over the truth.

See, Proverbs 21:2 says: *"Every way of a man is right in his own eyes; but the Lord weighs the hearts."*

Kal-Kal justified his actions with no remorse. He didn't understand the difference between business and brotherhood—two entirely separate worlds that ran on different axes. But Kal-Kal didn't care. In his heart, he'd let hatred fester—all for the love of money.

Kal-Kal wanted to be the HEAD NIGGA IN CHARGE. *Period.*

Later That Night
Brentwood, Dothan, Alabama

When Cartier Jay pulled up to his stash spot, he immediately knew someone had violated his space.

He didn't panic at first. Whoever it was couldn't have gotten much, he thought. His drugs were hidden extremely well. For anyone to find them, they'd have to be either an expert, desperate, or know exactly what they were looking for.

But the reality was worse than he imagined. Cartier Jay had his bricks neatly stacked up in the attic, alongside a black short-barreled AR-15 with a drum magazine. He also had a medium-sized safe installed in his master bedroom closet.

Cartier Jay wasn't on Google or Forbes or nothing, but his street value had climbed to $1.8 million. He was the walking definition of a young hood rich nigga. But now, all that was gone.

Tears of anger rolled down Cartier Jay's face as he realized he'd made a grave mistake: putting all his eggs in one basket. He couldn't wrap his mind around the loss.

"Argh!"

BOOM!

Cartier Jay punched a hole in the hall closet, his fury never breaking stride. He stomped toward his master bathroom, desperate to confirm one thing—the most important thing.

Under the sink. That's where it would be.

From his adolescent days breaking and entering, Cartier Jay knew that most people forgot to check under the bathroom sink, leaving all kinds of valuables hidden there. And sure enough, his recording security box was still in place.

T-Face, however, had been one step ahead. A B&E vet himself, T-Face had found the box but deliberately left it behind. It was a message—a blatant sign of disrespect. He wanted Cartier Jay to see for himself that if he wanted to touch him, he could.

T-Face took the money and dope because he had zero respect for Cartier Jay. In T-Face's eyes, Cartier Jay wasn't even on his level. Just a kid. And to make it worse, T-Face genuinely believed Cartier Jay was behind his missing Crip homies. On top of that, word had gotten to T-Face that Cartier Jay and Boo-Boo had fucked his baby mama. This was payback.

Cartier Jay watched the security footage four times, each viewing more painful than the last. He saw his entire life savings walk out the door, carried by five Schoolyard Crips.

"I'm gon' cut that fuck nigga into pieces, bruh. On God, boy!" he roared.

No one in the neighborhood had seen or heard a thing. If Cartier Jay could've been anything else in that moment, he would've been a fire-breathing dragon.

Cartier Jay vowed to cut T-Face into pieces—and he wouldn't stray from that path for anything.

Early the Next Morning
The Inner City
Dothan, Alabama
The horrid sound ricocheted throughout the Sprinter van when Cartier Jay smacked T-Faces baby momma so hard that blood sprayed from her mouth.

"How the fuck you don't know, *Bitch?*" Cartier Jay barked, his voice laced with fury. Blood leaked from her mouth, dripping onto the tarpaulin beneath her.

"Huh?" *SMACK!* He hit her again, just as hard, if not harder this time.

T-Face's baby momma's mascara was streaked and ruined, her face a mess of tears and makeup. She sat bound, hands and feet tied together. The crying hadn't stopped since she realized this wasn't some sick, twisted foreplay. It wasn't one of those erogenous moments she'd foolishly thought it could be at first. Like *The Weeknd* said in his song, *Save Your Tears for Another Day*. "Because we ain't *to*-fuckin'-*getter* no more, Jay!" she croaked pitifully, her words barely audible through the sobs. She knew she was in trouble, but the kind of trouble that led to death? That was the furthest thing from her mind. By now, Cartier Jay was sure she didn't know where T-Face was laying his head. As Boo-Boo chauffeured them through traffic, Cartier Jay leaned back in his seat and thought for a moment. But then his face twisted with suspicion.

This bitch is lying like a motherfucker. He started thinking harder. *How the fuck she don't know where her own kids' father at? Yeah right.* Cartier Jay's mind spiraled into anger again. Closing his eyes briefly, he let his thoughts sharpen into a conclusion.

T-Face got this bitch spying for him. Had to be.

"Alright. I believe you," Cartier Jay finally said, his tone calm, almost chilling.

Cartier Jay stepped over her, going towards the front of the van, but not before giving her a look—cold and mischievous.

"Untie me, Jay! My arms hur—"

Her plea was cut short. Blood burst from her neck bone like ribbons falling from the sky. Her head tumbled to the floor with a dull *thud*, rolling about a foot away from her now-slumped corpse.

Cartier Jay stood there with a Samurai sword—a Katana—in both his hands. He exhaled evenly, his breath steady like he hadn't just decapitated a human being. The sword gleamed under the van's interior lights, so sharp it had sliced clean through her neck muscle and bone like a butter knife sliding through warm butter.

"Y-you vic-vicious b-boy!" Boo-Boo said, catching the aftermath in the rearview mirror before turning onto Webb Road.

Unbeknownst to them, Kal-Kal followed them from a distance.

Cartier Jay crouched down, taking a moment to slice T-Face's baby momma's tongue from her lifeless mouth. He held it up, staring at the two vibrating tongue rings piercing it, flicking them playfully with his finger.

T-Face think shit a fucking game, Cartier Jay thought. *I'mma murk this peasant's whole family with his lame ass.* He wiped the sword clean with a rag, his expression dead serious.

Cartier Jay couldn't wait to find T-Face. If T-Face thought the club shit was serious. It was *picayune* to what Cartier Jay had in store for him over the life savings he had stolen.

Boo-Boo turned off Webb Road into the hog farm, driving all the way around to the back. Two minutes later, Kal-Kal passed by in the distance, still tailing them unnoticed.

Chapter 28

A Few Days Later
Grady Hospital
Atlanta, Georgia

Sitting in the small hospital room, Freak Zeenie soliloquized while Levi's chest rose and fell silently. Levi was comatose and had made little to no progress, if any. That didn't stop Freak Zeenie from talking to himself, going back and forth, asking and answering his own questions.

"I'm telling you, lil' bruh. When you wake up, you need to go 'head and marry Remy Red, boy!" he said. "For real, bruh, you gon' marry her?" He paused, then answered himself, "Yeah, you gon' marry her." He laughed lightly before his tone turned serious. "If not, then you a crazy-ass nigga, 'cause that girl crazy 'bout you, boy."

Freak Zeenie kept talking, determined to push Levi toward Remy Red when he got better. He truly believed Levi needed to betroth her.

But Levi couldn't hear a damn thing Freak Zeenie was saying. The steady beeping sound of the monitor was the only indication Levi was even still alive. Levi was in bad shape.

Freak Zeenie needed his lil' brother to come back around. He hated seeing Levi like this—in such a vulnerable condition. Freak Zeenie sat there for a moment, trying to think of all the things he needed to get done after visiting hours, when the nurse walked into the room.

"Hi. How you doing, Mr. Barber?"

"I'm alright," Freak Zeenie replied, eyeing her closely.

"Sorry to bother you, but I need to get Levi cleaned up before my shift ends, so if y—"

"Understood," he cut her off, getting to his feet and stretching. "You think he gon' come back around?"

The nurse looked at Freak Zeenie with a mix of admiration and sympathy. She wished she could give him some assurance, but under hospital policies, she wasn't allowed to speculate. "I sure hope so, Mr. Barber," she said softly, her voice hopeful but cautious, trying to ease the doubts swirling in Freak Zeenie's mind about Levi's recovery.

Freak Zeenie nodded, standing there quietly, weighing her words. The vibration of his phone broke the silence. "Alright, 'preciate it. I gotta take this," he said, pointing to his phone. Freak Zeenie stepped out into the hall before answering.

"What's up?" he said, picking up. "Girl, tell me something I need to hear so I can get in motion." He was eager, hoping for some good news.

Meanwhile, in Another Hallway—

Chucky stood silently, his face twisted into a lugubrious expression as he listened to the doctor. Delivering grim news was the hardest part of the doctor's job, and it showed in his somber tone.

"I'm sorry," the doctor said. "It's stage 3 pancreatic cancer. Six months or less." He patted Chucky on the shoulder before rushing off to answer a call over the intercom.

Chucky stood there for a moment, stunned. His baby sister—just 14 years old—was dying of cancer. Way too young. Chucky clenched his fists, anger and sorrow warring inside him. He turned to leave, promising himself he'd visit her every day until the end.

But as he headed toward the exit, his blood ran cold. His eyes widened to the size of avocados.

He thought he saw a ghost.

It couldn't be. Freak Zeenie was *dead*—unless Freak Zeenie had a twin. Chucky's heart raced as Freak Zeenie came into full view. The devastating news about his sister momentarily vanished under the weight of this new revelation. Seeing Freak Zeenie alive brought a whole new set of problems for Chucky.

While Freak Zeenie talked on the phone, oblivious to him, Chucky's mind raced. He shifted nervously, sizing up the situation, his hand slipping to the pistol tucked in the small of his back.

But then Chucky froze. He thought Freak Zeenie had spotted him—or maybe Freak Zeenie already knew who he was. Either way, Chucky wasn't taking chances. He moved quickly toward the exit, deciding to make a quiet escape.

Today, Chucky was alone. But now that he knew Freak Zeenie was alive, he planned to round up the Paisas. Next time, they'd catch Freak Zeenie slippin'—and they'd Swiss-cheese him with uncountable holes.

Freak Zeenie noticed Chucky fleeing and immediately rushed off in the same direction.

Same Time
Zacatecas, Mexico

The Bronco crept to a slow crawl before stopping completely on the macadam roadway.

Remy Red raised a pair of binoculars to her eyes, studying the massive estate. She scanned its foundation, looking for any cracks in the fortifications. But from what she could see, there was no chance of getting onto the property without being detected—or killed.

Remy Red had been in Zacatecas, Mexico, for almost two weeks. She wasn't entirely sure this was Zacatecas' place, but her intuition told her it was. The estate was the largest she'd seen since arriving in town, and she'd twice followed a limo from an uptown car wash straight to the property.

After a few moments, Remy Red backed the Bronco up and headed back toward town. She'd just gotten off the phone with Freak Zeenie minutes ago. He'd promised to be there within 72 hours.

Remy Red thought she had the same fortitude Freak Zeenie did when it came to taking down Zacatecas. But the enormities Freak Zeenie had planned were far more lurid than anything she'd imagined.

The Next Day
Somewhere in the Gulf of Mexico

Zacatecas sidestepped, then took three quick steps before swinging his leg like a soccer player in the World Cup. His kick sent Chucky's severed head flying into the ocean as if it were a soccer ball.

Throwing his arms into the air, Zacatecas celebrated his gruesome "goal" like he'd just won the championship. Chucky's decapitated head splashed into the water, bobbing on the surface like a fishing bobber.

Zacatecas had been stewing all day, frustrated by Chucky's most recent news. Chucky had called yesterday, swearing he'd seen Freak Zeenie alive and well at Grady Hospital in Atlanta. This came right after news that two black guys had been snooping around Zacatecas' Gwinnett County tire shop—right before the fire that claimed the lives of Tito and his brother.

Zacatecas asked Chucky if funeral arrangements for Freak Zeenie had been made. Chucky gave the wrong answer. Zacatecas played it cool, though, inviting Chucky to his yacht to "discuss details."

When the helicopter dropped Chucky off in the middle of the Gulf of Mexico, Zacatecas greeted him with a firm handshake and brotherly hug. But as soon as Chucky sat down, two brawny Paisas grabbed him, holding him in place.

Chucky struggled, but his small 5'1" frame was no match for them. Zacatecas had one Paisa hold Chucky still while the other restrained his head. Suddenly, Zacatecas turned toward one of the Paisas holding Chucky down. "Fetch me the chainsaw," he said coldly, his voice void of emotion.

The brawny Paisa obeyed without hesitation, quickly bringing the heavy tool back to Zacatecas. Zacatecas grabbed it, his face betraying a flicker of frustration as he yanked the starter cord. The chainsaw sputtered twice before roaring to life, its jagged teeth spinning wildly. Then the Paisa that had fetched the chainsaw went back to holding Chucky down.

Zacatecas gripped the handle tightly, letting the violent hum of the chainsaw fill the air. He swung it drunkenly, the blade tearing clean through Chucky's neck in one gruesome motion. Blood sprayed everywhere as Chucky's head tumbled to the deck, landing with a wet thud.

But Zacatecas didn't stop there. His unsteady swing caught the Paisa's forearm, slicing through muscle and bone with ease. The injured Paisa screamed in agony, clutching the bloody stump where his arm used to be.

Without missing a beat, Zacatecas turned to the other Paisa. "Shoot him," he ordered, nodding toward the screaming man. The second Paisa pulled out his pistol and fired a single shot into the injured man's head, silencing him forever. Both bodies were discarded before Zacatecas returned to entertain his Colombian connect.

"I didn't mean for you to see this side of me," Zacatecas said in English, taking a seat with small splotches of Chucky's blood and DNA of the dead Paisa on his shirt. "But you know how business operates, yes?"

"Sí, my friend, sí," the Colombian replied softly, sipping his drink.

Before the night ended, Zacatecas issued orders for an all-out massacre targeting Freak Zeenie and his family. He knew it was Freak Zeenie who'd caused the death of his little brother, Flocko.

I underestimated you once, but not again, puta, Zacatecas thought drunkenly as his heavy eyes finally closed.

The Same Time
18th Street, Downtown
Atlanta, Georgia

Freak Zeenie tossed and turned for the remainder of the night, haunted by a strange feeling that something bad was coming. If he only knew.

Chapter 29

Two Days Later
The Inner City
Atlanta, Georgia

Today, Freak Zeenie left Grady Hospital after visiting Levi earlier than he usually did. Even with the sun high in the sky, shining so bright that sunglasses were a necessity, Freak Zeenie felt like a hurricane was brewing. It was as if a huge dark cloud hovered over him, weighing him down. Just today alone, Freak Zeenie had already sent up three prayers, and the day was still fairly young. He couldn't put his finger on it, but there was an eerie feeling he couldn't shake. At first, he thought it was because he was scheduled to leave for Mexico tomorrow, but he quickly dismissed that idea. Deep down, Freak Zeenie knew the trip had nothing to do with the unsettling sense he felt. His mind was locked on Zacatecas and how he couldn't wait to cancel the man's macabre existence for the hideous attempt he'd made.

At a traffic light, Freak Zeenie glanced down at his phone. His brows folded inward as he read a message that popped up. The pipes on his recently purchased Dodge Durango—snatched from Gucci Mane—growled loudly, vibrating through the air. Freak Zeenie opened the text:

Kal-Kal! What's up big bruh? A buck fifty. Are you ready for me?

Freak Zeenie stared at the text but didn't respond. *Fuck did this nigga get this number from?* he thought. He knew there was only one way Kal-Kal could have gotten it. *This nigga gotta be the one responsible for the B&Es.*

The light finally changed, and Freak Zeenie eased off the brakes, tapping the gas to make the truck shoot forward in a blur. Another light turned red ahead, forcing him to stop again, his irritation growing with every second.

Same Time
Webb Road, Webb, Alabama

Cartier Jay and Boo-Boo had just finished feeding the hogs another victim—this time a member of the Schoolyard Crips. The dude didn't know shit about T-Face's whereabouts, but he had been responsible for hitting Cartier Jay's stash spot. Last time they were out here, dumping T-Face's baby mama, they had heard the distinct sound of crackling twigs and leaves nearby. Cartier Jay figured it was probably a wild animal stalking the hogs, so he decided to set a medium-sized bear trap at the edge of the woodline earlier today

"Bet this stops they ass, boy!" Cartier Jay said, sprinkling some pine straw over the trap to hide it from plain sight. The spiked jaws of the trap gleamed for a moment before disappearing beneath the straw. "Let that fucker come back tonight," he muttered as he finished up.

Just as he was done, his phone chimed. "This Pops," Cartier Jay said, pulling out his phone. "Damn, wonder what he on? You know his old ass don't be textin' a nigga like that."

Cartier Jay opened the message while Boo-Boo stayed quiet, his thoughts lingering on the trap. Boo-Boo, high as a kite off the pills, couldn't stop thinking about how the trap would crush whatever got caught in it.

"Man, Pops said if we see Kal-Kal, hold his ass hostage until he shows up—don't matter what, just hold that nigga down. Pops' words," Cartier Jay said, reading the message aloud.

Hearing that, Boo-Boo's ears perked up like a startled deer. "N-now wh-what th-the f-fuck h-he d-done d-did?" Boo-Boo stammered, heading out of the woods toward the van parked nearby.

"Shit, I'on't know," Cartier Jay replied, following behind. "But whatever it is, Pops want him snatched up. Now that I think about it, though, the nigga has been acting kinda strange lately, ain't he?" Cartier Jay said, sending a text to Kal-Kal. When no reply came back, he frowned.

"H-hell y-yeah!" Boo-Boo said, scratching at his neck. "H-he b-been like th-the moon—d-distant as fuck, c-cuz. Y-you h-hear m-me?"

Cartier Jay nodded in agreement, tossing the severed heads of the corpse they had just fed to the hogs into a plastic bag. With that, they climbed into the van and pulled off from the hog farm, leaving nothing behind but the faint smell of blood and the gleeful squeals of the well-fed hogs.

Back in Atlanta

Right after Freak Zeenie sent another text, he shot up the highway, only to get caught at another red light. "Damn! What's up with all these fuckin' lights, man?" he muttered in frustration.

Freak Zeenie was heading to the hardware store to grab a few much-needed items he wanted to take with him to Mexico. He glanced in the rearview mirror first, then checked both side mirrors when he heard the loud, roaring sounds of motorcycles closing in fast. Before Freak Zeenie knew it, two motorcycles blocked him from the front while another pulled up alongside his driver's side. The two bikes in front had someone strapped to the driver by a thick leather belt, facing Freak Zeenie's windshield. The bike on his left also had a passenger sitting backward, aiming directly at him.

Freak Zeenie's heart started pounding a mile a minute as he realized he was face-to-face with the reaper. He scanned for a way out, but traffic was too thick. Rapid gunfire erupted, riddling his SUV, causing it to rock violently from the force of the assault weapons. Hoping to survive, Freak Zeenie leaned over and shielded his face with his arms.

The windshield cracked into a spider web pattern, but none of the bullets penetrated the bulletproof glass. Freak Zeenie punched the gas to the floor, and the bikes sped off in front of him, staying close enough to keep him boxed in. The bike alongside him kept pace effortlessly, still firing at the driver's side window. Freak Zeenie sat back up, adrenaline coursing through him, staring at his cracked windshield. He veered hard to the left, trying to swerve the bike off course, but the rider moved like a pro, dodging every attempt while continuing to dump rounds into his SUV.

The two bikes in front were now aiming at the engine block, unloading massive rounds of lead. Freak Zeenie clenched the wheel, thanking God the Dodge Durango had been one of his best investments yet—fully bullet-proof. Not one bullet had pierced the SUV so far. Realizing this, one of the bikes in front slowed down, and the passenger unstrapped themselves from the driver.

Seeing this, Freak Zeenie slammed the gas again, the SUV roaring forward in a blur. Just as he was about to ram the motorcycle, the passenger did the unexpected—leaping from the bike onto the hood of Freak Zeenie's truck. The motorcycle sped off, putting distance between itself and the SUV.

"Fuck!" Freak Zeenie spat, jerking the wheel hard to the right, causing the back end of the SUV to slide, trying to throw the assassin off. But the assassin clung to the hood's crease with one hand while pointing a mini assault weapon directly at Freak Zeenie.

Thinking fast, Freak Zeenie tried some TV stunt shit— snatching up the emergency brake while slamming the regular brakes with both feet, cutting the wheel sharply to the left. The SUV spun in a 360-degree circle, and the sudden momentum launched the assassin off the hood. The assassin slammed headfirst into a light pole, their skull busting open like a dropped watermelon, spraying brains across the grass like spaghetti.

Freak Zeenie barely had time to regroup before he spotted two more motorcycles closing in—this time with a pickup truck full of Mexicans trailing behind them.

"Fuck!" Freak Zeenie growled, dropping the emergency brake and slamming the gas, shooting past the oncoming bikes. Police sirens howled in the distance as Freak Zeenie desperately tried to escape the neighborhood and make it back to the main highway alive.

One of the bikes pulled up on Freak Zeenie's driver's side, still with a passenger strapped to the back, unloading shots at his windowpane. Suddenly, a car pulled out from a driveway into the street, forcing Freak Zeenie to swerve just in time. The motorcycle wasn't as lucky, smashing into the car head-on. The impact ripped both the driver and passenger in half, their torsos flying over the car and landing fifty yards away.

Freak Zeenie saw the police cars entering the neighborhood but couldn't stop. Blowing past three patrol vehicles, Freak Zeenie's heart pounded as the last bike sped past the first patrol car, spraying it with bullets. The officer in the passenger seat was killed instantly, and the driver was critically injured.

The other two patrol cars weren't quick enough to avoid the pickup truck barreling toward them. The truck, with a massive guardrail welded to the bumper, plowed into the lead patrol car, sending it spinning into the one behind it. The gang of Paisas in the back of the truck ducked low, avoiding being thrown out. The truck never slowed, hellbent on one mission: kill Freak Zeenie.

Finally, Freak Zeenie gained enough time to reach into his stash spot and grab his pistol. Cracking the window—barely, since it could only crack slightly—Freak Zeenie mumbled a quick prayer, "Please, God," as the bike came full force, still firing.

Leaning up, Freak Zeenie stuck the gun's barrel out the crack, squeezing off shots. By the grace of God, he caught the biker dead through the bike's windshield. The motorcycle rolled forward, carrying the corpse before jumping the curb and slamming into a building, throwing the body off.

Looking in the rearview mirror, Freak Zeenie saw the truck gaining fast. Yanking the steering wheel hard to the right, he narrowly avoided another patrol car. The truck wasn't so lucky, smashing into the side of the patrol car, killing both officers on impact. The force ejected the truck's driver, sending him flying over the patrol car and killing him instantly. By the end of the crash, there were no survivors.

Breathing heavily, Freak Zeenie heard the distant hum of helicopters. Blue lights flashed behind him as he tried to find a way out. Spotting an underground parking lot, he veered into it.

Jumping out, Freak Zeenie quickly wiped down the SUV, inside and out. The Dodge Durango had served him well, but it was going back to Gucci Mane. Freak Zeenie had never registered it, so he trusted that Gucci would know exactly what to say if the time came. After all, Gucci Mane was off papers now—he'd be GUWOP for sure.

Hearing police sirens closing in, Freak Zeenie sprinted out of the parking lot.

Later That Night
Atlanta Airport

Freak Zeenie had contacted Remy Red earlier, speeding up their plans. The only thing he wanted to know before leaving was whether she was positive Zacatecas was still in town. Remy Red assured him he was, and that conviction was all Freak Zeenie needed.

Funk dropped Freak Zeenie off at the airport, dapping him up before pulling off in his Maybach. Freak Zeenie boarded the plane under false identification, just as he had instructed Remy Red to do.

As the plane prepared for takeoff, Freak Zeenie sat back, gripping his armrest. This was a one-way trip to Zacatecas, Mexico.

Same Time
First Baptist Church, Birmingham, Alabama
Pastor Barber slept curled up on a pew inside the empty church. "We gon' boycott Freak Zeenie's ass, bruh! Boycott 'em," he mumbled in his sleep, replaying the earlier conversation he'd had with his brother, Chief Duke.

Chief Duke had been sentenced to six months in the FBOP.

Chapter 30

Halloween Night
The Fair
Dothan, Alabama

Cartier Jay and Boo-Boo both were dressed up in *Scream* masks and Dickies mechanic jumpsuits. Earlier in the day, they had been cruising the streets, hoping to catch T-Face slipping or one of his gang members. With no luck and running on sheer faith, it was now nighttime, and they'd yet to run into anyone.

Cartier Jay was flaming mad because Uncle James had called, needing him to go back to Smokey Pigs to pick up more meat and bring it to the Fairgrounds. Uncle James wasn't someone you denied—he rarely asked anyone for anything. So when he called for help, you honored it, no questions asked. But that didn't change the fact that Cartier Jay was irritated as hell about it. The errand had distracted him from his mission of handling T-Face.

The trailer was hitched to the back of the Urus SUV as Cartier Jay pulled back into the Fairgrounds with the .408 rifle across his lap.

"Man, Unk knew dog on well he was gon' need more food than he brought in the first damn place!" Cartier Jay bellowed, his frustration clear. He wanted Boo-Boo to chime in, but Boo-Boo stayed quiet, knowing it wasn't his place to comment.

***

Across the Fairgrounds—

T-Face was at the Fair, enjoying time with his kids, who had begged him to take them out for Halloween. At first, he'd resisted—too much money was on the line for him to be out in public like this. But his kids were persistent and didn't take "no" for an answer. Eventually, they wore him down, and here they all were.

T-Face hadn't heard from his baby mama in a minute and he had good mind to kick her ass real good once he caught up with her. But before he could even process his anger, an unexpected call came in. It was his baby mama's mother, frantic and upset, claiming she'd already contacted the police after finding her daughter's tongue in her front yard. She recognized it from the tongue rings.

"Yeah, Dad! Look, no hands! Weee!" one of T-Face's kids hollered from the Ferris wheel as it spun them around.

T-Face wasn't on the ride with his kids, but he threw his arms up, pretending to mimic their excitement. He wore a smug expression, but his mind was elsewhere. *Damn, Shann. You left me to raise two lil' girls on my own. How the fuck am I supposed to do that?* he thought, contemplating how to explain to his kids that they would never see their mother again. The thought hit hard enough to almost bring a tear to his eye—but T-Face didn't cry.

Same Time: The Fairgrounds—

After getting uncle James situated. Cartier Jay and Boo-Boo strolled through the fair. Coming upon the Ferris wheel, Cartier Jay blood, shot up enormously sighting T-Face. Cartier Jay begun perspiring under the mechanic suit as he had a melee with his self-control.

"Look, nigga!" Cartier Jay growled, motioning in T-Face's direction with his head. He was ready to murk T-Face right there in the middle of the fairgrounds, anger clouding his judgment. "I'm 'bout to mop this bitch nigga! Fuck it."

"Nawl, cuz," Boo-Boo said quickly. "W-we c-can't d-do t-that. W-we w-won't n-never g-get t-the h-hell o-outta p-prison, nigga!" Boo-Boo stuttered, his nervousness glaring. "I-if w-we d-do t-that, y-your b-bread i-is a-as g-good a-as gone, n-nigga!"

The two stood there debating, their heads constantly on a swivel to ensure T-Face really was alone.

Cartier Jay contemplated the outcome. He wanted T-Face dead right now, and knowing that they was masked up had gave Cartier Jay that much more confidence to blow T-Face clean across the yard of the fair. Right in front of his kids too. The battle within caused Cartier Jay to grit his teeth. "A'ight. We'll just follow him from a distance, 'cause one thing fo'sho—he got to take them ugly ass kids of his home. Then it's a wrap!" he said, his tone still heated. "Until then, let's have some fun!" With that, Cartier Jay took off running towards T-Face.

T-Face walked his kids towards the concession stand. The three of 'em were ready to get their grub on. Cartier Jay was running full speed when he jumped into the air, bumping into T-Face hard, damn near knocking T-Face down. Before T-Face could react, Boo-Boo did the exact same thing, barreling into him from the opposite direction.

As they ran past, T-Face heard one of them mutter, "Trick or treat!"—or maybe it was "Bitch, you weak!" He wasn't sure. But T-Face scoffed at the idea of anyone thinking he was weak.

"H-hey you lil' mother fuckers!" T-Face bellowed behind them. "Ya-yall b-better watch th-the f-fuck out! K-knock m-my k-kids d-down, a-and I-I k-know s-somethin'!" he hollered after them.

T-Face assumed they were just teenagers horsing around, chasing each other through the fairgrounds. He focused back on the menu posted on the side of the food truck.

Unbeknownst to Cartier Jay or Boo-Boo, they weren't the only ones watching someone. While they'd been riding 'round all day looking for T-Face, Kal-Kal was watching them. Kal-Kal was behind a killer clown mask tonight.

Kal-Kal's patience with Freak Zeenie was wearing thin. On top of that, Cartier Jay and Boo-Boo hadn't led him to anything useful. Frustrated, Kal-Kal began plotting his next move. *Fuck it,* he thought. *I'll just go out to Kinsey, Alabama, and break into Freak Zeenie's house. Ain't no way he moved all that shit. It's way too much.*

"Who gon' know?" Kal-Kal muttered to himself, his thoughts becoming more sinister by the second. At this point, his mind was clear—laser-focused. Kal-Kal began crafting his plan to rob Freak Zeenie blind and skip town. *Yeah, that's it! I'm 'bout to send all y'all fuck niggas to prison. And in less than a year? Tops. I'm that nigga*, he thought, grinning behind his mask.

Kal-Kal's thoughts spiraled further. *Hell yeah. Y'all stupid-ass niggas 'bout to end up on death row at Holman like that nigga from that movie,* "Just Mercy." He chuckled darkly, trailing behind Cartier Jay and Boo-Boo as they followed T-Face.

"Um hum," Kal-Kal murmured, a wicked smile creeping across his face.

***

3:33 a.m.
T-Face's Crib
Ozark, Alabama

"You thought shit was sweet over here, huh, pussy-ass nigga?" Cartier Jay bellowed, his voice cold and menacing. He slapped T-Face hard across the bridge of his nose, bussing it open and breaking it on impact.

"Argh . . . Fuckk! Shittt, mann!" T-Face shrieked in pain, trying to lean forward, but the ropes binding him to the chair wouldn't let him budge. This time, he'd been caught with his pants down for real. As soon as T-Face had made it home, he'd put his kids to bed, but just as he was pulling back the covers to lay down, he'd heard the front door crash in. Thinking it was the Feds, he froze—now, he realized how wrong he was.

Boo-Boo strolled into the bedroom. "E-everything o-on p-point, b-bruh," Boo-Boo stuttered, letting Cartier Jay know he'd tied up T-Face's kids and the female T-Face had over for the night.

Cartier Jay nodded, his face a mask of fury. "Where that shit at, fuck nigga? I want it all, pussy! Play, and you lay!" Cartier Jay's voice boomed.

T-Face still didn't know who was behind the masks, but the stuttering voice sounded too familiar for comfort. His stomach sank.

Outside the House—
Kal-Kal sat patiently in his car, parked a few houses up the street. He'd followed Cartier Jay and Boo-Boo here, and now he was second-guessing himself. Kal-Kal knew things were looking grim for T-Face, and though he hated to lose the money T-Face brought in, he hated the thought of being connected to whatever was about to happen even more.

Man, I hope them niggas don't hurt those innocent kids, Kal-Kal thought, his anxiety mounting. He kept his eyes locked on the house as his mind began racing. *Fuck, man. What if this shit goes sideways?* He grabbed his phone, debating what to do. "Fuck it," he muttered, pressing "9" and then "1," but hesitated before pressing the final "1."

Back Inside the House—
Boo-Boo dragged T-Face's baby girl to the bedroom where her dad was bound at. She was kicking, squirming, and crying trying to break free of his grip. Boo-Boo snatched her up then dropped her hard on the floor in front of T-Face.

BLOCKA!

Cartier Jay fired a shot from the .408 rifle. The massive bullet exploded through T-Face's kneecap, blowing his entire lower leg clean off.

"Arghhh! Oh fuck! Oh Shit! Nooo!" T-Face howled, his screams deafening. Blood gushed from his mangled stump, pooling on the floor. His daughter's terrified shrieks filled the room as she wet herself, frozen in horror at the sight of her father's severed leg lying across the room. More so, the blast had temporarily deafened her

T-Face's screams turned into guttural cries, his body convulsing in shock from the blood loss and sheer agony. Boo-Boo, unbothered, bent down and pulled out a blowtorch, igniting it with a cold precision. He pressed the fiery torch to T-Face's bleeding stump, cauterizing the wound. The smell of burning flesh filled the air as T-Face let out a blood-curdling scream, so loud Kal-Kal thought he heard it outside in his car.

Cartier Jay let out a menacing, petulant laugh, his patience wearing thin. "Fuck nigga, where that shit at?" he barked, his voice laced with fury. "I ain't shit to play with, bitch-ass nigga!"

Cartier Jay glanced at T-Face's sobbing daughter, his eyes narrowing. "Is this pussy?" he sneered, pressing the barrel of the .408 against the side of the little girl's head. "I'm 'bout to blow this lil' bitch's head the fuck off, fuck nigga!" He nudged her head roughly with the rifle, his finger tightening on the trigger.

"Th-think I'm fuckin' playin'?" Cartier Jay growled, his anger boiling over.

"O-ok o-okay! W-wait!" T-Face stammered, his voice slurred as his eyes rolled back. He was on the verge of passing out from the blood loss, pain, and sheer terror. Boo-Boo, already prepared for this, quickly pulled out a syringe filled with a lethal cocktail of melted cocaine and meth. He tied a belt tightly around T-Face's arm, found a vein, and plunged the needle in, pressing the plunger all the way down.

Cartier Jay cursed under his breath, frustrated. He wished he hadn't shot T-Face so soon—the .408 was too powerful, and now it looked like T-Face might die before giving up his stash. "Fuckin' nigga pushed me to it," Cartier Jay muttered. "All that petty-ass lyin' and stalling."

T-Face's body jerked violently as the drug cocktail surged through his veins. His eyes shot wide open, his pupils dilated to the size of dimes. He gasped, his breathing becoming erratic. Boo-Boo stepped back, watching as T-Face's body went limp for a moment before convulsing.

"Get his ass up," Cartier Jay barked, his frustration simmering beneath the surface.

Boo-Boo and Cartier Jay yanked T-Face upright, tying a garbage bag tightly around the bloody stump where his leg used to be. Blood seeped through the makeshift tourniquet as they prepared to move him.

Twenty-five Minutes Later—
A Storage Building Somewhere in Ozark, Alabama
Cartier Jay had Boo-Boo trailing him and T-Face in T-Face's Trackhawk. Finally, Cartier Jay was starting to feel a small sense of relief as he and Boo-Boo worked diligently, loading both trucks with Cartier Jay's money along with all the money T-Face had stacked up since being put on by him.

T-Face sat bound and gagged in the front seat of the SUV. He ground his teeth from the super-strong potency of the drug surging through his system as he struggled against the restraints. He couldn't feel pain at the moment, but tears streamed down his cheeks as he helplessly watched his entire life savings—his money and his drugs—slip right out of his grasp. *I hope my lil' girls are good*, he thought, though his tears were not for them. They were for the loss of everything he'd worked for, not for the children left tied up and terrified back at his crib.

Kal-Kal shook his head in disbelief. From where he was hiding across the street, he could see everything going down, using the darkness to his advantage. Though he couldn't make out the exact items being moved, Kal-Kal knew what it was. *Where the fuck twelve at?* he thought, his head swiveling nervously as he scanned for any sign of police lights. But there wasn't a single patrol vehicle in sight.

T-Face, on the other hand, was still convinced he was going back home to untie his kids and assure them they were safe. That hope quickly faded when he saw his crib blur past as they sped through the purlieu. A new kind of worry clawed its way into his chest, and he began silently praying he could somehow plead his way out with the masked man who sat beside him, staring straight ahead into the darkness. T-Face wasn't used to being the one begging—he'd spent most of his life in control, treating himself like a god in his hood. But Cartier Jay had every intention of showing T-Face that he was as mortal as anybody else.

First Down
Webb Road
Webb, Alabama

Fog crept across the ground as Cartier Jay turned into the hog farm. T-Face's head swiveled, his eyes darting around as he tried to make sense of his surroundings. His skin was pale now, his body trembling from blood loss, and for the first time in years, real fear clawed at him. He turned to the masked driver beside him.

"I-I th-thought y-you w-was g-gon' l-let me g-go if y-you g-got what y-you w-wanted, c-cuz?" T-Face stuttered, desperation in his voice. "I-I g-gave y'all e-everything, e-everything y'all a-asked f-for!"

T-Face thought his cooperation would earn him freedom. That hope was short-lived when Cartier Jay yanked off his mask, revealing his face.

T-Face's body tensed, and a hot stream of defecation seeped into his boxers, releasing a foul stench that filled the truck's cabin.

"I knew you was a ho', ol' bitch-ass nigga!" Cartier Jay bellowed, rolling the window down to let out the smell.

T-Face's mind raced as the night replayed in his head. From the moment the two masked men bumped into him, to now, he realized it had all been planned—they had been stalking him the entire time, using Halloween as a cover.

Cartier Jay's face twisted into an expression that left T-Face at a loss for words.

"What?" Cartier Jay sneered. "What? That big mouth ain't got no slick shit to say now, huh? Do you, pussy?" Cartier Jay laughed as T-Face remained silent. "Soft-ass fuck nigga!" he spat, knowing that without his Schoolyard Crip homies, T-Face was just another inglorious hood nigga.

In the Woods—

It took Cartier Jay and Boo-Boo twelve minutes to get T-Face strapped down on the ground. Meanwhile, Kal-Kal parked further down the road and made his way through the woods, his phone in hand, recording every second. He planned to send the footage to his other phone back at his granny's house for safekeeping. The cool November air chilled him, and he shoved his hands deep into his pockets as he moved.

Cartier Jay grabbed a saber saw and went to work on T-Face's remaining good leg, slicing through the patella with ease.

"Arghhh!" T-Face's scream ripped through the quiet night as the serrated blade tore through flesh and bone. He was feeling every bit of the pain, because the drugs had start to wear off.

Cartier Jay stepped back once he was done, watching as T-Face's severed leg dropped to the ground.

"There. Now you back at an even height, pussy-ass nigga!" Cartier Jay said with a venomous grin.

Boo-Boo slapped T-Face hard across the face. "Sh-shut th-the f-fuck u-up, b-bitch a-ass n-nigga! Y-you t-took th-that b-bread a-and sh-shit l-like a m-man, s-so t-take th-this li-like o-one!" Boo-Boo snarled, picking up the severed leg and tossing it into the hog pen. The hungry pigs fought over the piece of meat, but it was hardly enough to satisfy them.

Cartier Jay methodically sawed off T-Face's other limbs, one by one. Blood pooled on the ground as T-Face's screams grew weaker. By the time Cartier Jay reached his neck, T-Face had already bled out, his lifeless head rolling to the side as it detached from his body.

"Got damn," Kal-Kal whispered to himself as he recorded the entire gruesome spectacle. He moved to his right to get a better angle.

CLOW!

The bear trap snapped shut around Kal-Kal's leg, the steel teeth crushing his patella and nearly severing the limb entirely. His phone flew from his hand, landing a few feet away.

"*Arghhh!*" Kal-Kal's scream echoed through the woods, piercing the cold night air.

Boo-Boo was the first to reach him, gun drawn, his heart pounding. Cartier Jay arrived seconds later, his face twisted in anger when he saw who it was. Recognition turned to disappointment, and then to rage.

"What the fuck you doin' out here, stupid-ass nigga!?" Boo-Boo demanded, his voice rising in panic.

Kal-Kal's only response was more screaming. "My leg!" he shrieked.

Then Boo-Boo's eyes locked onto Kal-Kal's phone lying nearby, still recording. His expression darkened.

"This nigga twelve, cuz!" Boo-Boo yelled, uncharacteristically free of his stutter as he pointed his gun at Kal-Kal's head.

"*Nawl, boy!*" Cartier Jay barked, knocking Boo-Boo's aim off just in time.

BLOCKA!

The shot missed Kal-Kal's head by inches, hitting the dirt beside him.

"Pops, man! Pops!" Cartier Jay snapped, reminding Boo-Boo of the bigger picture. Boo-Boo stormed off, frustrated, while Kal-Kal continued to writhe in pain.

Later That Same Night
Dothan, Alabama

Cartier Jay paid a veteran extra to come patch up and cast Kal-Kal's mangled leg—and to keep his mouth shut about what he'd really seen. Kal-Kal lay on a soiled mattress that sat in the far corner of the dark room. He was chained to a thick bolt anchored into the floor, with a 15-foot chain that allowed him just enough slack to reach the bathroom. Kal-Kal laid there dead still, knocked out cold from the morphine coursing through his system.

Cartier Jay had just finished texting Freak Zeenie. He laid the phone down on the table. "This bitch ass nigga boy!" he bellowed, his voice dripping with anger. He and Boo-Boo still couldn't believe the video footage Kal-Kal had secretly recorded of them committing those heinous crimes. Just the thought of Kal-Kal's betrayal turned Cartier Jay's stomach.

After running the stacks of cash through the money counter, Cartier Jay took back what was rightfully his and split the rest down the middle with Boo-Boo. At first, Boo-Boo tried to protest, but he quickly lost that argument.

As Cartier Jay counted his portion, his mind drifted back to a conversation he'd had with his dad, Freak Zeenie, about a year ago. Freak Zeenie had warned him: "It'll always be the niggas closest to you who cross you out, sell you out, and hate you the most when the time comes. The ones you can't see ain't as much of a threat, 'cause they can't watch your moves to plot against you." That warning now played on a loop in Cartier Jay's head. Before retiring for the night Cartier Jay and Boo-Boo taped signs to the decapitated heads of their latest victims. Each sign read: YOU REAP WHAT YOU SOW! Under the cover of darkness, they slung the gruesome trophies across power lines throughout the small city, and went home.

Chapter 31

Months Later
The Car Wash
Zacatecas, Mexico

Freak Zeenie thought he'd never get his chance to catch up with Zacatecas since he'd been in town—until one night when Freak Zeenie decided to enjoy some Mexican Choca at a Spanish strip club. The moment he spotted Zacatecas, he had to ease his way right back out, hoping not to be discovered.

Freak Zeenie initially thought he could murk (murder) Zacatecas that very night, but reality hit different—it was too many Paisas around for him to make a clean getaway. That night ended in vain.

Knowing that pussy had power, Freak Zeenie sent Remy Red to audition for a spot at the strip club. But she got declined, thanks to the blatant racism radiating through the establishment. The employers and the audience were prejudiced against anyone who wasn't Mexican. That plan was a DUB (*duh, you bogus*).

The carwash, however, was a long shot that Freak Zeenie was willing to take. Twice a week for the past few months, Remy Red had witnessed the black limo rolling through, picking up prostitutes for sexual favors. She played her position and patiently waited for the perfect opportunity.

Freak Zeenie could never get up on the limo without being spotted, and frustration was beginning to take its toll. But Freak Zeenie banked on the element of surprise, knowing it was his best shot.

Another day couldn't pass with Zacatecas still breathing. Freak Zeenie was ready to end Zacatecas' putrid life and finally move on with his own. Slipping inside the carwash garage as the limo went through its automatic cleaning, Freak Zeenie made his move.

The driver was looking down at porn on his phone when he saw the shadow—too late. Freak Zeenie was in the driver's seat within seconds, leaving the chauffeur's lifeless body crumpled inside the garage. Breathing hard, Freak Zeenie let an evil grin creep across his face.

Inside the limo, Zacatecas was receiving some of the best black head of his life from Remy Red while the vehicle slid through the carwash. The deluxe package wasn't just for the limo; Zacatecas was getting one too.

He opened his eyes. "Suck that dick, puta!" he growled, trying to choke her with his prick, but Remy Red wasn't fazed. She was in control, giving him a blowjob out of this world, then switching to slow neckin' him. Suddenly, the limo jerked, causing her teeth to scrape the head of his dick.

"Siss . . . shit! Take it easy, Maricón!" Zacatecas hissed, tensing up and banging on the partition, cussing out the "chauffeur."

Remy Red knew it was showtime.

"Relax, baby. Let me handle that, big daddy," she cooed, boosting his already overinflated ego. Zacatecas laid his head back, eyes closed in pure bliss.

The limo exited the carwash and sped out onto the desert highway, the momentum slinging both passengers across the seat into the door violently.

"¡Si, si, si! Hey, puta! Maricón!" Zacatecas banged on the partition again, his words dripping with venom.

Remy Red saw her opening and seized it. She lunged, plunging a hypodermic syringe into his neck, pressing the plunger down forcefully until the needle snapped off in his flesh.

"Argh!" Zacatecas shrieked, backhanding Remy Red so hard she saw stars. Woozy from the blow, she still smirked—her job was done.

The venom worked instantly, leaving Zacatecas paralyzed from the neck down. The partition lowered slowly after Remy Red tapped on it twice.

"Anybody can be touched, Zacatecas, even you," Freak Zeenie said, his voice cold as ice. "You should've killed me when you had the chance. Sending kids to do a man's job was your mistake."

Zacatecas' wide, unblinking eyes betrayed no fear, even as Freak Zeenie pulled the limo to the side of the road. Time was running out—Freak Zeenie had left the chauffeur's dead body in the carwash garage, and someone would find it soon.

"This is for Khashia and her family. And me. You can't kill what's already de—"

Psst! Psst!

Two muffled .40mm bullets tore through Zacatecas' cranium, spraying brain matter onto the bullet-proof rear window of the limo.

"Come on, we gotta go!" Freak Zeenie bellowed, jumping out of the car.

Dust clouds rose in the distance as the roar of approaching vehicles echoed through the desert. Freak Zeenie and Remy Red could hear the exhaust pipes growling and gaining on them rapidly.

"We need to get to the border! How far is it?" Freak Zeenie asked, panting.

Remy Red pulled up Grande Rio and Tijuana on Google Maps. With only 50% battery left on both their phones, Freak Zeenie shut his off to save power for emergencies.

"We gotta move!" Remy Red said, panic creeping into her voice as the sounds of the pursuing Mexicans grew louder.

They stumbled into the backyard of a nearby house. Freak Zeenie's eyes landed on a hauntingly beautiful four-wheeler parked near the shed. He ran to it.

"Damn! Where the fuck's the key?" he yelled, his eyes scanning frantically. He spotted a can of Ready Sealer, grabbed it, and ran back to the four-wheeler. Holding the can upside down, he sprayed it into the ignition. Within ten seconds, the green light popped on, and the engine roared to life.

"Hell yeah! Come on!" he hollered, but Remy Red was already climbing on.

As they sped off, a pudgy woman ran out of the house, brandishing a big-boy .357 Magnum.

BOOM! BOOM!

Two shots rang out as Freak Zeenie floored the throttle, the bullets barely missing them.

"Which way?" Freak Zeenie yelled over his shoulder.

Remy Red fumbled with her phone. "Um, keep going straight!" she shouted.

"Go, Freak Zeenie, go!" Remy Red screamed, glancing back to see two 4x4 trucks cresting the hill, their truck beds full of armed Mexicans. Shots erupted as the pursuit began.

***

Meanwhile—
Birmingham, Alabama

Pastor Barber was trying to stay free until his brother Chief Duke got out. Chief Duke only had a few more days to go before his release, so Pastor Barber lied when Agent Simpson personally came to take him to jail.

Pastor Barber claimed that he was about to get the mother load from his nephew Freak Zeenie. He also explained to Agent Simpson the reason for Freak Zeenie's absence was because he was picking up the load now, and that's why Freak Zeenie wasn't answering him at the moment. Agent Simpson was so thirsty to get Freak Zeenie that he went for the okey-doke once again. Pastor Barber had finessed for a little more free time.

But life was still a mess for Pastor Barber. His wife had filed a civil suit against him. He'd graduated from sniffing cocaine to smoking roc' (crack). And to top it off, he was no longer preaching at First Baptist Church. Instead, he was sneaking into the church late at night to raid the kitchen for food and then crashing on the pew until morning.

Pastor Barber sat on the back of First Baptist Church.

"God. Please forgive me!" said he muttered, saying a quick but powerful prayer. He put the flame to his crack pipe, inhaling deeply. When he exhaled, he was as high as Trump Tower.

"See, Proverbs twenty-six, verse one says—" Pastor Barber begun preaching right in the backyard of his old church. No one was there but him, the graves, and God.

***

Later that Night
Somewhere in Mexico
Freak Zeenie and Remy Red had to stop the four-wheeler. The lights were too much of a giveaway, and the gas was running low. Freak Zeenie found a nearby deserted house and siphoned some gas.

With only one gun and limited bullets, Freak Zeenie and Remy Red were taking serious risks being out in the wilderness alone in the dead of night. If the Cartel didn't find you, the coyotes or dehydration might.

"Look, get some sleep, 'cause you gone have to drive tomorrow," Freak Zeenie said. "I'll stay up and be on P' (point)."

They laid low inside a house made entirely of dirt, with no doors or windows. It looked like a giant sand castle.

Remy Red didn't argue about Freak Zeenie's plan at all. She was exhausted and drifted off quickly.

The Next Day—

Freak Zeenie and Remy Red had ditched the 4-wheeler hours ago, because it simply broke down. They had walked so far that the both of them were drenched in sweat. But the good news was was the chasing had stopped today, and they had managed to blend into a large group of migrants.

Freak Zeenie glanced around. Everyone in the group was equally drenched in sweat, inching toward the border under the scorching heat. This was one of the hottest years on record, and it wasn't even summer yet.

Suddenly, chaos erupted. The whole crowd began running, falling, and screaming with fear towards the river. Freak Zeenie head swiveled from the roaring of the engines that raced their way out the blue.

"Wh–"

Before Freak Zeenie could finish his sentence, gunshots cracked the air. They were being chased by the Paisa Cartel who now governed the passage across the Grande Rio, charging admission to and fro. Zacatecas had them issue green wrist bands going out and yellow ones to come into their country. If you didn't have one visible, then you were in violation and enormity would be brought upon you with great effort.

"Oh shit!" Freak Zeenie yelled, ducking as bullets whizzed past. He and Remy Red saw a mother and her child fall dead a few steps in front of them. Never breaking stride, Freak Zeenie and Remy Red high-stepped over the two corpses, hot-tailing it to the river along with the panic-stricken migrants.

The Paisa Cartel unleashed hundreds of rounds into the river, gunning down as many unpaying migrants as they could. Freak Zeenie and Remy Red dove underwater, swimming like Olympic champions.

When they came up for air, they found themselves slowed by the large orange floaters designed to stop intruders from crossing into the U.S. temporarily.

On the U.S. side, border patrol agents waited at the river's edge on horses, four-wheelers, and in trucks. Migrants who made it to land scattered in all directions, trying to evade capture. Freak Zeenie and Remy Red ran for their lives, the border patrol hot on their heels.

"Come on, come on, get yo' ass up!" Freak Zeenie yelled, helping Remy Red back on her feet after she had tripped over them.

The minor setback created a major problem. Border patrol closed the gap and were right on top of them. Just when they thought it was over, the officers sped past them to catch a family of five. That gave Freak Zeenie and Remy Red enough time to escape.

But their relief was short-lived. Other border patrol officers came speeding toward them on a four-wheeler, yelling for them to stop in Spanish. Freak Zeenie and Remy Red kept running, but exhaustion began to set in, and panic caused them to accidentally split up.

"Damn, girl!" Freak Zeenie cursed in his mind as he realized they were separated.

Border patrol was gaining quickly; they had locked in on Remy Red. Remy Red was standing hunched over with her hands on her knees. Remy Red had given up. Tears slid down her face, mixing in with her sweat as she thought about going to jail. Remy Red finally looked up, but couldn't see far ahead or behind her—either due to how much dust was in the air from all the commotion taking place. Not knowing where Freak Zeenie was at made Remy Red even sadder.

Border patrol wasn't far from Remy Red as they were coming over the hill full speed.

"Freeze! Freeze I s—"

Freak Zeenie step out from behind a cactus clothes, lining the officers from off the 4-wheeler. Remy Red was still hunched over, taking in heaps of air into her lungs. She was a nervous wreck and didn't look back when she heard the 4-wheeler revving right behind her.

"Let's get it!" Freak Zeenie bellowed out, his head swiveling as he prepared to make their escape.

Remy Red finally turned around and saw the 4-wheeler first, then she looked at the driver

"Freak?" she asked, her voice shaky.

"Yeah! Now get the fuck on!" Freak Zeenie barked.

Remy Red gave a weak smile, grabbed his hand, and climbed onto the ATV.

Freak Zeenie made the tires throw dirt up as he mashed down on the throttle.

Four Hours Later
The Bottom of Texas

The 4-wheeler was out of gas, and both Freak Zeenie and Remy Red's phones were dead. They were trekking through Texas on foot, stranded with no clear plan. Every so often, a vehicle would pass by, and they'd stick their thumbs out, trying to hitch a ride, only to be ignored. But as long as they were free, they kept walking. That's all that mattered.

"I can't wait to see my baby, you know?" Remy Red said, trying to make small talk so she could keep her mind off the fact that her feet were killing her.

"Hum huh," Freak Zeenie mumbled, distracted. He knew that this journey wasn't short, but it wasn't going to get any easier either.

After three hours of walking, the night finally swallowed them whole. Exhausted, their feet screaming in pain, they somehow kept moving. A truck passed by but unexpectedly pulled over a short distance ahead.

Freak Zeenie approached the passenger door cautiously. "Nawl, thank you, but we good," he said, patting the door, signaling for the driver to move along.

"No problemo, my man. I don't mind helping!" the small Spanish man said, showing a mouth full of rotten teeth.

Freak Zeenie hesitated. He was skeptical. But his feet were on fire, and they still had the pistol if things went south. "Alright. How far is the Greyhound bus from here?" he asked.

"It's about twenty miles north of here, señor, and I'm heading that way anyway. Get in," the man said.

Freak Zeenie and Remy Red exchanged looks, then climbed into the 4x4 truck. Within five miles, they were both fast asleep, so exhausted they didn't even feel the syringes plunge into their arms. The small Mexican man had drugged them with a heavy dose of sleeping meds.

The Next Day
Unknown—
When Freak Zeenie and Remy Red woke up the next day, confusion hit them like a ton of bricks. Their memories were fuzzy, their bodies aching, and their stomachs growling from hunger. Bound to chairs with their hands tied behind their backs and their feet strapped to the chair legs, they looked around the small room, trying to make sense of their situation.

"Huh?" Freak Zeenie muttered, squinting at the unfamiliar surroundings. "Where the fuck we at?"

His confusion turned into frustration, then panic. "H–"

The door swung open, cutting off his sentence. Freak Zeenie and Remy Red's mouths dropped in disbelief as the man entered.

"Missed me?" The man stood there with his arms spread out like a scarecrow.

"ZA-CA-TECAS?" Freak Zeenie exclaimed, his voice filled with more disappointment than anger.

Zacatecas nodded, smirking. Freak Zeenie shook his head in defeat, realizing how bad the situation was.

"I'll be right back. I got something for you," Zacatecas said, turning to leave the room. As soon as he stepped out, a flood of Paisas entered, every one of them looking exactly like Zacatecas—his plastic surgery doubles.

"Huh, what the fuck?" Freak Zeenie said, baffled, while Remy Red remained silent, her face pale.

Seconds later, rapid gunfire erupted just outside the room.

The Paisas rushed out to investigate, only to be met with a hail of bullets. The gunfire was relentless, tearing through them. Freak Zeenie and Remy Red heard the chaos and quickly tilted their chairs over, pretending to be dead as blood splattered across the room. The blood soaked them, but it was the only thing that kept them alive.

The Martinez Cartel had arrived, catching the Paisas slipping. They were out for revenge, seeking blood for blood after the murder of their leader. The entire building turned into a war zone, with the Paisas being cut down one by one in a brutal display of cartel violence.

When the gunfire finally stopped, the room was silent except for the sound of dripping blood. Freak Zeenie struggled against his restraints until he managed to free himself. He untied Remy Red, and they stumbled out of the building, finding themselves in the middle of nowhere.

Chapter 32

Four Days Later
Kinsey
Dothan, Alabama

It was evident that Freak Zeenie was overjoyed today. With Zacatecas dead, Freak Zeenie didn't have to watch his back. Freak Zeenie knew he'd just won the game—a game where the only rule was that there were no rules. Now that he was officially out the game, Freak Zeenie needed to strategize how to get rid of all the bricks (drugs) still stashed at his house in Kinsey, Alabama, and out at the tree farm. Once those were gone, he planned to dive headfirst into his new role in the *Change of Heart* program.

Freak Zeenie had also made new plans to start his *Enigma* podcast coast to coast. The date for its launch was locked in—set in stone. He had talked about it so many times with his cousin Funk that he'd lost count.

But there was still one wish hanging over his head: he wanted Levi to wake up. Freak Zeenie wanted Levi to leave the streets behind too. And when Levi woke up, it was going to be on. Levi would be Freak Zeenie's co-host on his *Enigma* podcast, 'cause who in the hell could out talk the two of them together? Nobody.

Though Freak Zeenie had been ignoring Pastor Barber's calls, he figured since he was free to do as he pleased now, he might throw his uncle six or seven bricks free of charge. Let him bounce back. Freak Zeenie was tired of Barber's constant pestering and thought maybe this would finally shut him up.

Moving around the house, Freak Zeenie's thoughts raced. He wondered how his uncle Chief Duke and his wife were doing. Glancing at his watch, he realized it was too late to call, so he made a mental note to check on Duke the next day.

As Freak Zeenie laid down that night, his thoughts drifted to Kal-Kal. Cartier Jay and Boo-Boo had filled him in on Kal-Kal's police tactics, but they hadn't given him the details. After De'shawn's basketball game tomorrow, Freak Zeenie planned to go see what Kal-Kal had going on. But as he closed his eyes, he tossed and turned, unable to find any sleep.

The Next Day
Dothan High School
Dothan, Alabama

It was the first Friday after spring break. Dothan High was jam-packed. De'shawn, the lead scorer on the basketball team, was the reason for the crowd's turnout. His freshman year had been lit thanks to the popularity he gained from his victory at the Fairgrounds the previous summer. Since then, he'd been averaging 22 points a game.

Outside the school, De'shawn was crossing Cartier Jay and Boo-Boo up on the court as they tested his skills. Freak Zeenie stood on the sidelines, proud of De'shawn. When the game was over, Freak Zeenie planned to tell De'shawn the truth—that he was his father.

Freak Zeenie's phone chimed, interrupting his train of thought.

"How you doing M—"

"Deacon, what in the world have you done son?" Mama Lois hysterically yelled through the phone cutting Freak Zeenie completely off mid-sentence. "Awl, Deacon! What you done went and done? H–"

"What?" Freak Zeenie asked, panic creeping into his voice. "What, Mom? What you talking 'bout? What I do?" Freak Zeenie was trying to see what his mom knew that he didn't. With all he'd done, she could have been talking about anything.

"Deacon! It's a massive worldwide manhunt out for your arrest, son!"

"Whattt!" Freak Zeenie shrieked, his head swiveling and his eyes scanning the area. "For what? For what, mom?" His heart raced, pounding a thousand beats a minute.

"Duke called, talking 'bout how you all over the TV. I turned it on, and you all over the news for a murder in Mexico! And the U.S. Marshals been over here too," she said. "They won't say what they want but want me to contact them if you show up! Why, Deacon? Why?" Mama Lois was in tears now.

At a loss for words, Freak Zeenie's panic was written all over him, alerting Cartier Jay and Boo-Boo. Both instinctively clutched their weapons, sensing something was wrong. Freak Zeenie's mind raced, trying to figure out where he'd slipped up and how he'd made such a colossal mistake. His feet started moving before his brain caught up.

Cartier Jay and Boo-Boo left De'shawn to see what was up with Freak Zeenie. De'shawn hadn't noticed anything, 'cause he was in a zone thinking 'bout winning the game as he continued dribbling the ball through his legs in the opposite direction. Cartier Jay caught up to Freak Zeenie.

"What's up, Pops?" Cartier Jay asked. Freak Zeenie only gave him a one-minute finger, signaling for him to wait. Cartier Jay didn't like what he saw; Freak Zeenie's body language screamed trouble. He didn't know, but Cartier Jay wanted to know as bad as a hog wanted slop.

"A'ight, Mom. Be cool," Freak Zeenie finally said, trying to calm her down. "I'm gon' take care of it. I promise!" He hung up.

Freak Zeenie tried to remain calm, noticing everyone looking from their phone directly at him. Freak Zeenie's phone chimed again. Without glancing at the caller ID, he answered, still scanning the area for an escape route.

"Hello?"

Same Time
Grady Hospital
Atlanta, Georgia

BEEP! BEEP! BEEP!

Levi's heart monitor sped up like crazy. His body jolted as he began thrashing his head violently from side to side.

"Huh-huh-huh! Um! Na!" Levi mumbled, his voice weak and disoriented.

Remy Red, who had been staring blankly out the window at the parking lot, snapped out of her thoughts when she heard Levi stirring.

"Levi!" she gasped, rushing to his side. But before she could do anything, a team of doctors and nurses burst into the room, forcing her to step back.

"Is he alright? Is he okay?" Remy Red asked frantically, repeating the question in different ways. Her only response was the slam of the door in her face. Tears streamed down her face, timid but uncontrollable.

A Few Moments Later—

A nurse emerged from Levi's room, and Remy Red perked up instantly, her heart in her throat.

"Is he okay, Ms.?" Remy Red asked fearfully.

"Oh yes, dear. He's finally come out of the coma!" the nurse replied, her voice brimming with relief. "Right now, the doctors are just checking to make sure everything is still intact and stable. Honey, God is a great God!"

"Yes, He is. All the time," Remy Red whispered to herself. She pulled her phone out and immediately dialed Freak Zeenie.

Back in Dothan

Freak Zeenie listened carefully to Remy Red's update, but his eyes never stopped scanning the crowd. He could feel the public's stares, hear their whispers, and see them pointing in his direction.

"Bet that up! God is good! Check it out though—I gotta run! Shit real!" Freak Zeenie deaded the call before Remy Red could say another word.

"Aye, Cartier Jay, listen up. Here's what I need from y'all," Freak Zeenie started as he began explaining their tasks.

Before he could finish, a black Dodge Charger turned the corner at the top of the street, creeping slowly.

De'shawn was practicing his dribbling, edging closer to the curb where the Charger was headed. He was about to head to the gym for warm-ups with his team.

Freak Zeenie's eyes darted around, catching sight of an identical Charger creeping in the opposite direction. His senses heightened, and he instinctively began looking for De'shawn.

"D—" Before he could call out to De'shawn—

BLOCKA!

Rapid gunfire erupted from both Chargers, cutting through the air like thunder. Freak Zeenie ducked low, running in a crouched position toward De'shawn. Cartier Jay and Boo-Boo whipped out their guns, returning fire, but the storm of bullets coming at them forced them to take cover.

The parking lot descended into chaos. People scrambled, running for their lives and screaming as bullets tore through cars and shattered windows.

SKURRR!

The shooting stopped suddenly. Freak Zeenie lifted his head, and what he saw made his heart skip a beat before it sped up dangerously.

"De'shawn!" Freak Zeenie screamed, bolting after the black Charger as it sped away, its tires screeching around a corner on two wheels. De'shawn's legs were hanging halfway out of the backseat, but before Freak Zeenie could get any closer, the door slammed shut, locking the boy inside.

The Chargers disappeared into the distance. Freak Zeenie stopped, panting heavily, his chest heaving in frustration.

"Damn! Fuck, man! They got my boy!" he shouted, pacing erratically. He couldn't stop moving, his adrenaline spiking uncontrollably, until the sound of approaching police sirens assaulted his ears.

"I gotta go!" Freak Zeenie yelled, sprinting toward his car, seemingly fueled by raw energy.

"What about De'?! Pops, what about De'?" Cartier Jay called after him, but his words fell on deaf ears.

Same Time
Grady Hospital
Atlanta, Georgia

Levi was barely conscious, his body weak, but he managed to mumble a few words here and there.

Remy Red, ecstatic, couldn't stay still. Her nerves were on edge, but her joy was overwhelming. She stood by the window, glancing out into the night as she drew the curtains closed.

"Cartier Jay and them will be here in the a.m.," she said to Levi. "Boot and Freak Zeenie send their love too, nigga!"

Levi blinked weakly in response.

"You gon' ma—" Remy Red's sentence trailed off as her eyes grew wide with terror. At least 15 armed Mexicans were storming into the hospital with machetes, pistols, and assault rifles.

"Oh fucking shit!" she blurted out, panic gripping her as she desperately tried to formulate an escape plan.

Levi noticed the fear in her voice. "What?" he croaked weakly.

Kinsey, Alabama

No one could have ever prepared Freak Zeenie for what he saw when he pulled into his driveway. His house had been riddled with bullets. The front door was completely off the hinges.

Freak Zeenie's two Bull Kutties laid slain across the yard. The massive storage house, as far as he could tell, had been emptied completely Freak Zeenie's eyes darted around, taking in the destruction.

Rushing inside, Freak Zeenie took the stairs two at a time, heading straight to the basement. When he reached it, he fell to his knees.

It's said that what you put into the universe, you get back.

"Fuck naw, man!" he screamed, his voice raw with pain. "Hell fuckin' naw!"

The safe was cleaner than a freshly polished 1991 Fleetwood Lac'.

Placing both hands on his head, Freak Zeenie's body began to tremble.

***

A Few Minutes Later—

Freak Zeenie tried to steady his thoughts, searching for a way through the disaster, but his phone interrupted him. The screen read RESTRICTED, and Freak Zeenie instinctively pressed ignore, thinking it was another unwanted prison call.

The phone chimed again almost instantly.

"Yeah?!" Freak Zeenie yelled into the phone.

"Freak Zeenie… I'm disappointed," the voice drawled. It was Zacatecas.

"Why didn't I get to tell you last week? Oh, right—because we were interrupted by all those fake attempts on my life," Zacatecas continued. "They missed me, as you can see. How could you think so little of my eminence, Freak Zeenie?"

Freak Zeenie clenched his jaw, silent rage brewing within him.

"You like the little message I sent y'all?" Zacatecas taunted. "You missed me. My rivals missed me too. But unfortunately, you did manage to get one of my closest men. I'll give you that. But I'm a man of power, Freak Zeenie. Power beyond your little longitude and latitude."

His voice turned darker. "Running off on the plug will get your sockets blown out," Zacatecas chortled menacingly. "I'm about to murder your whole family—starting with your young son, De'shawn. And oh yeah . . . Levi should be dead too, as . . . of . . . *now!*"

CLICK.

"Bitch-ass motherfucker! I'ma ki—" Freak Zeenie screamed, but Zacatecas had already hung up.

Freak Zeenie's thoughts spiraled as he processed Zacatecas' words. *That fucking Migo got a rabbit's foot up his burrito-eating ass*, he thought bitterly.

Snatching his keys, Freak Zeenie ran out of the house, dialing Mama Lois' number. No answer. He tried again. Still no answer.

"Fuck! Come on, Mom, answer!" he yelled, trying over and over again. He tried Cartier Jay's number next. No answer. Then he called Remy Red. No answer.

Kicking up a cloud of dust, Freak Zeenie sped out of his driveway. The fire burning inside him couldn't be extinguished—not by anything short of death or a lifetime prison sentence.

Chapter 33

Grady Hospital
Atlanta, Georgia

The first floor of Grady Hospital was in total shambles. The Paisas shot everything that moved in their path. They weren't there to play games—they were there to kill Levi, and whoever got in their way was just collateral damage.

Remy Red struggled to help Levi into the wheelchair.

"I got you!" Remy Red said, struggling with Levi because he was like dead weight. Plus she was trying not to cause any more damage to Levi's injuries at the same time.

"Argh!" Levi grunted out an agonizing sound in pain. The good drugs that Levi was on was still no match for the pain he felt.

Remy Red pulled her Glock 27 from the small of her back, checkin' it quickly She cursed herself for not bringing the extended clip but knew she'd have to make do with the standard mag.

"We got to get the fuck out of here!" Remy Red bellowed, pushing the wheelchair towards the door with urgency.

The door swung open before Remy Red reached it.

"Oh my God! I heard guns –" a nurse began, but her sentence was cut short when she saw the compact pistol in Remy Red's hand. The nurse ducked instinctively, almost losing her head because Remy Red almost squeezed that trigger out of reflex.

"What are yo—"

"Is there a safe way out of here?" Remy Red cut the nurse off sharply. The nurse froze, stunned into silence.

"We all are in grave danger!" Remy Red snapped again. "We need a safe way out!"

The nurse jumped into action. "Yes, the employee elevator! It only works with a key or keycard," she said hurriedly.

"Where's the key?"

"Follow me!"

The nurse led them to the elevator, and the gun sounds could be heard getting closer as screams of death echoed throughout. The nurse quickly scanned her key card.

"What's taking so long?" Remy Red asked impatiently, putting her back to the wheelchair and holding her gun up to cover their six..

The doors on the elevator finally opened.

BLACKA!

Rapid gunfire ricocheted off the wall right beside Remy Red's head.

BLOCKA! BLOCKA! BLOCKA!

Dropping to one knee, Remy Red unleashed a volley of shots, her aim steady despite the chaos.

"Argh! Puta!" one of the Mexicans cried out as a bullet tore through his abdomen, causing him to drop his weapon.

More shots whizzed by as three additional Paisas rounded the corner, spraying bullets wildly. Remy Red braced herself and shoved the wheelchair backward into the elevator with her hip, firing off more rounds to suppress the advancing gunmen. None of her remaining shots found their target, but she focused on survival rather than precision.

She jammed the keycard to close the elevator doors, but just as they sealed shut, she saw red mist explode from the nurse's head. The back of her skull blew out, and chunks of brain and blood sprayed across the wall like ribbons. The nurse staggered for a brief moment before collapsing in a lifeless heap.

On the first floor two more Paisas stood at the base of the elevator, frantically pressing the buttons, trying to get in on the work. Remy Red had her gun up and ready to skeet off, taking no chances. The Paisas had become tired of waiting. They turned to leave until they heard the faint *ding* of the elevator bell.

The elevator door slowly opened.

BOOM! BOOM!

Remy Red didn't hesitate, firing two perfectly aimed shots. Each bullet punched a clean, 50-cent coin-sized hole through the throats of the two men, dropping them instantly.

Scanning her surroundings, Remy Red's eyes darted ubiquitously across the massacre the Paisas had left behind. Blood pooled around lifeless bodies scattered everywhere. Her breath quickened, but she didn't freeze.

Remy Red bolted toward the front exit, weaving between the corpses that littered the floor.

Police sirens wailed in the distance, faint but growing louder. Just as she stepped outside, she spotted a patrol car parked by the curb. Relief washed over her briefly—until she noticed the blotch of blood smeared across the windshield and the officer slumped lifeless inside the car. Her moment of hope shattered instantly.

"We gotta keep movin'!" she muttered, preparing to make a break for her own vehicle. But when she glanced back at the hospital, her stomach sank. More Mexicans were rushing toward her position, and there were far too many for the ammo she had left.

Thinking quickly, she yanked the back door of the patrol car open and flipped Levi out of the wheelchair, tossing him into the back seat like a sack of potatoes.

"Arghhh!" Levi bellowed in pain, his body writhing as he hit the seat.

"I k—"

BLOCKA!

Shots ricocheted off the patrol car, sending sparks flying. The back window shattered as Remy Red slammed the driver's door shut. Luckily, Levi had fallen flat across the seat, avoiding the storm of bullets that sprayed through the broken glass.

Dropping the patrol car into drive, Remy Red floored the gas pedal, causing the car's back end to fishtail wildly.

A Mexican stepped into her path, aiming a short-barrel AR-15 and squeezing the trigger. Bullets riddled the car, spider-webbing the front windshield and blowing out the remnants of the rear window.

Remy Red ducked low, gripping the steering wheel tightly while keeping her foot planted on the accelerator. A bullet whizzed past her head, missing her skull by centimeters.

"Arghhh!" she screamed, the deafening gunfire pounding in her ears.

The Paisa continued firing, unrelenting as he stood his ground, believing in his shot. At the last second, he tried to jump out of the way, but the patrol car plowed into him with the force of a freight train, running him down like a speed bump.

Once the shooting stopped, Remy Red straightened up in the seat, just in time to turn out of the parking lot on nearly two wheels.

Levi groaned in the back seat, too weak to move, but he and Remy Red both knew one thing—they had narrowly escaped death. For now, they were alive, but life on the run wasn't much of a life at all.

Chapter 34

Same Time
Brentwood
Dothan, Alabama

Death loomed over Kal-Kal. Kal-Kal. He was slipping in and out of consciousness, the oxygen deprivation making his vision blurry and his mind foggy. His feet squirmed in desperation as he saw the reaper creeping closer, its bright red, menacing eyes glaring at him from over Freak Zeenie's shoulder.

Freak Zeenie had damn near lost everything that mattered to him and was blaming Zacatecas and Khashia for his shortcomings. Freak Zeenie was filled with indignation. All Freak Zeenie had wanted in the beginning was to come home from prison and be a productive citizen, take his mama Lois to church, and take care of his progenies.

"You wanna steal from niggas who feedin' you, motherfucker?" Freak Zeenie hissed through gritted teeth, choking the life out of Kal-Kal. "Yeah, bitch! You gon' die lookin' me in my eyes, fuck nigga!" His hands tightened like vice grips around Kal-Kal's neck, squeezing harder and harder, feeling the last remnants of life seeping out of him.

"You goin' straight to hell, pussy!" Freak Zeenie spat. "You hear me? Hell! 'Cause we don't want your kind in heaven! Yo' kind is boycotted, nigga!"

Kal-Kal tried to squeal, gasping as his windpipe threatened to collapse. Freak Zeenie released him suddenly, letting him slump forward, coughing violently, desperate to suck in air.

"*Cough, cough!*" Kal-Kal coughed violently, trying to suck in as much air as he could. Kal-Kal's hands were bound behind his back, keeping him a prisoner to the chair. "Argh!" He squealed out in excruciating pain. Again as Freak Zeenie donkey-kicked Kal-Kal's injured leg with all his might, sending a wave of agony surging through his body.

Freak Zeenie turned away, walking over to Cartier Jay and Boo-Boo, who stood nearby, their faces expressionless, as if the torture they'd just witnessed was an everyday occurrence. Freak Zeenie knew he should've been furious with them for bringing Kal-Kal in, but he couldn't bring himself to be mad. Kal-Kal had been someone Freak Zeenie had known for over 20 years.

Cartier Jay and Boo-Boo didn't flinch. They remained nonchalant, knowing better than to interrupt Freak Zeenie's fury. Boo-Boo, however, was tired of the back-and-forth. If only Freak Zeenie knew but he didn't, because Cartier Jay didn't explain a lot of things to his pops for many reasons. The main one was, his uncle Levi had told him to never go to the hog farm without him in the first place.

"W-what's u-up? W-we w-will g-get rid of th-that r-rat a-ass n-nigga, u-unk!" Boo-Boo said, tired of the games. He was ready to push Kal-Kal's noodles out right then and there. Boo-Boo snatched his gun out with lightning speed.

Freak Zeenie knew he had to lay low, because he was a wanted man. Not just in the bounty but in Mexico too. Freak Zeenie was not willing to go back to anybody's prison for nothing. Especially not before he found De'shawn, and not before he pushed Zacatecas' top back. That's when Freak Zeenie had a rational thought.

"Nawl. keep that bitch ass nigga alive and healthy," he said. "I just might be able to use him after all." Freak Zeenie left the parable in the air. Cartier Jay and Boo-Boo didn't have the slightest clue what Freak Zeenie was talking 'bout.

Freak Zeenie left and headed out to the tree farm, because it was probably one of the safest places for him at the moment. Cartier jay and Boo-Boo left right behind Freak Zeenie after securing Kal-Kal back shackled in the room.

Dothan, Alabama

The streets were smothered with police officers after the discovery of the decapitated heads hanging from the power lines throughout the community. Right now the streets weren't safe. The city was on edge. If Freak Zeenie could just make it to the tree farm, then that's where he planned on spending the rest of the night until sunrise.

Freak Zeenie drove through the backroads, his mind racing. His thoughts drifted to De'shawn, the son he hadn't seen in too long.

"Father God, please! Please! Super please be a light and guide for lil' De'shawn. Let him be alright and come up from under this devious act," he prayed out loud, his voice cracking with desperation. "In Jesus' name, amen."

Tears streamed down Freak Zeenie's face as he thought about the destruction Zacatecas had inflicted on his life. Rage built in his chest like a volcano about to erupt.

"Arghhh!" he hollered, pounding the steering wheel. "I'm gonna kill you, bitch! On God!"

The rest of the drive to the tree farm was spent in a haze of anger, prayer, and paranoia. Freak Zeenie stuck to backroads, his eyes scanning every shadow and corner for threats.

The Next Morning
The Tree Farm
Dothan, Alabama

The sun gave off an ambience so brilliantly, that the rays broke through the tinted windows of Freak Zeenie's jeep. Freak Zeenie stirred from out a tiresome, uncomfortable sleep. If times had been different, Freak Zeenie would have loved to be up this early, moving about, but reality told only the truth. Freak Zeenie knew that closing his eyes back wouldn't make his situation vanish, even though he wanted and needed it to.

With two weeks' worth of beard matted on his face, and a George Jefferson taking place upon his cranium, Freak Zeenie managed to get moving and climbed out the jeep. Retrieving the shovel, Freak Zeenie went and found his mark, and he slowly began working.

It was spring, not summer, and the dirt was like digging through asphalt with a spoon. Even with the sun steadily elevating promising hot record breaking temperatures. The trees blocked as much sun as they could for as long as they could.

"Got damn! Shit!" Freak Zeenie, muttered, dropping the shovel in frustration. "It's too early for this stupid shit man! *Damn!*" The ground was concrete stiff, and even a bulldozer would have a hard time with it at that time of day.

SHRUSH! SKRUSH!

The faint crackle of a walkie-talkie shattered the silence.

"Black Jeep with a—"

Freak Zeenie's ears perked up, his body snapping to attention.

"Fuck!" he hissed, his head swiveling in search of an escape route.

"*Freeze! Police!*" an officer yelled, drawing his weapon. Freak Zeenie bolted, running through the woods like a gazelle being chased by a lion.

BOOM! BOOM!

The police officer let two rounds fly behind Freak Zeenie that were meant to kill, as he continued the hot foot pursuit.

"Suspect running through the woods!" the officer barked into his radio. "Headed east out at the tree farm!"

Although Freak Zeenie was getting out the police officer's sight, the officer picked up his pace and was gaining on Freak Zeenie.

Same Time
Outside Mama Lois' House
Dothan, Alabama

Mama Lois moved fast towards the front of her house, cocking a shell into her shotgun.

BOOM!

The slug tore through the door, hitting the Mexican on her porch square in the chest, blowing him off his feet. Six carloads of Paisas pulled up and poured outside Mama Lois' house, moving in fast, guns drawn. Mama Lois ratcheted another round into the shotgun, her face set in grim determination.

***

Back at the Tree Farm

Freak Zeenie did a quick zig zag tactic hoping to avoid being killed in the thickness of the woods. Refusing to give up even though he was tired, Freak Zeenie kept it moving. He was tempted to look back to jug the gap but he didn't. Instead, he ran hard for his life.

Patrol cars screeched to a halt, blocking off the eastern edge of the woods. Uniformed officers spilled out, weapons drawn and ready to fire, their barrels trained on the tree line. They were ready to blow Freak Zeenie's soul clean out of the atmosphere if he slipped up. Freak Zeenie took a chance, he turnt around and let off three concurrent shots.

BOOM BOOM BOOM!

The bullets hit their mark. The lead officer went down hard, collapsing like a lumberjack's freshly-felled tree. His service weapon flew from his grasp as he hit the dirt. He gasped for air, blood gushing out of a jagged wound in his neck. Freak Zeenie didn't hesitate. He sprinted over to the officer, standing over the man as his eyes pleaded for mercy.

"No mercy, pig!" Freak Zeenie spat, his voice venomous.

BOOM!

A single shot to the head ended the officer's suffering, splattering crimson across the leaves. Freak Zeenie didn't flinch. He took off running again, moving like Diggs breaking for a game-winning touchdown—smooth, fast, and unstoppable. The officer who had tried to take him down now lay lifeless, a monument to the cost of chasing the wrong man.

Freak Zeenie changed directions and came out on the westside of the woods instead of the east. His instincts told him to avoid the side the officers were most likely monitoring. His gut was right—he didn't see a single patrol car until it was almost too late. Sprinting blindly out of the woods and into the street, Freak Zeenie collided with fate.

The police cruiser came out of nowhere, its tires screeching as it skidded sideways in a desperate attempt to avoid him. The vehicle slammed into him anyway, knocking him off his feet and sending him flying backward into the ditch he'd just climbed out of.

"Argh!" Freak Zeenie grunted, the air knocked clean out of him. He tried to scramble upright, but his body refused to cooperate.

The cruiser's driver's door flung open, and a figure leapt out, sprinting toward him. Freak Zeenie's vision blurred, the edges of reality closing in as he tried to make sense of what was happening. He blinked hard, trying to focus.

"Freak!" A familiar voice pierced the haze.

Freak Zeenie fluttered his eyes trying to process the recognition. He knew that voice.

"Re-Remy R—" His words were slurred, weak.

Before he could finish, everything went black. Freak Zeenie's body slumped back into the dirt, unconscious.

Police sirens grew louder, their wails rounding the corner, closing in on their location. The officers were getting closer—too close. This wasn't the end; it was just the beginning. For Freak Zeenie and Remy Red, survival meant one thing: they'd have to live life on the run.

To Be Continued . . .
RAN OFF ON DA PLUG 3:
LIFE ON THE RUN!

Coming Soon . . .

Lock Down Publications and Ca$h Presents
Assisted Publishing Packages

Due to an increase in the price of services we have increased our prices. The prices below reflect the price increase as of 11/1/24.

BASIC PACKAGE	UPGRADED PACKAGE
$699	**$1000**
Editing	Typing
Cover Design	Editing
Formatting	Cover Design
	Formatting
	Upload eBooks to Amazon
	Upload Paperback to Amazon
ADVANCE PACKAGE	**LDP SUPREME PACKAGE**
$1,400	**$1,700**
Typing	Typing
Editing (line editing/content)	Editing (line editing/content)
Cover Design	Cover Design
Formatting	Formatting
Copyright Registration	Copyright Registration
Proofreading	Proofreading
Upload eBooks to Amazon	Set up Amazon Account
Upload Paperback to Amazon	Upload eBooks to Amazon
	Upload Paperback to Amazon
	Advertise on LDP's Amazon and Facebook Page

***

Other services available upon request.
Additional charges may apply

Lock Down Publications
P.O. Box 944
Stockbridge, GA 30281-9998
Phone: 470 303-9761
Email: lockdownpublications@gmail.com

Submission Guideline

Submit the first three chapters of your completed manuscript to ldpsubmissions@gmail.com. In the subject line add **Your Book's Title**. The manuscript must be in a Word Doc file and sent as an attachment. Document should be in Times New Roman, double spaced, and in size 12 font. Also, provide your synopsis and full contact information. If sending multiple submissions, they must each be in a separate email.

Have a story but no way to send it electronically? You can still submit to LDP/Ca$h Presents. Send in the first three chapters, written or typed, of your completed manuscript to:

LDP: Submissions Dept
P.O. Box 944
Stockbridge, GA 30281-9998

DO NOT send original manuscript. Must be a duplicate.
Provide your synopsis and a cover letter containing your full contact information.

Thanks for considering LDP and Ca$h Presents.

NEW RELEASES

BLOODLINE OF A SAVAGE 1-3
THESE VICIOUS STREETS 1-3
RELENTLESS GOON 1-3
BY PRINCE A. TAUHID

THE BUTTERFLY MAFIA 1-3
BY FUMIYA PAYNE

A THUG'S STREET PRINCESS 1&2
BY MEESHA

CITY OF SMOKE 3
BY MOLOTTI

GET IT IN SLUGS 1 &2
BY B. STALL

STANDING ON HER BUSINESS 1&2
BY DG SANTANA

STEPPERS 1,2&3
THE REAL BADDIES OF CHI-RAQ
BY KING RIO

THE LANE 1&2
BY KEN-KEN SPENCE

THUG OF SPADES 1&2
LOVE IN THE TRENCHES 2
CORNER BOYS
BY COREY ROBINSON

TIL DEATH 3
BY ARYANNA

THE BIRTH OF A GANGSTER 4
BY DELMONT PLAYER

PRODUCT OF THE STREETS 1-3
BY DEMOND "MONEY" ANDERSON

NO TIME FOR ERROR
BY KEESE

MONEY HUNGRY DEMONS 1-2
BY TRANAY ADAMS

HUB CITY MENACE 1-3
BY J. WHITE

A THUGGISH PASSION 1&2
LAND OF DA HOOLIGANZ 1-4
KILLAZ ON STANDBY 1&2
BY IRA B.

FO'EVA ROLLIN 1&2
BY ASSA RAYMOND BAKER

THE LEVEL UP 1&3
BY LUXURY KING

Coming Soon from Lock Down Publications/Ca$h Presents

IF YOU CROSS ME ONCE 6
ANGEL V
By Anthony Fields

A THUGS STREET PRINCESS 3
By Meesha

CORNER BOYS 2
By Corey Robinson

THA TAKEOVER
By Keith Chandler

BETRAYAL OF A G 2
By Ray Vinci

SAVAGE FAMILY EMPIRE 1&2
SOULLESS GOON 1,2&3
THE DIRTY SIDE OF MONEY 1,2&3
By Prince

FOR MY ENEMY'S SAKE
AMBITIONS OF A SLIDER
FRESH OFF DA PORCH
By IRA B.

THE TRUCKLOAD 1-4
TIPPIN' THE SCALES 1-3
BAD BITCHES WIT GUNZ 3
PROBLEM SOLVED 2
By Christopher "Diesel" Hornezes

Available Now

RESTRAINING ORDER 1 & 2
By **CA$H & Coffee**

LOVE KNOWS NO BOUNDARIES 1-3
By **Coffee**

RAISED AS A GOON I, II, III & IV
BRED BY THE SLUMS I, II, III
BLAST FOR ME I & II
ROTTEN TO THE CORE I II III
A BRONX TALE I, II, III
DUFFLE BAG CARTEL I II III IV V VI
HEARTLESS GOON I II III IV V
A SAVAGE DOPEBOY I II
DRUG LORDS I II III
CUTTHROAT MAFIA I II
KING OF THE TRENCHES
By **Ghost**

LAY IT DOWN I & II
LAST OF A DYING BREED I II
BLOOD STAINS OF A SHOTTA I & II III
By **Jamaica**

LOYAL TO THE GAME I II III
LIFE OF SIN I, II III
By **TJ & Jelissa**

IF LOVING HIM IS WRONG…I & II
LOVE ME EVEN WHEN IT HURTS I II III
By **Jelissa**

PUSH IT TO THE LIMIT
By **Bre' Hayes**

BLOODY COMMAS I & II
SKI MASK CARTEL I, II & III
KING OF NEW YORK I II, III IV V
RISE TO POWER I II III
COKE KINGS I II III IV V
BORN HEARTLESS I II III IV
KING OF THE TRAP I II
By **T.J. Edwards**

WHEN THE STREETS CLAP BACK I & II III
THE HEART OF A SAVAGE I II III IV
MONEY MAFIA I II
LOYAL TO THE SOIL I II III
By **Jibril Williams**

A DISTINGUISHED THUG STOLE MY HEART I II & III
LOVE SHOULDN'T HURT I II III IV
RENEGADE BOYS 1-4
PAID IN KARMA 1-3
SAVAGE STORMS 1-3
AN UNFORESEEN LOVE 1-3
BABY, I'M WINTERTIME COLD 1-3
A THUG'S STREET PRINCESS 1&2
By **Meesha**

A GANGSTER'S CODE 1-3
A GANGSTER'S SYN 1-3
THE SAVAGE LIFE 1-3
CHAINED TO THE STREETS 1-3
BLOOD ON THE MONEY 1-3
A GANGSTA'S PAIN 1-3
BEAUTIFUL LIES AND UGLY TRUTHS
CHURCH IN THESE STREETS
By **J-Blunt**

CUM FOR ME 1-8
An LDP Erotica Collaboration

RAN OFF ON DA PLUG 2 | PAPER BOI RARI

BLOOD OF A BOSS 1-5
SHADOWS OF THE GAME
TRAP BASTARD
By **Askari**

THE STREETS BLEED MURDER 1-3
THE HEART OF A GANGSTA 1-3
By **Jerry Jackson**

WHEN A GOOD GIRL GOES BAD
By **Adrienne**

THE COST OF LOYALTY 1-3
By **Kweli**

BRIDE OF A HUSTLA 1-3
THE FETTI GIRLS 1-3
CORRUPTED BY A GANGSTA 1-4
BLINDED BY HIS LOVE
THE PRICE YOU PAY FOR LOVE 1-3
DOPE GIRL MAGIC 1-3
By **Destiny Skai**

A KINGPIN'S AMBITION
A KINGPIN'S AMBITION II
I MURDER FOR THE DOUGH
By **Ambitious**

TRUE SAVAGE 1-7
DOPE BOY MAGIC 1-3
MIDNIGHT CARTEL 1-3
CITY OF KINGZ 1&2
NIGHTMARE ON SILENT AVE
THE PLUG OF LIL MEXICO 1&2
CLASSIC CITY
By **Chris Green**

A GANGSTER'S REVENGE 1-4
THE BOSS MAN'S DAUGHTERS 1-5
A SAVAGE LOVE 1&2
BAE BELONGS TO ME 1&2
A HUSTLER'S DECEIT 1-3
WHAT BAD BITCHES DO 1-3
SOUL OF A MONSTER 1-3
KILL ZONE
A DOPE BOY'S QUEEN 1-3
TIL DEATH 1-3
IMMA DIE BOUT MINE 1-6
DYING FOR LIKES
By **Aryanna**

A DOPEBOY'S PRAYER
By **Eddie "Wolf" Lee**

THE KING CARTEL 1-3
By **Frank Gresham**

THESE NIGGAS AIN'T LOYAL 1-3
By **Nikki Tee**

GANGSTA SHYT 1-3
By **CATO**

THE ULTIMATE BETRAYAL
By **Phoenix**

BOSS'N UP 1-3
By **Royal Nicole**

I LOVE YOU TO DEATH
By **Destiny J**

I RIDE FOR MY HITTA
I STILL RIDE FOR MY HITTA
By **Misty Holt**

LOVE & CHASIN' PAPER
By **Qay Crockett**

TO DIE IN VAIN
SINS OF A HUSTLA
By **ASAD**

BROOKLYN HUSTLAZ
By **Boogsy Morina**

BROOKLYN ON LOCK 1 & 2
By **Sonovia**

GANGSTA CITY
By **Teddy Duke**

A DRUG KING AND HIS DIAMOND 1-3
A DOPEMAN'S RICHES
HER MAN, MINE'S TOO 1&2
CASH MONEY HO'S
THE WIFEY I USED TO BE 1&2
PRETTY GIRLS DO NASTY THINGS
By **Nicole Goosby**

LIPSTICK KILLAH 1-3
CRIME OF PASSION 1-3
FRIEND OR FOE 1-3
By **Mimi**

TRAPHOUSE KING 1-3
KINGPIN KILLAZ 1-3
STREET KINGS 1&2
PAID IN BLOOD 1&2
CARTEL KILLAZ 1-3
DOPE GODS 1&2
By **Hood Rich**

THE STREETS ARE CALLING
By **Duquie Wilson**

STEADY MOBBN' 1-3
THE STREETS STAINED MY SOUL 1-3
By **Marcellus Allen**

WHO SHOT YA 1-3
SON OF A DOPE FIEND 1-4
HEAVEN GOT A GHETTO 1&2
SKI MASK MONEY 1&2
By **Renta**

GORILLAZ IN THE BAY 1-4
TEARS OF A GANGSTA 1/&2
3X KRAZY 1&2
STRAIGHT BEAST MODE 1&2
By **DE'KARI**

TRIGGADALE 1-3
MURDA WAS THE CASE 1-3
By **Elijah R. Freeman**

SLAUGHTER GANG 1-3
RUTHLESS HEART 1-3
By **Willie Slaughter**

GOD BLESS THE TRAPPERS 1-3
THESE SCANDALOUS STREETS 1-3
FEAR MY GANGSTA 1-5
THESE STREETS DON'T LOVE NOBODY 1-2
BURY ME A G 1-5
A GANGSTA'S EMPIRE 1-4
THE DOPEMAN'S BODYGAURD 1&2
THE REALEST KILLAZ 1-3
THE LAST OF THE OGS 1-3
By **Tranay Adams**

MARRIED TO A BOSS 1-3
By **Destiny Skai & Chris Green**

KINGZ OF THE GAME 1-7
CRIME BOSS 1-4
By **Playa Ray**

FUK SHYT
By **Blakk Diamond**

DON'T F#CK WITH MY HEART 1&2
By **Linnea**

ADDICTED TO THE DRAMA 1-3
IN THE ARM OF HIS BOSS
By **Jamila**

LOYALTY AIN'T PROMISED 1&2
By **Keith Williams**

YAYO 1-4
A SHOOTER'S AMBITION 1&2
BRED IN THE GAME
By **S. Allen**

TRAP GOD 1-3
RICH $AVAGE 1-3
MONEY IN THE GRAVE 1-3
CARTEL MONEY 1&2
By **Martell Troublesome Bolden**

FOREVER GANGSTA 1&2
GLOCKS ON SATIN SHEETS 1&2
By **Adrian Dulan**

TOE TAGZ 1-4
LEVELS TO THIS SHYT 1&2
IT'S JUST ME AND YOU
By **Ah'Million**

KINGPIN DREAMS 1-3
RAN OFF ON DA PLUG
By **Paper Boi Rari**

THE STREETS MADE ME 1-3
By **Larry D. Wright**

CONFESSIONS OF A GANGSTA 1-4
CONFESSIONS OF A JACKBOY 1-3
CONFESSIONS OF A HITMAN
CONFESSIONS OF A DOPE BOY
By **Nicholas Lock**

I'M NOTHING WITHOUT HIS LOVE
SINS OF A THUG
TO THE THUG I LOVED BEFORE
A GANGSTA SAVED XMAS
IN A HUSTLER I TRUST
By **Monet Dragun**

QUIET MONEY 1-3
THUG LIFE 1-3
EXTENDED CLIP 1&2
A GANGSTA'S PARADISE
By **Trai'Quan**

CAUGHT UP IN THE LIFE 1-3
THE STREETS NEVER LET GO 1-3
By **Robert Baptiste**

NEW TO THE GAME 1-3
MONEY, MURDER & MEMORIES 1-3
By **Malik D. Rice**

CREAM 2-3
THE STREETS WILL TALK
By **Yolanda Moore**

THE STREETS WILL NEVER CLOSE 1-3
By **K'ajji**

LIFE OF A SAVAGE 1-4
A GANGSTA'S QUR'AN 1-4
MURDA SEASON 1-3
GANGLAND CARTEL 1-3
CHI'RAQ GANGSTAS 1-4
KILLERS ON ELM STREET 1-3
JACK BOYZ N DA BRONX 1-3
A DOPEBOY'S DREAM 1-3
JACK BOYS VS DOPE BOYS 1-3
COKE GIRLZ
COKE BOYS
SOSA GANG 1&2
BRONX SAVAGES
BODYMORE KINGPINS
BLOOD OF A GOON
By **Romell Tukes**

CONCRETE KILLA 1-3
VICIOUS LOYALTY 1-3
BLOODY MONEY BAGS
By **Kingpen**

THE ULTIMATE SACRIFICE 1-6
KHADIFI
IF YOU CROSS ME ONCE 1-3
ANGEL 1-4
IN THE BLINK OF AN EYE
By **Anthony Fields**

THE LIFE OF A HOOD STAR
By **Ca$h & Rashia Wilson**

NIGHTMARES OF A HUSTLA 1-3
BLOOD AND GAMES 1&2
By **King Dream**

GHOST MOB
By **Stilloan Robinson**

HARD AND RUTHLESS 1&2
MOB TOWN 251
THE BILLIONAIRE BENTLEYS 1-3
REAL G'S MOVE IN SILENCE
By **Von Diesel**

MOB TIES 1-7
SOUL OF A HUSTLER, HEART OF A KILLER 1-3
GORILLAZ IN THE TRENCHES
OOPS CRY TOO 1&2
THE DAUGHTER OF A CARTEL BOSS
By **SayNoMore**

BODYMORE MURDERLAND 1-3
THE BIRTH OF A GANGSTER 1-4
By **Delmont Player**

FOR THE LOVE OF A BOSS 1&2
By **C. D. Blue**

KILLA KOUNTY 1-5
TENDER
By **Khufu**

MOBBED UP 1-4
THE BRICK MAN 1-5
THE COCAINE PRINCESS 1-10
STEPPERS 1-3
SUPER GREMLIN 1-4
A GANGSTA'S SON
By **King Rio**

MONEY GAME 1&2
By **Smoove Dolla**

A GANGSTA'S KARMA 1-5
By **FLAME**

KING OF THE TRENCHES 1-3
By **GHOST & TRANAY ADAMS**

BAD BITCHES WIT GUNZ 1&2
PROBLEM SOLVED
By **"Christopher Diesel" Hornezes**

QUEEN OF THE ZOO 1&2
By **Black Migo**

GRIMEY WAYS 1-3
BETRAYAL OF A G
By **Ray Vinci**

XMAS WITH AN ATL SHOOTER
By **Ca$h & Destiny Skai**

KING KILLA 1&2
By **Vincent "Vitto" Holloway**

BETRAYAL OF A THUG 1&2
By **Fre$h**

COUNTDOWN OF A KILLA 1&2
SEX, MURDER AND GOD 1&2
GUNS DOWN, BOTTOMS UP 1&2
By **Lo-Life**

THE MURDER QUEENS 1-7
By **Michael Gallon**

FOR THE LOVE OF BLOOD 1-4
By **Jamel Mitchell**

RAN OFF ON DA PLUG 2 | PAPER BOI RARI

HOOD CONSIGLIERE 1&2
NO TIME FOR ERROR
By **Keese**

PROTÉGÉ OF A LEGEND 1,2&3
LOVE IN THE TRENCHES 1&2
By **Corey Robinson**

THE PLUG'S RUTHLESS DAUGHTER 1&2
By **Tony Daniels**

BORN IN THE GRAVE 1-3
CRIME PAYS
By **Self Made Tay**

MOAN IN MY MOUTH
By **XTASY**

TORN BETWEEN A GANGSTER AND A GENTLEMAN
By **J-BLUNT & Miss Kim**

LOYALTY IS EVERYTHING 1-3
CITY OF SMOKE 1-3
By **Molotti**

HERE TODAY GONE TOMORROW 1&2
By **Fly Rock**

WOMEN LIE MEN LIE 1-4
FIFTY SHADES OF SNOW 1-3
STACK BEFORE YOU SPLURGE
GIRLS FALL LIKE DOMINOES
NAÏVE TO THE STREETS
By **ROY MILLIGAN**

PILLOW PRINCESS
By **S. Hawkins**

THE BUTTERFLY MAFIA 1-3
SALUTE MY SAVAGERY 1&2
By **Fumiya Payne**

THE LANE 1&2
By Ken-Ken Spence

THE PUSSY TRAP 1-5
By **Nene Capri**

DIRTY DNA
By **Blaque**

SANCTIFIED AND HORNY
by **XTASY**

BOOKS BY LDP'S CEO, CA$H

TRUST IN NO MAN
TRUST IN NO MAN 2
TRUST IN NO MAN 3
BONDED BY BLOOD
SHORTY GOT A THUG
THUGS CRY
THUGS CRY 2
THUGS CRY 3
TRUST NO BITCH
TRUST NO BITCH 2
TRUST NO BITCH 3
TIL MY CASKET DROPS
RESTRAINING ORDER
RESTRAINING ORDER 2
IN LOVE WITH A CONVICT
LIFE OF A HOOD STAR
XMAS WITH AN ATL SHOOTER